It Started with a Note

Copyright © 2022 by Meg Easton

Cover Illustration: Blue Water Books

Interior Design: Mountain Heights Publishing

Author website: www.megeaston.com

Nestled Hollow Romance

Coming Home to the Top of Main Street

Second Chance on the Corner of Main Street

Christmas at the End of Main Street

More than Friends in the Middle of Main Street

Love Again at the Heart of Main Street

More than Enemies on the Bridge of Main Street

The Royal Palm Resort

A Kiss at Midsummer

A Kiss at Christmas

How to Not Fall

How to Not Fall for the Guy Next Door

How to Not Fall for the Wrong Guy

How to Not Fall for Your Best Friend

How to Not Fall for Your Ex

A Mountain Springs Christmas

The Christmas Pact

The Christmas Bet

Love Started

It Started with a Sunset

It Started with a Note

It Started with a Glance

Coming Home to Silver Leaf Falls

For my husband, Lance

It Started with a Note

It Started with a Note

MEG EASTON

*A*very Parks was pretty sure that she was the most boring person on the planet.

Her boss, Grant, the associate director of admissions processing, was walking by her desk on the way back to his office, so Avery motioned at the paper on her desk and asked, "Why do we need to write bios about ourselves?"

"The university wants them all on the website. That way, when students are applying at Lake Baldwin State University and need to contact someone, they can click on the Admissions tab, see your smiling face and engaging bio and feel like you are a real person who's ready to help them. It's not meant to be hard."

But it was. She couldn't think of a single interesting—or engaging—thing to say. This kind of task only landed on her desk in the slower spring semester, never the busier fall semester. She suddenly longed for the busyness of fall. Since she had fewer student employees she was over during the spring semester, her workload was still substantial.

Her coworker, Joy, came out of her office, the same paper in one hand and a mug of coffee in the other. "What is it about writing a bio that makes you feel like you're the most boring person ever?"

Yes. Someone who understood. "I'm realizing that I don't go on nearly enough adventures." Avery always really felt more alive when she went off and did something new and fun and interesting and out of the ordinary. But she just didn't do that enough. Why didn't she? "If I did, then maybe I'd have something interesting to put."

Joy nodded. "And I've realized that I need an interesting hobby. Something that looks good on paper."

"Right?" Avery said. "Because I don't feel like I can write 'Avery can pick up things with her toes, never wears striped shirts for no particular reason at all, and is bad at karaoke,' unless I also say that I have a trophy with the words 'Most Boring' on it."

One of the student employees, a quiet girl named Julia, came over to her desk, tablet in hand, asking her to sign off on a reimbursement of an application fee for someone who came in to tour the school. After Avery signed it, Julia said, "You could always write in your bio that you have a pretty epic-looking signature."

Avery smiled at Julia. "You are currently my very favorite employee."

Julia grinned as she headed back to her workstation.

She looked back down at her blank bio and sighed before looking back at Joy. "I think I rely on others to plan things too much—I need to get better at instigating fun things myself. Like Summer does," she said as she motioned to her coworker across the half wall that separated the admissions department from the Welcome Center.

"Aww," Joy said, as they both looked at Summer. "I swear she's been glowing ever since she got engaged on Friday. I wish I could've been there to witness it."

Summer glanced over at Avery and smiled and waved before she went back to talking with someone at her office door. Avery turned back to Joy. "It was an amazing proposal. There were a lot of people at that game, and plenty of them posted about it on social media if you want to see a video."

"I already saw it on Instagram and heart-ed it. It was kind of hard to miss."

"That's what I want in my life—big, exciting things. I don't want to be the person whose life is so boring and predictable that she can't even think of something interesting to put in her bio. Or at least something more interesting than the fact that I keep my desk clean but my bedroom's a mess. I want to be someone who can put on their bio that they like to. . . I don't know, wrestle alligators."

"Yeah," Joy said, "South Dakota isn't quite known for its abundance of alligators."

"Okay, then, for my ability to ride a mechanical bull for more than four seconds. Or how fast I am in a giant hay bale rolling competition."

Grant walked out of his office, his arm full of some file folders and his laptop, looking like he must be headed to a meeting, and stopped in front of her on his way out. He tapped two fingers on her desk. "I know I already asked you to compile a list of deferment stats ASAP, but I have a meeting to discuss admissions scholarships tomorrow. Will you get me all the info on our application numbers and the numbers of applicants who qualified for each type of academic scholarship, as well as a projection for our needs for next year?"

Avery's eyes went wide. The deferment stats was already a huge project, and she didn't know how she would find the time to work on the scholarship one, too, especially with all her other duties. But she put on a smile and said, "Sure!"

She could feel Joy's eyes on her before Joy said, "Actually, I've got some free time. I can get that for you."

Grant nodded, then headed out for his meeting.

"Well," Joy said as soon as the door had closed behind him, "you can always put on your bio that you're a people pleaser who can't say no to any request for help, even if your plate is full."

"Ha, ha. And thank you for taking over on that project." Avery glanced at her phone as it lit up with a text from her sister, Riley, asking if she could cover her turn of making dinner tonight. She flipped the phone over. She'd tell her yes when Joy wasn't looking. "Seriously, though," Avery said, "what am I going to put on this bio?"

Cameron, another of her student employees, said from where he was sitting, staring at a computer screen, "You wear cardigans a lot. You could put that."

"And you're very punctual," Rashaad called out from his workstation at the other side of the open area.

"See?" Avery said, holding her hands out as evidence. "Boring."

"Don't forget 'predictable,'" Cameron said.

Avery shook her head, laughing. "Okay, okay. So I should put—she cleared her throat—'Avery Parks is known for her wearing of cardigans and her punctuality. She excels at picking things up with her toes, keeping her desk clean, and signing her name on things. She is bad at karaoke, keeping her room clean, and the ability to say no when asked to do more than she can do.' Did I cover it all?"

"And you don't wear stripes," Julia said.

Avery nodded. "And I don't wear stripes."

"I think you've got yourself a winning bio," Rashaad said.

"All right, done!" She joked. "Now we can all get back to doing our piles of work."

Laughing, her employees all went back to work. If nothing else, at least they all seemed to enjoy the bonding and joking around.

But since she was standing, motion on the Welcome Center side of the half wall caught her eye and she looked over at the same time as Joy did. Brock walked past Summer on his way to his office but paused to give Summer's hand a little squeeze, then he winked at his now-fiancée and they both seemed to blush.

"I want that," Avery said at the same time Joy did.

Avery looked at her coworker. "Oh, yeah? Do you think things will get that serious with the guy you're dating?"

"He *is* pretty great." Joy took a sip of her coffee and shrugged. "But I think it's too soon to tell. Is there anyone on your radar?"

A mental image of Nicolas Servais, the foreign exchange student Avery's family had hosted when she was a junior in high school, immediately came to mind before she shoved it away. "Nope," she said. Nicolas just happened to be a super sweet, good-looking guy who offered to let her stay at his grandpa's flat in Brussels if she ever came to visit, and she only thought about him because she'd been talking with Summer about taking Nicolas up on his offer. Nicolas had a serious girlfriend *and* he lived 4367 miles away. (She'd checked.) They'd been good friends, but no. She was definitely not interested.

"If I date anyone right now, I'll only attract someone who's also boring and predictable. I want to become someone who is bold and daring and tries new things first."

"And who is willing to stand up for herself," Joy added.

"Okay, *and* willing to stand up for myself. Once I get those things figured out, *then* I can think about dating or being in a relationship."

Deja's desk was just on the other side of the half-wall, out in the open area, so she piped up, "Girl, you are lovable just the way you are."

"Aww," Avery said, "thanks, Deja."

"But you really should keep that goal of standing up for yourself more."

―――

AVERY WAS STANDING at the counter in the kitchen, dumping the carrots, celery, and onions into the simmering pot of chicken broth on the stove when the front door opened and both of her roommates walked in, which rarely happened. Their schedules were so different that they could rarely guess when all three of them would be home at the same time.

"Avery," her sister, Riley, said as she hung her purse and coat on the hooks by the door, "you are a godsend. I know I've been slacking on making meals when it's my turn, so I'm going to take you both out for dinner tomorrow." She brushed away from her eyes the same medium brown hair with the ever-so-slight reddish tint that could only be seen in bright sunlight that Avery had. "Your choice of restaurant, Avery. Where do you want to go?"

Avery pushed the chopped chicken from the cutting board into the soup with the knife, then set the knife down, turned around, leaned against the kitchen counter, facing her roomies. Their apartment might have three decently-sized bedrooms, but the kitchen and living room were roughly the size of a napkin. So even though the table and couch were between her and them, it felt like they were in the same room.

"I don't know," Avery said as she dumped the seasonings she'd already measured out into the soup. "You both like Bald Man Subs. Oh, and Shelly, you like that Indian place in Golden Springs, right? We could go there."

Riley held up a hand as she walked into the kitchen. "Stop. I asked where *you* want to eat. You. Avery. If you were eating alone, where would you choose? You're the one who has been making dinners way more than your share lately. It's *your* choice."

Avery didn't usually stop to think about where she wanted to eat. Honestly, she had no idea. But that wasn't the important thing right now. "I'll think about it and tell you tomorrow. But in bigger news, I've decided that I'm going to do bigger and bolder and more daring things. And that I am going to start being the instigator on them."

"Oh, yeah?" Shelly asked. Shelly was her calmer roommate. Her blonde hair was almost always up in a messy bun or ponytail. It was only February, yet she already had the beginnings of a tanned face, even though she didn't ski. Not that she had the build of a skier—she took care of plants and had a build closer to a willow tree.

"Yep. And I decided I'm going to start by going to Belgium." The words just spilled out of her, like they could no longer be contained now that someone was in the room to hear the words.

Avery had grown up on a farm, and the only places outside of South Dakota that she'd traveled to was Minnesota (she lived twenty miles from the border) and Iowa and Nebraska (which were each less than 140 miles away). So traveling to another country was something huge. And scary. And maybe life-changing. And definitely big and bold and daring. And expensive. But at least if she went to Belgium, she'd have a place to stay for free.

"For real?" Riley asked.

Avery grinned. "Go big or go home, right? And I figured I do enough going home. It's time to go big."

"So you're going to contact Nicolas?"

Okay, that was the hard part. She was the one who helped people—she wasn't the one who asked for help. Ever. It was uncomfortable and she was not good at it at all. Sure, Nicolas had been the one to offer, but she still had to ask to take him up on that offer, and that was going to be tough.

But she'd already decided to be tough. Hard, uncomfortable, it didn't matter. She was determined. "I am. If I get things lined up with him, will you go with me?"

"Ave, I've told you that if you go, you'd have a hard time getting me *not* to go with you."

That was good. She wasn't sure she could plan something that big if she didn't have a buddy to go with her. She turned to her other roommate. "Shelly?"

She shook her head. "There's no way I can get away." Shelly was a manager at a nursery, and the spring and summer—Avery's least busy time of the year at work—was Shelly's busiest time. It was handy to be able to cover for each other when cleaning the apartment or cooking, but much less handy when it came to doing anything that required taking time off work.

Shelly walked to the stove and peeked into the pot, breathing in deeply the scent of the soup. "Someone needs to stay here to feed Floaty and clean his bowl and make sure the toilet doesn't spontaneously overflow." Their monthly rent split three ways was great, and so were the three bedrooms, but their apartment wasn't exactly a five-star resort. "Besides, I could never go that long without seeing my seedlings. And if I went, I wouldn't meet my financial goals. You two go. I'll hold down the fort."

They had daydreamed about actually taking Nicolas up on his offer a few times—back before she'd decided she needed better "bio" material and hadn't thought she'd ever be bold and daring enough to plan the trip—so she'd already known that Shelly's answer would be no. She was just glad her friend seemed perfectly fine with not going. Maybe she was excited to have the whole place to herself.

"We'll finish making dinner," Riley said. "Message Nicolas right now."

"I don't know." Avery picked up the spoon and stirred the simmering soup, watching the chicken, vegetables, and seasonings swirl around the pot. Why was she suddenly worried about the enormity of the trip? Her bravado from seconds ago needed to make its way back to her ASAP. She put the spoon down and turned back to her roommates. "What if he offered me his grandpa's place to be nice, never expecting me to take him up on his offer? What if it's a huge imposition for him?"

Riley folded her arms. "That's not what Nicolas is like, and you know it."

"Okay, so that's not what he's like. But he never really talked much about his grandpa when he lived with us. Maybe he's not as generous as Nicolas is. What if it causes conflict between the two of them?"

"Then Nicolas wouldn't have offered."

"What if his girlfriend wouldn't be okay with the two of us coming and him showing us around a bit? He didn't have a girlfriend back when he offered to have us come visit sometime."

"You'll never know unless you ask. The two of you were closer than he or I ever were when he lived with us, and you've kept in touch with him much more than I have over the past ten years, but"—Riley pulled her phone out of her pocket— "if you don't message him, I will."

Avery held up a hand. "No. I'll do it." It had to be her. Letting Riley wasn't a very bold or daring thing at all.

Riley looked at her expectantly.

"Well, I'm not going to do it right now with you both watching. Besides, I think I'd rather write him a note and mail it." It was going to take a lot of thought to get the wording just right, and she didn't want the pressure of having the two of them looking over her shoulder. The only trips she had planned before now were baby small. This was mammoth large.

But her life wasn't going to change as much as she wanted it to by taking small baby steps.

Shelly grabbed a spoon out of their silverware drawer,

scooped up some broth, then blew on it. "I don't know. Writing him a note kind of just sounds like a way of procrastinating the asking." She put the spoon in her mouth, then said, "Mmm. I think it needs a pinch of dill."

It wasn't like they'd been daydreaming about the trip for *that* long. Okay, she'd first had the thought back in September, but it had just been a wish back then. She hadn't started thinking about it like it might be a possibility until she was at the LBSU basketball game last Friday night, right before Brock had proposed to Summer. During the pre-game, Summer had asked Avery to picture what she would feel like after having taken such a leap.

She still remembered the feeling that had washed over her like it was just happening. She'd felt powerful. Like if she took this giant leap, she could accomplish any goal. Like it would get her in a place where she felt more confident about taking risks, instead of just taking the comfortable route on things.

She was going to keep reminding herself of that feeling until she took all the steps to get to Belgium. Because in the five months between first thinking of it in September and last Friday, the only step she'd managed to take was going along with Riley when she'd practically forced her to get her passport. She was ready to take more steps now.

"Writing him a note isn't procrastinating. It's. . . sweet. Nicolas stayed with our family the year he and I were both juniors in high school and Riley was a freshman. During my senior year, we used to mail each other handwritten notes all the time. When he gets a handwritten note from me, it'll remind him of our connection more."

"Aww, that *is* sweet," Shelly said. "Yes, do that."

They'd written each other notes a lot that year after he went back to Belgium, but in the nine years since they'd graduated high school, they hadn't been communicating nearly as much. Only a few times a year now. She needed any extra bit of connection with him that she could get.

Riley shook her head. "I still think you should just message him because it's instant. You won't have to wait."

But maybe she wasn't ready for an instant response. What if the answer he gave was a no? Going on a trip like this was still a fledgling little dream. She didn't want it stomped on yet.

Since they were both watching her, Avery pointed to the box of pasta that was on the counter. "There's the noodles for the soup." Then she went to the tiny desk that sat against the wall between the kitchen and the living room that was mostly used as a flat spot for the mail. She pulled a pad of notepaper from the drawer, waved it in the air as if it was a response to Riley's comment, and headed into her room to write the note without an audience.

The next morning, she stopped by the outgoing mail slot for her building, envelope in hand. She had rewritten the note four times before she felt like it was right. And it did feel like it was right. So why was she still standing at the slot, letter in hand, not dropping it in?

Be brave and take the leap, she told herself.

Then she dropped the letter in the slot.

———

AVERY HURRIED into her apartment when she got home from work and closed the door behind her, giving a full-body shiver from the below-freezing temperatures outside.

"Cold?" Riley asked from where she was sitting on the couch, flipping through a magazine about wedding flowers.

Avery shook off her coat and hung it on the hook. "So cold. And windy. With no sun. Any mail for me?"

"Not anything from Nicolas. Do you know if he even got your letter?"

Avery sighed. "No."

"See?" Riley said, closing her magazine and setting it on the coffee table. "This is why you use Messenger instead of snail mail. It's instantly there *and* it lets you know when he's seen it. None of this coming home every single day for three weeks, hoping you've gotten a response."

Okay, so Riley may have been right. This waiting and not knowing was killing her. "I could reach out over Messenger to see if he got it. But what if he did and things aren't going to work out, and he decided that ghosting me was a kinder response than telling me what the reason was? Then I'll just make things awkward. Besides, it's not like I can't do something else big and daring." Although she really *really* wanted to do something as big as that.

Riley studied her for a long moment like she was trying to decide how to put something delicately. But Riley never said things delicately—she just said it like it was. "Avery, I get that you like things peaceful and free of conflict and all that. And that you never want to ask for anyone's help, probably because you don't want to put them out at all."

Avery nodded.

"But if you want to be the kind of person who takes risks and takes control of your life so you can be the person you want to be before you find your dream man? Start by doing this."

She just looked at her sister for a long moment before she said, "Okay. If he hasn't responded by next week, I will message him."

Chapter Two

NICOLAS

Nicolas was in his own world as he poured the milk chocolate over the rest of the shell and the filling in the bonbon mold—the final step in the process. He'd come into the kitchens at Oma Servais long before any of the chocolatiers arrived, but as he worked, they'd all trickled in. Their chatter felt so far away, yet fueled him as he worked. He loved that they got such an early start in this department.

He'd come up with the flavors and ingredients for this one himself, but he used the techniques that his Grandma Servais had taught him before she passed away. And it was something her grandma had taught her. There was a distinct comfort in using a tradition that had been passed down for generations.

After he scraped the excess chocolate off the mold, he

stuck it in the chiller while he cleaned up his work area. He didn't have much time before he needed to be in building A, where the executive suites were located. He put away the colored cocoa butters, took his mixing bowl and kitchen utensils to the wash station, and threw away his used piping bags.

The moment the chocolates were cooled enough, he pulled them out of the chiller, excited to see the finished product, when he felt more than heard someone step up behind him. Without looking, he knew it was Jean-Pierre, the Chief of Product Development at Oma Servais. Jean-Pierre wasn't always in this building—he spent half of his day in the executive building with Nicolas. Nicolas ignored his colleague's presence, flipped the mold over, then tapped on it with the wooden mallet before lifting the mold.

"Breathtaking," Jean-Pierre said.

Nicolas smiled. He had painted a stripe of perfectly plum-colored cocoa butter in the bottom of the mold, followed by a partially crossing stripe of deep brown. Then, before the stripes had set too much, he'd lightly touched each mold with a cotton ball with gold cocoa butter on it. It fanned out the stripes just a bit and added a look of almost marbled gold across everything. With the perfectly tempered milk chocolate poured in after, it left each half-sphere bonbon looking like a shiny golden brown and plum treasure.

"I don't think we've had anyone who has mastered the ability to make a bonbon look so exquisite since you left this department when you were eighteen."

He smiled at Jean-Pierre's compliment. Ever since Nicolas had moved on to other departments at Oma Servais, he'd come here to play with new looks and tastes whenever he was feeling stressed. It helped to calm him and focus him like nothing else.

For years, though, Jean-Pierre had seemed to view Nicolas as a threat. Like he would try to take over Jean-Pierre's position if he wasn't careful. But now that the man was only months from retirement, he no longer seemed threatened by Nicolas's presence.

Nicolas grabbed a paper towel from the rack beside him, folded it in fourths, then placed one of the bonbons on it. He held it out to Jean-Pierre. "Would you like a taste?"

He practically held his breath as he watched the product developer's face while he bit into the chocolate. After creating the milk chocolate shell, Nicolas had piped in a plum filling, sprinkled on some unflavored pop rocks, then finished filling it with a chocolate hazelnut ganache with the perfect amount of cardamon and the barest hint of ginger. Then he'd sealed the bonbon with the same tempered chocolate, making the outer shell appear seamless.

Jean-Pierre made a few moaning sounds of pleasure as

he ate that Nicolas wished he hadn't heard. When the man finished his bite, he studied the rest of the bonbon in his hand, looking at the filling. "It. . ." His face appeared thoughtful like he was trying to decide how to describe it. "It gave me the distinct feeling of being at a celebration with colleagues or friends at a high-class venue. Yet at the same time, it also came with. . . nostalgia, almost. A yearning for my childhood."

Nicolas's smile spread across his face. That was exactly the range of emotions that he'd hoped the bonbons would evoke. It was one of the reasons he loved making chocolates—it wasn't just about the taste. It was about the feelings he could bring out in someone else. Almost like the flavors created a story filled with emotions.

Jean-Pierre looked at his smile. "You planned that. How?" He placed the rest of the bonbon in his mouth.

Nicolas grabbed the cloth and wiped down the stainless steel countertop. "I just pulled together tastes you would likely only enjoy the combination of with an adult palette, which made the pop rocks feel like a burst of champagne. But I also put in subtle hints of childhood with tastes reminiscent of peanut butter and jelly, so the pop rocks would also remind you of the fun of being a kid."

Jean-Pierre wiped the bit of chocolate that had melted onto his fingers with the paper towel. "Such talent. You have an innate sense of what flavors can be combined to make something truly exquisite. Would you mind if we tried these out in Servais First?"

Servais First was their flagship store, attached to the kitchens in this building. It was the one location of their hundreds of stores in Belgium alone where they tested new flavors to see if customers liked them enough to roll out nationwide or even internationally.

"Go ahead. I'll take a few of them back to A with me, but I'll leave the rest." He reached across to the shelf at the edge of the workspace to a paper he'd been scribbling on and handed it to Jean-Pierre. "Here's how I made them." And then he quickly boxed up the ones he was taking with him.

Jean-Pierre looked down at the paper, nodding as he read it. "They'd be smart to put you here when I retire." He looked back up from the paper to meet Nicolas's eyes as Nicolas took off his apron, hung it on the hook, then grabbed his suit coat from the hook next to it.

Once Nicolas slipped it on, he clapped the man on the shoulder. "You know that'll never happen. My path has been laid out for me since before either of us started working here."

The man nodded.

"Thanks for letting me come take over a workstation unannounced," Nicolas called out as he headed out of the kitchens holding three small boxes, each containing two bonbons.

"Anytime," Jean-Pierre said, which was way better than the response he used to give Nicolas back when Nicolas was a twenty-year-old who thought he knew everything and Jean-Pierre had just taken the job as Chief of Product Development.

Nicolas stepped out into the chilly morning air and headed to Building A, feeling much more ready to start his day than he'd been when he'd woken up at five. He glanced down at his watch. He should even make it into his office before nine.

Nicolas walked into the ridiculously opulent building that housed all the executive offices and conference rooms and said hello to Ines, the receptionist. He knew that his mother and his grandfather had both felt that this building showed clients and other people they met with that Oma Servais was a powerhouse, but Nicolas didn't think they needed to be quite so extravagant to accomplish that. Their product and their stores spoke for them.

As soon as he stepped into his office suite, his assistant, Finn, stood up from his desk and followed Nicolas into his office. Finn was a lean, trim man who always wore a suit and tie with the top button done up no matter how late they worked and rarely broke his ultra-professional exterior. Even his slightly curly hair was tamed and never out of place.

Nicolas's office was big enough that it still felt spacious, even with his massive desk, a conference table, and a seating area. His favorite part of the whole thing, though, was the floor-to-ceiling windows that spanned an entire wall. He would never tire of the view of the city of Brussels to his right and the woods at his left.

He set the boxes of bonbons on his desk as Finn told him about the day's schedule. It was a schedule that consisted mostly of meetings and brainstorming sessions with the public relations team, the marketing team, and the brand strategist. He'd held a lot of different positions at this company over the years, each one more challenging than the previous. Some he liked better than others. Being the Chief of Marketing was a huge challenge, but he liked it.

This was Nicolas's first position on the executive team and was the position that most closely fit with his college degree. His parents' goal wasn't that he be an expert at every position—it was just that he know the ins and outs of the company well. He liked being on the executive team because what he did made a difference. He could effect change.

"Oh," Finn said, "and your mother would like to remind you that you need a suitable date for the International Royal Chocolatier Awards reception next month."

To Nicolas's mother, "suitable" didn't mean "someone you liked spending time with and got along with well." It meant "someone who will make a good wife to a future

CEO. Someone with good family connections that will help with alliances." *Good breeding* and *good schooling* and *looked good while dressed in black tie apparel* were also a given.

He shook his head that his mother relayed this information through his assistant when she was just down the hall from him in the CEO's office. She could've just as easily summoned Nicolas to her office or shown up at his.

"And she said she didn't need to remind you that her retirement—and therefore the time when the board will be choosing who will replace her as CEO—is closing in and that your spot isn't guaranteed just because your grandfather is Chairman of the Board."

Nicolas stood a little straighter. "So, if I don't bring someone 'suitable,' I can get out of being CEO?"

He'd meant it as a joke, and he liked to think that Finn cracked a smile on the inside, even if he didn't show it on the outside.

Finn cleared his throat. "She also said to remind you that being CEO was what you were raised for and something about your lifelong plan. She said if you can't find someone appropriate, she'll line up someone for you."

Nicolas paused for a moment. "Is it Fleur?" Fleur wasn't a bad date to go with. The two of them were good friends, and she was every bit as uninterested in a relationship with him as he was with her. They might not ever be each other's first choice, but if they were single, they both would always say yes to each other if asked. It helped that they were each accepted by both sets of their parents.

"Yes. But your mother has a Plan B, too. Or I guess *Plan C* since you getting your own date is Plan A."

"Is Plan C one of the Benali sisters?"

Finn nodded.

"Gaëlle or Ophélie?"

"She said to threaten you with whichever one I thought you'd least like to take since she hopes you'll be a good son and find your own date." He paused. "Or, in her words, 'get back together with Sophie already.'"

For some reason, his mom ranked "good breeding and good connections" over "not cheating on the guy you're engaged to." Nicolas didn't.

He ran his hands over his face. "You can assure my mother that I will be responsible, as usual, and that she can count on me to find my own date. Oh, and take her a box of these when you do." He grabbed a box of the bonbons he'd made and handed them to Finn. Not as any kind of reward for the little jabs she'd managed to get in, but because he took any chance he could get to subtly remind his mother that he was good at product development. Not that it would change anything, but he still wanted the reminder there.

Finn nodded. "Will do."

"These are for you," he said as he handed another box

to Finn. Then he handed the third and last box to him. "And these are for whoever it is that you're sneaking texts to that makes you smile down at your phone." As much as Finn seemed to be hiding his texting, Nicolas knew he wasn't ready to talk about this person yet.

Finn blushed and looked down, smiling. A rare show of emotion for the stoic assistant.

"Yeah, that's the smile. Tell whoever it is that I like that they make you happy."

"Thank you. I will."

As Finn gathered his things, Nicolas picked up a letter that had been set on his desk. A glance at the top corner told him that it was from the host family he'd stayed with in America the year he'd been an exchange student. The letter looked like it had been through *a lot*. From what he could tell by inspecting the envelope, it had originally been sent to his place two addresses ago, then forwarded to his previous address where, based on the postmark, it stayed a while.

Then, whoever lived there now must've realized who he was and forwarded it to Oma Servais headquarters, where it eventually made it to his desk. There were so many postmarks and scrawled messages and fold marks and smudges on the envelope that it looked years old, even though it had only been sent three or four weeks ago.

He opened the envelope and recognized Avery's handwriting immediately. He scanned through the note quickly enough that he was able to stop Finn before he got to the door. "Hold on. Will you also check to see when my grandfather's flat here in Brussels won't be in use and get back to me with the dates?"

"Will do," Finn said before exiting Nicolas's office.

Then Nicolas sat down at his desk to fully read every word in Avery's note, a smile spread across his face the whole time.

Chapter Three

AVERY

very parked in the employee parking lot at Lake Baldwin State University, slipped the strap of her bag onto her shoulder, then pulled her hood up over her head. The second she opened her door, the wind bit into her, blowing already fallen snow against her exposed face.

During a normal year, there were several days in March in Lake Baldwin, South Dakota that were a few degrees above freezing and sunshiny, which made it feel like it was practically shorts weather. Why couldn't they get a few days like that this March instead of all the well-below-zero temperatures and windy weather?

She ducked her head to avoid most of the snow-filled wind and ran across the campus sidewalks toward the Student Center, where she worked. The faux fur on her hood obscured her view of most everything else, so she was surprised when she realized that her friend and co-worker, Pavani, was reaching for the door handle at the same time as her.

They both hurried into the building and shivered as the doors closed, blocking all the wind and allowing the warmth of the building to wash over them.

"Oh my Hello Kitty it's freezing out there!"

"You know how some people say that washing their car causes it to rain?" Pavani asked as she shook the snow off her.

Avery nodded brushing the snow off her own coat.

"I think we need to figure out what makes it sunny, and then we should all do that."

Avery laughed and then glanced at her friend as they headed down the hallway. Pavani had seemed not quite her usually happy, energetic self lately. Maybe she was feeling like Avery was. "Pavani, have you ever felt like you were exactly where you were supposed to be, but also that you were meant for bigger things?"

Pavani looked up at the ceiling, considering the question as they walked down the hallway to the chatter of the college students surrounding them. "No."

"Oh."

"But I think that's what my older brother, Rajiv, was feeling. He was living in Hillsboro, Oregon, which is where almost all of my family lives. He had a good job, but he just felt like there was something more for him, so he moved to Seattle." Pavani paused for a moment, then said, "I don't know why I'm telling you this—it's not the same situation as yours at all." She laughed and placed a hand on her forehead. "I've been feeling a little sick lately, and I swear it makes me not think straight."

That was what she'd been noticing in her friend—not sadness or another emotion, but physical illness. "Uh oh. Do you think it has anything to do with your appendix rupturing last fall?"

Pavani shook her head as they neared the Welcome Center. "It doesn't seem the same at all. I'm just feeling run down and, I don't know, kind of all-over *blah*. I'm sure I'll get past it soon. But I've kind of been feeling the opposite of the way you've been feeling lately. Like I belong somewhere else, but I love it here way too much to even let myself consider what that might mean."

Avery's eyes flew to Pavani. "You're thinking of leaving LBSU?"

"No, of course not! Like I said, I love it here too much," Pavani said as they reached the doors to the Welcome Center and came to a stop. "But what about you? What's your gut telling you? What do you feel like you *should* be doing?"

Avery glanced a dozen feet further down the hallway to the door to Admissions and shook her head. "I don't know. I haven't felt like I should leave here." Actually, the only thing she really felt like she should do was to go to Belgium. Which was crazy. It wasn't like a trip to another country was going to change her life. She wasn't going to live an unfulfilled life if she didn't go, and thinking otherwise was just nonsensical. She simply needed to broaden her horizons. Push herself to try new things.

"But you also feel like you should be doing something else?"

Avery shrugged and then hiked her bag onto her shoulder a bit better. "I'm sure the feeling will go away. Just like your illness."

Pavani gave Avery's shoulder a bump with hers. "I think if the feeling goes away, that means you've given up."

Avery laughed off her comment, but she couldn't stop replaying that sentence in her head. *I think if the feeling goes away, that means you've given up.*

"Wait," Pavani said, "this has to do with going to Belgium, right?"

"I mean, I don't know. Logically, these feelings have nothing to do with Belgium. But it also kind of feels like it all has to do with going there."

"And you know a guy from there?"

"Yeah, Nicolas. If it weren't for him offering me a place to stay, I'd never be able to afford to go there."

"And he's a good guy?"

"He's the best. He was an exchange student who

stayed with my family our junior year." She smiled as a memory hit her that would explain to Pavani the type of person Nicolas was. "Almost that entire year of school, I was dating this guy, Travis, but we broke up about four weeks before junior prom. Travis and I had planned to go together pretty much the whole time we'd been dating, so I'd already bought my dress.

"Now maybe four weeks was enough time for some people to find a new date, but that wasn't how things worked for me. Most of the girls in my school were in love with Nicolas, so he could've asked anyone. But he hadn't yet. So he asked me, knowing how much I wanted to go."

"That's so sweet!"

"That's what I thought! So we drove to prom in my beat-up Toyota Corolla. And the dance was amazing. So much more fun than if Travis and I had still been dating and had gone. And Nicolas was friends with everyone. So while we were there, he got it worked out with another group who had arrived in a limo for us to ride home with them, because he wanted me to have that experience.

"So we pulled up to my house in it, and Nicolas got out and walked me to my door—which was also his door, since he lived there, too—like a perfect gentleman. He told me again how beautiful I looked and thanked me for joining him, and then he lifted my hand and kissed it. It was the sweetest thing. The others took him back to the high school to get my car, after, and then he drove it home."

"Oh my goodness," Pavani said, putting her fingers on her chest, "I think my heart just melted a bit. Girl, go to Belgium. See your old friend again. And then go off and figure out why you've been feeling like you should go there."

When Avery got back to her desk, she set her bag down and turned on her computer before sitting down. It had been close enough to a week since she'd told Riley she would contact Nicolas. And she wasn't ready to give up.

She picked up her phone and went into the Messenger app, ready to scroll down to his name, which was probably quite a way down, since it had been a few months since she'd last messaged him.

But his name was on top. In bold. It took her brain a moment before it processed that he had sent her a message. And seven hours ago, even! How in the world had she made it to nine a.m. without checking?

She tapped on the message, holding her breath while her heart beat erratically.

The message from him started with a picture. As she squinted to see it better without tapping on it, she realized it was the note she'd sent him. But with tons of writing and postmarks on the envelope. And so many bends and crinkles that it looked like it had been through a war zone. A message from Nicolas was right below the image.

Nicolas: This took a while to find me.

Avery shook her head. Okay, so maybe Riley had been right—mailing a message hadn't been the best option. There wasn't any more to his message, though. He was seven hours ahead of her, so he was probably close to the end of his work day. She quickly typed in a response.

Avery: And it looks like it got to see quite a bit of
the world on its way.

She told herself to set the phone down. He'd sent his message so long ago—it wasn't like he was still there with his phone open, waiting for her response. He was probably busy working. Maybe he even had chocolate all over his hands.

But she didn't put her phone down. She kept holding it like it was the lifeboat and she'd just fallen overboard. It only took a few seconds before she saw the dots, indicating that he was typing.

Nicolas: It had quite the adventure. I don't want
to chance a repeat by mailing a letter back, though,
so if it's okay with you, I'll just respond here.

Before she got a chance to reply, though, he sent another message that contained one word: *WAIT*.

So she waited. Her screen darkened three times and she tapped to keep her phone screen from turning off every time. She only had to remind herself to breathe three or four times, which she thought was pretty good.

Then an image came through and she immediately tapped on it. It was a note, handwritten in the same slanted handwriting that she immediately recognized as Nicolas's.

Avery,

Thank you for your letter. I loved seeing your handwriting after all this time. I almost typed this message but realized that would be taking the easy way out, and I wanted to honor the time you spent on a note to me.

I would love to have you and Riley visit Brussels! Things are busy at work right now, so I won't be able to show you around as much as I would like to, but I'll make sure to at least get a day or two off to show you Ghent, where I live. I promise you'll love it even more than Brussels. And I'll make sure you have everything you need to enjoy your stay even when I'm not available.

*I've checked on my grandfather's flat and verified
that he won't be using it the last two weeks in
April. Would that work for you? If not, let me know
and I'll find additional dates.*

Nicolas

She let out a breathy laugh as she read. Partly out of relief that he'd finally gotten her letter and seemed so willing to have her visit. And partly because it made her soul happy to see his handwriting again after all this time. He always had the best handwriting. It looked much like his hair had when they'd been in high school—carefully crafted, but with the appearance of casual indifference, with just the right amount of uniqueness and personality. He still curved the line on his lowercase a's and d's, l's and t's, giving them a little swirl up at the end.

Her favorite parts, though, were the few places where he'd messed up and scribbled out a word, writing a small "ignore me :)" just above it. It made those 4300 miles between them seem to disappear.

She read through the letter a second time, excitement building. As soon as she got to the end again, where it said the dates his grandpa's place was available, she practically leaped out of her office chair, almost knocking it over as it rolled away, and ran to Grant's office. The middle of April was only five weeks away.

His door was open, and he looked up in alarm at her sudden appearance and the breathless look on her face. "Does the last two weeks of April work for me to go on vacation?" They'd already discussed her taking time off, just not when.

He pulled up something on his computer. "The last two weeks of April. . . So right before finals."

"Which is one of our least busy times."

He kept looking at his computer screen, slowly nodding. Then he looked back at her. "As long as Joy can cover for you that—"

Avery didn't even wait for him to finish the sentence before she stepped to the doorway of Grant's office and called across the hallway toward Joy's open office door. "Joy." Her coworker swiveled in her chair to see Avery through the glass wall of her office. "Can you cover for me the last two weeks of April so I can go to Belgium?"

Her eyebrows rose. "He said yes?"

Avery grinned.

"Yes!" Her gaze shifted to Grant. "Yes! Of course! Yes!"

Avery turned back to Grant, sucking in a huge breath that made her feel like she was floating.

He shook his head, but he had a smile on his face. "Request granted."

"Holy frijoles. I can't believe this is happening. Thank you!" she shouted as she turned and raced back to her desk. With trembling fingers, she managed to type out a message to Riley.

AVERY: Nicolas says we can stay at his grandpa's flat the last two weeks of April. Does that work?

Riley responded with a string of emojis that included clapping, smiling, laughing, cheering, sunglasses, dancing, and way more thumbs up than she had on her person. Then she texted, *Let me check with Sara.*

Sara was Riley's business partner at Under the Arch, their wedding flower shop, and the person who would have to cover both of their positions with Riley gone.

It took way too long for Riley to respond. Avery drummed her fingers on her desk, logged into her computer, drummed her fingers some more, opened her texting app to make sure she hadn't missed anything, and went into her work email on her computer before Riley responded.

RILEY: We have a massive wedding we are doing the flowers for the last week of April, but Sara and I decided it'll be fine if we just hire some temporary help. As long as she's overseeing everything, it'll work out great. I'm in!!

Avery sent Riley back her own string of happy emojis,

then responded to Nicolas to thank him profusely and let him know that those dates worked out great and that she would get their plane tickets scheduled tonight and let him know the details.

Then she leaned back in her chair in an exhausted state of happiness. She didn't know what she would find in Belgium, but now that she knew she was going, everything felt. . . *right*. She took a minute to picture the trip.

Nicolas's grandpa's flat could be the size of a closet and contain only a single cot that she and Riley would have to take turns sleeping on, using a rolled-up sweatshirt as a pillow. They could be staying in a sketchy part of the city and wouldn't be able to be outside after dark. They could get horribly lost anytime they tried to get anywhere.

It wouldn't matter. Because for the first time in months, she didn't feel like something wasn't right or that she was supposed to be doing something different. Which didn't make any sense—all she did was plan a vacation. It wasn't like a vacation could change her life.

But still, it suddenly felt like the path that she had stepped on was the path she was supposed to be on. She didn't know where that path would lead, but she was finally there, stepping on it. She could choose to stay in her comfort zone forever, or she could choose to take a leap and go bigger.

She was choosing to go bigger.

Chapter Four

NICOLAS

After walking out of work for the day, Nicolas got into his car parked under the covered parking beside Building A, pulled out his phone, and smiled as he tapped on the message from Avery.

AVERY: I am moments from leaving work early to head for the airport. Are you still planning to leave us a list of any sites you think that Riley and I should see while we are there? Or one we should start with?

NICOLAS: The list will be waiting for you at my grandfather's flat.

He'd asked Finn to make a list for him. Nicolas had

grown up in Brussels, so nothing in the city was new to him, and his growing-up years weren't exactly spent doing the most touristy things. But Finn had just moved to the city three years ago, so his perspective was much fresher. Nicolas had been tweaking the list Finn had made, adding his own suggestions and commentary. It had turned into a list he thought they'd love.

NICOLAS: Let's see. . . The first site your family took me to right after I moved in as a foreign exchange student was The South Dakota State Agricultural Heritage Museum. I will be sure to find something for you and Riley to do that is equally entertaining.

He chuckled to himself, just thinking about how Avery would react to his message. The name of the museum alone hadn't made it sound like the most exciting place to be, but he remembered being fascinated by it. He had just immersed himself into a state and a culture that was so different from the one he'd grown up in, and the museum visit had grabbed his attention and helped to pull him into that world.

Plus, it had been great to see Avery's dad, Dalton, get so excited about everything. His own father was on the terse side, so it had also been mind-blowing to see a dad so talkative and animated. Especially about farm equipment and farming techniques—things Nicolas had known nothing about.

AVERY: Hey! Don't knock the Ag Heritage Museum—it's one of the coolest things we have around here. Which means your list should contain the coolest site in Brussels.

AVERY: Besides, we also took that weekend trip to the other side of the state to see the Badlands and Mount Rushmore while you were here. That was pretty epic. And so was Falls Park in Sioux Falls.

There had been nothing about the nine months he'd spent in Lake Baldwin, South Dakota that hadn't seemed epic to him. But he had especially loved Falls Park and Mount Rushmore.

NICOLAS: True. I'll make sure to include something equally epic. Like *Manneken Pis*.

AVERY: That sounds pretty impressive, and like it's an important part of Brussels.

NICOLAS: It totally is.

AVERY: Nice try. The Manneken Pis is a two-foot-high statue of a little boy peeing.

NICOLAS: You knew that already, huh?

AVERY: My parents have been texting Riley and me facts they Googled about Belgium every single day for the past few weeks. You'd be surprised how much random knowledge I have now.

NICOLAS: But the statue IS an important part of Brussels. He's beloved here, and there are even costumes that they put on him several times a year.

AVERY: According to my parents, he has 1046 costumes, and there's even a museum displaying them.

NICOLAS: That is impressive knowledge. Okay, I will make sure that the list I leave for you is worthy of a couple of my favorite people who have much random knowledge.

AVERY: You're the best.

AVERY: Oh! I've got to run. There was an issue with the batch of application fees I just ran and

I've got five minutes to fix it before I have to leave
all this to Joy. Catch you in Brussels!

He smiled as he started his car and backed out of his
parking space. He wished he would have more time to spend
with Avery while she was visiting, but it was kind of a crazy
time at work, especially with the IRC Awards coming up.
Chatting with Avery always lifted him and left him happy and
feeling more fortified to deal with all he needed to deal with.

And since he was heading through the city and to the
other side of Brussels—the side opposite from the direction
of his apartment in Ghent—for his weekly dinner at his
parents' house, being fortified was very much what he
needed right now.

He'd always wondered what a relationship with Avery
would be like. He'd been pulled to her from his very first
day in South Dakota. But he'd known even back as an
almost seventeen-year-old that it would never work. They
came from two worlds that were so vastly different that
they couldn't coexist.

And he wouldn't want to pull Avery from her world.
He really liked that world. So maybe it was a good thing
that she and Riley were coming at such a busy time for
him—it would be a lot easier for him to keep from wanting
a relationship with her if he didn't see her much.

Nicolas's phone rang, and the screen on his dashboard

showed that it was his brother, Maxim. He pressed to answer the call, and as soon as Nicolas said hello, Maxim said, "It's a girl!"

"Ah, congratulations! And everything looked good?"

"Yep. The ultrasound tech said she's as perfect and healthy as could be. And Léa's due date didn't change much at all—it's still the end of August."

"That's great news, brother. The two of you are going to make the best parents. I'm thrilled for you both. And for me—I can't wait to be an uncle."

"It's the greatest feeling, isn't it?" Maxim let out a breath that just sounded. . . happy. Maxim's life hadn't been easy. Nicolas was glad that it had taken him to this place where he was married to someone perfectly suited to him and that they were expecting their first child.

"Are you going to let our parents know they're going to be grandparents?" The moment the words were out of Nicolas's mouth, he knew he shouldn't have said them. The elated feeling they'd been sharing immediately nosedived.

"Tell me this. Are you allowed to bring up my name in conversation yet?"

He hadn't tried recently, but he still knew the answer. "No."

After a brief pause, Maxim said, "I wasn't just disowned—I was erased from their lives."

"But they'll have a grandchild. Maybe that'll make things change."

"Maybe at some point, Léa and I will tell them. When both us and they are ready. I can't see it being anytime soon."

Nicolas and Maxim had always been close. When Nicolas was thirteen and Maxim was eighteen—just graduating from secondary school—Maxim had announced that he had somehow managed to switch to the Vocational Secondary Education track for his last two years of school and had been studying carpentry. It was still baffling to Nicolas that he'd managed to keep something so massive from their parents.

But what sent their parents over the edge was the fact that Maxim had also announced that he wasn't going to continue with the optional extra specialization year, which would leave him with a diploma that wouldn't allow him to pursue higher education.

Nicolas and Maxim had stayed close even through the hard days that followed as their parents cut Maxim off completely and dropped all the responsibility of running the family business on Nicolas.

Part of the fallout of Maxim's choices meant that Nicolas's parents started watching Nicolas's education like a hawk, controlling everything.

Well, everything except the part where he went to South Dakota. They'd decided that he needed a base in international business before heading off to university and planned to send him to New York for his third cycle—his junior year in American high school. They didn't find out that Nicolas had switched the location from New York to a school smack in the middle of farm country until it was too late. It had been his one glorious rebellion.

A rebellion he'd been even more glad that he made all over again over the past five weeks since he and Avery had started messaging so frequently. At the realization of exactly how glad he was for it, he knew how hard he was going to have to work at being careful around her. It seemed like she had a direct line to his heart, so he knew he was in more than a little trouble.

Chapter Five

AVERY

"Oof, that's a heavy one," Avery's dad, Dalton, said as he hefted her suitcase into the trunk of their car. Then he picked up Riley's suitcase. "This one, too."

"We have no idea how big Nicolas's grandpa's flat is." Avery walked around to the back driver's side door. "It's not his home—it's just a place where his grandpa stays maybe one week a month. It might be just a teeny tiny room, so Riley and I decided we better pack everything we need into one carry-on suitcase so it won't take up much space."

He shifted the suitcases in the trunk, pushed the trunk closed, then rubbed his hands together to brush off the dirt that had gotten on his hands from the dusty car. "Did you have to stand on each other's suitcases to hold everything down while you zipped them up?"

"Don't be silly, Dad," Riley said as she opened her car door. "We sat on them."

Once they were all in the car and their dad was starting the engine, their mom, Jody, said, "Did you pack your underthings at the very bottom? I'd hate to see either of you getting your luggage flagged by airport security, and when they unzip it, have your unmentionables go flying every which way."

"I think our 'unmentionables' are safe, Mom," Riley said.

They headed down I-29, in the slow lane, of course, passing by all the flat, open farmland that was finally free of snow and beginning to have small green plants poking up through the soil everywhere.

Getting to the point of having everything planned and heading toward the airport had felt like such a monumental task, and months ago, Avery had felt like it was impossible. But here they were, on their way. The excitement of what lay ahead of them fluttered around in her chest like wild butterflies. She hadn't stopped smiling in days.

Her dad motioned to a field on their right. "It looks like we got our first set of acres planted before the Coulters. Our oats are already popping up."

"Oh, Dalton," her mom said, reaching out to put a hand on his thigh. "You don't know that this field isn't their second set of acres."

"Maybe. But I'm going to live off the high of having two planted and two ready to go. It's a thing of beauty, girls," he said, glancing at them in the rearview mirror. "I can't wait for you to see it all when you get back. I can feel it in my bones that we are going to have the perfect amount of cool weather, which is going to give us nice, heavy oats."

"They don't want to hear about oats," Avery's mom said. "They're about to head out of the country for the first time. Oh, I'm just so excited and nervous for you! You girls are so much braver than I."

"Speaking of which," her dad said, "I hear they have the best mussels and frites in Belgium. They're practically famous for it. Frites are fries, just so you know. Now, I couldn't tell you what mussels are, but based on the pictures, I think they're seafood. Like a clam. And I don't know if you're supposed to eat the fries with the mussels or if they are two separate things, but you should try them and let us know."

"I'll put it on the list," Avery said. But the only thing she could currently think of that was on her list was seeing Nicolas. They had sent so many messages back and forth over the past five weeks as she prepared for this trip that he'd started taking up a bigger and bigger spot in her thoughts, which was very problematic. She was very committed to her *break from dating* plan. This trip was only about broadening her horizons and gaining new experiences. That was it.

Her mom turned in her seat a bit toward Avery and Riley. "Riley, you're okay leaving and missing that extravagant wedding coming up? It's the biggest one Under the Arch has ever done, right?"

"Yes, because Sara and I still planned everything together and I got to do all the ordering and prep work. We've hired some temp help already, and Sara said if she makes it through everything she'll emerge from the other end with superpowers, so she's excited about that. It would be great to be there for all of it, but not better than going to Belgium!"

Just hearing the word "Belgium" made Avery's stomach and heart get all fluttery. Nicolas was just so much fun to talk to, which made her feel like she was kind of falling for him, which led to her having to stop those feelings in their tracks repeatedly. She couldn't be pining over a man who wasn't available. And even if, by some miracle, he was available, they still had not only more than half the United States between them, but also an entire ocean.

She just needed to stop thinking of him. This trip was about going to Belgium, not about going to see Nicolas.

"Oh, Nicolas was such a sweet kid, wasn't he?" her mom said.

Yeah, that wasn't helping Avery to stop thinking of him.

"Remember how he was in the chore rotation just like you two were? Half of the time when I came in from the farm, the two of you hadn't finished your chores, but Nicolas always had his done."

Riley laughed. "Yep, always making us look bad."

"I remember when he first moved in with us," her mom continued, "I assigned him to clean the main bathroom that week, and he asked me to show him exactly how I would like it cleaned. So thoughtful. And he was so attentive the entire time I was showing him. He just made you feel good about yourself, didn't he? Avery, you and he always got along so well. You should see if there's anything between the two of you while you're there."

"Mom!" Avery said, really needing her to stop singing Nicolas's praises. "He has a girlfriend. It's been a long while since he's told me, but if I'm remembering correctly, he's also engaged to her." Which meant that she probably shouldn't have been messaging him as much as she had been. Sure, she always made sure to keep things in the friend zone, but he was so easy to talk to that it was sometimes hard to remember that he was taken.

"A long while, huh?" her dad asked. "Are you *sure* he still has a girlfriend?"

"We've chatted a bunch, and he's never mentioned them breaking up, so yeah. I'm sure.

Even if he broke up with her and forgot to tell me, I'm not going to Belgium to find a man."

"That's right," her dad said as he glanced to his left at someone passing him. "There are plenty of available men right here in South Dakota. So, Jody, don't be trying to get our little girl married off to someone so far away."

"You're right, you're right." Her mom said, then turned to Riley and whispered loudly, "Riley, I'm assigning you to find out Nicolas's relationship status and report back."

"Look how fast that guy is going!" her dad said as he held a hand out in the direction of the Honda Accord passing him in the left lane. "I bet he's going eighty miles per hour!"

"Dad," Riley said, "the speed limit on this road is eighty miles per hour."

"The speed *limit*. As in 'for emergencies.' Forty is the speed for non-emergencies. Crazy driver. Avery, you can find a guy right here at home, right?"

Avery rubbed her forehead and stared out the side window, willing the scenery to go by faster than it was so they would get to the airport more quickly. Her dad was more used to driving a combine than he was a car, which had a max road speed of somewhere around 17 miles per hour, so his "uncomfortably fast" highway speed was considerably slower than the other cars on the road. She was used to it, but with the way the conversation was going, all of her was wishing for more speed.

She did want to find a partner in life who was right for her and she right for them. But not until she figured out her life and career and which direction she wanted to head.

When they finally got to the airport, her dad helped them to get their luggage out of the trunk, then her mom hugged her, squeezing tight and not letting go for a long time. Then she pulled back, keeping her hands on Avery's shoulders. "Have a safe flight, okay? Call us often and let us know how you are. Especially call us to let us know you've arrived safely, you hear?"

"I will, Mom."

Then their mom hugged Riley and their dad put an arm over Avery's shoulder, giving her a side hug. "Stay away from sketchy-looking alleyways while you're there."

She nodded.

"And any food establishments that look like they might not always obey safety regulations."

She laughed. "We will."

After quite a few more safety suggestions from her dad and quite a bit of "did you remember to pack" from her mom, they gave them both a second round of hugs before her parents got back into their car, waving as they drove off. Her mom even turned in her seat to keep waving until they were out of sight. Then Avery walked with Riley into the Sioux Falls Regional Airport and on to their adventure that would hopefully be as life-changing—and not in a bad way—as Avery dreamed it would be.

Chapter Six

NICOLAS

*N*icolas pulled into the circular drive in front of his parents' estate and strolled up to the door. He normally just walked in, but Philippe seemed to always be watching for him and made sure he had the front door open before Nicolas could even reach for the knob.

"Welcome, sir," Philippe said, opening the door wide then closing it behind Nicolas.

"Hey, Philippe," Nicolas said as the man took his coat. "How is that granddaughter of yours?"

Philippe smiled widely. "She was just elected president of her primary school."

"Oh, right on! Tell her I said congratulations."

"I will." He held his arm out in the direction of the

hallway just past the grand staircase. "Your parents are waiting for you in the sitting room."

Nicolas said hello to the maid, Amandine, on his way to the sitting room, where his parents each had a drink in hand and were discussing some issue in the legal department at Oma Servais that Nicolas hoped they wouldn't keep talking about. His father may be a brilliant lawyer, but he hadn't passed any of those genes onto Nicolas.

His mother set her drink down as she stood to greet him. "You're late," she said as she put a hand on each of his shoulders and pretended to kiss him on each cheek. It wasn't exactly a hug, but it was the closest he got from his mother. "Grégoire has had the meal ready for several minutes now."

Yeah, he hadn't planned to sit in his car messaging Avery for so long after work before heading here, and it honestly hadn't even occurred to him that it might make him late.

"Since you don't have cocktails with us here anyway," his father said, "let's head into dinner. It smells delicious."

That sounded almost like an acceptance on his father's part about Nicolas's unwillingness to drink. Family dinners tended to simulate traversing a minefield, and he needed a clear head for it.

They were only a couple of minutes into eating the amuse-bouche—a tomato soup that Nicolas always loved—

when his mother said, "We'd like to talk to you about something."

Of course, they did. It was the real reason they had these "family" dinners—to tell him what he should be doing but wasn't. Maneuvering around Mine Number One commenced.

"You're already twenty-seven," his mother said. "If you want to be able to have your first child by age thirty, you need to get serious about dating and not just date frivolously."

Nicolas had dated Sophie for a year and a half and they had been engaged to be married not long ago. And that hadn't even been his first serious relationship. It wasn't like he'd gone his whole life only dating *frivolously*. "Mother, it's only been five months since Sophie and I broke up. I haven't found anyone since that I want to date more seriously."

Although Avery popped into his head the moment he said that, he quickly forced the thought away—dreaming about impossibilities wasn't going to help him get through this conversation.

"But how hard have you been trying?" she asked.

"You're right. I should get on a dating app for the 'Rich and Socially Suitable.'"

His dad's lips quirked up ever so slightly, and he picked up his napkin and dabbed at his mouth to hide it. His mom's lips, though, hardened into even more straight of a line. She leaned slightly to the left as Grégoire took her bowl of soup and replaced it with an asparagus salad.

"Maybe if you can't find someone new," she said, "you should try again with Sophie. She has such a great family."

And there was Mine Number Two. "Mother, things will never work out between us again." He looked up at Grégoire as he took his bowl and replaced it with the salad, and said "Thank you."

"I just think you're being flippant about this whole thing. Marriage is serious business. Family is important."

"Like Maxim is?" Okay, so it probably hadn't been a smart comment to say if he was looking to keep the peace. Nor was it the most effective moment to test their reaction at hearing his brother's name if Nicolas's goal was to help heal the chasm between them, but he couldn't resist the opportunity to point out the hypocrisy in his mother's words. Even if it did mean that he brought Mine Number Three on himself.

The look on her face was immediate and resembled the look she might have if Grégoire had brought out a steaming pile of rotting rubbish instead of their actual dinner. Maxim had been right—they weren't ready for any kind of reconciling.

It also served as a reminder that if Nicolas didn't do what they wanted, he'd no longer be considered part of the family. As if he'd ever forgotten.

Because his mother always needed to control the

conversation and she most definitely didn't want to talk about Maxim, she steered it right back where she wanted it to be. "You have a date to the International Royal Chocolatier Awards reception, right?"

"Don't worry. I have a date."

She gave him a stare as if she could see right into his mind. He responded by spearing a vinaigrette-covered asparagus with his fork and popping it into his mouth.

"You don't have a date, do you?"

He swallowed his bite. "Mother, you can always count on me."

Maxim's biggest fear was being trapped doing something he didn't want to do. Nicolas had that same fear, too, but it definitely wasn't his top fear. His top fear was losing his support system. His family was dysfunctional, sure, but he still loved and needed them. The only company he'd ever worked for since he was a kid was Oma Servais, so much of his support system was there. Many of his extended family members worked there, too.

So everything was intertwined. He couldn't do what his brother did and walk away from all of that. He couldn't lose that much support.

His mother was still giving him that searching stare. Then she turned her focus back to her plate. As she held an asparagus spear perfectly in place with her fork, a knife in her other hand, she sliced through it with tightly controlled motions. "I want a folder on the person you're bringing on my desk by Friday, or I will be finding you a suitable date."

And there was Mine Number Four. "You're going to vet my date?"

"That's how important this is. You're never really going to be good at being the CEO of Oma Servais if you don't have a good spouse supporting you. I wouldn't be nearly as good at it if I didn't have the support of your father."

And then his dad added, almost like they'd choreographed it, "And I wouldn't be as good at my job if I didn't have your mother supporting me."

It was true. They did support each other well in their jobs. It just seemed like that was what their marriage was based on—supporting each other in their careers, not supporting each other as a whole person. That wasn't the kind of marriage he wanted for himself.

He endured the lectures and questioning of his life choices through the duck with Bordelaise sauce and spring vegetables, and then the apple tarte Tatin that Grégoire brought out once they'd finished, but only because he thought about Avery and their conversations anytime he came across another mine in the minefield.

By the time he got back to his apartment in Ghent, it was nearly eleven and he was exhausted. But it felt good walking into his own home. His apartment was nice and big but not extravagant. There were no cooks or maids or assistants anywhere because there never were.

He walked into his bedroom, loosening his tie, taking off his jacket, and smiling at his messy bed. That always made him smile. When he was a kid, he had a responsibility to make his bed before he went to school in the mornings. But even if he didn't, it was still made by the time he got home from school with a precision that only maids could do. And when he did make it before going to school, it was straighter than he'd made it by the time he got home.

Part of his desire to never make his bed as an adult might've been a bit of rebellion, just knowing it would bother his mother if she ever saw it. But the bigger part was that he liked the reminder that if he made a mess, it wasn't going to get cleaned up for him. He was responsible for his choices, and what he did mattered. He might keep every other bit of his apartment clean, but he would always keep his bed a mess.

He went to his closet and hung up his suit coat and tie, kicked off his shoes, unbuttoned a few buttons on his shirt, then pulled his phone out of his pocket and plopped onto his bed. Avery was an old friend. *Just* an old friend, he reminded himself. Nothing more.

Could he send her a goodnight text? Old friends did things like that, right? Maybe? It was only four p.m. for her, so it wouldn't be a goodnight text at all. More of a "checking how your travel is going" text. He was sure friends did that.

So he opened the Messenger app and typed in *I hope your trip to the airport and your flight have been uneventful in the best way. I just survived dinner with my parents which, let me assure you, is an impressive feat. I'll chat with you tomorrow.* Then, before he let himself think about it and analyze it, he tapped send.

He waited, sprawled on his bed, propped up on one elbow until her response came in.

AVERY: Congratulations! Consider me sufficiently impressed by your impressive feat. Our first flight —just an hour-long—was great. We are currently living our best lives during our layover in the St. Paul airport. Goodnight. Sleep well.

She had sent him a goodnight message.

"Friends do that," he said out loud in an effort to convince himself. *That's exactly what old friends do.*

Chapter Seven

AVERY

Avery and Riley took an hour-long flight from Sioux Falls, South Dakota to St. Paul, Minnesota, switched planes during their one-hour layover, then flew two and a half hours to New York. They wandered around JFK airport for their three-hour layover that was delayed and turned into a five-and-a-half-hour layover, then made it through their almost eight-hour flight to Brussels.

By the time they waited in their back-row seats until all 198 other passengers deplaned before them, Avery was exhausted. But strangely, not in an "I need to crash onto whatever cot is in Nicolas's grandpa's flat" way—the thrill of excitement that ran through her at being in Belgium after dreaming about it for so long was way too potent for sleeping.

Besides, with the seven-hour time difference and the long flight, it was only four-thirty p.m. And Avery's nervousness and excitement had been building with every minute of their travel. Landing at the airport made it all feel so real. As she stepped off the plane, she wondered what it had been like for Nicolas when he'd stepped back into this airport after living with her family for nine months.

Their flight had come in a few minutes earlier than the new, delayed arrival time that they'd given them back at the JFK airport, so she and Riley meandered into interesting-looking shops as they made their way toward baggage claim, pulling their wheeled carry-on suitcases behind them. She knew that the languages spoken in Belgium were primarily Dutch and French and that they'd be in the part of the country where they mostly spoke Dutch. Thankfully, most of the people working in the shops also spoke English—something very common in Belgium. But just hearing that English with a Dutch accent was magical. It reminded her of Nicolas.

As they walked out of a shop full of sunglasses and watches, Avery gasped and grabbed Riley's arm. "Oma Servais! That's Nicolas's family's business!"

They went into the chocolate shop and looked around at all the shelves and cases filled with the most beautiful chocolates she'd ever seen. There were so many colors and shapes, and the scent was intoxicating.

The person behind the counter walked over to them and said in highly accented but perfect English, "How may I assist you?"

Avery couldn't help the grin that spread across her face. "Our friend's family owns this business. It's so cool they have one right here in the airport." She'd known that his parents had a little shop that they ran not far from their home, and she had somehow always pictured their business as that single shop. How cool that they had expanded to the airport of all places?

The shop owner, not looking the least bit excited or impressed by their revelation, just raised an eyebrow. "So can I box anything up for you?"

Riley nodded. "How about a small box with a variety. Maybe some of your favorites?"

After they paid with the Euros that she'd exchanged back home, Avery walked out of the shop, her suitcase handle in one hand and the box of chocolates in the other. "They're just so pretty! When Nicolas lived with us and said his parents owned a chocolate shop, did you imagine them being this pretty?"

"Nope," Riley said as she licked chocolate from her finger. "Or this delicious. Why haven't we been asking him to ship us a box every week since he moved back?"

When they went down the escalator to baggage claim, Avery glanced around for someone who seemed like he or she might be looking for them. Nicolas had said not to worry about getting transportation from the airport to his grandpa's flat—he'd have someone there to pick them up. Somehow, she hadn't thought to ask what his friend looked like.

She was just pulling out her phone to send him a message when Riley grabbed her arm and nodded toward a man who was probably in his fifties, wearing a dark gray suit with shiny shoes and hat, holding a sign that read *Avery and Riley Parks*. "Nicolas sent a driver for us?"

Avery shrugged and walked toward the man. "I guess?"

When they reached him, Avery introduced herself and Riley.

The man smiled broadly, which made his round cheeks appear even more round. He tipped his head. "I am Jacques Dubois, at your service. I will be driving you to Master Servais's flat."

Avery glanced at Riley, and Riley mouthed *Master?*

Jacques gave a nod toward the luggage carousels. "Shall we pick up your luggage?"

"Oh, we already have it," Avery said, lifting the handle of her rolling carry-on just a bit.

The man's eyebrow quirked up slightly, but Avery couldn't tell if it was because he was impressed that they'd managed to squish everything they'd need into a single suitcase each, or if he thought they must have arrived super unprepared. And suddenly she wondered if she was super unprepared.

Jacques led them to his car and loaded their suitcases into the trunk. She looked around at the other cars waiting. She'd never been good at recognizing the makes and models of cars, but she was surprised to see that most of the cars within sight were very similar to the ones she saw back home. And she was surprised that they drove on the right side of the road.

As Avery slid into the backseat, she checked out the spacious area, running her fingers along the soft leather of the seats. It wasn't exactly a limo, but it sure had the feel of the one she'd been in with Nicolas the night of Junior prom.

As Jacques got into the car and pulled away from the curb, he said, "Nicolas wishes to apologize for not being able to pick you up but gives the warmest welcome to our country. He instructed me to take you to his grandfather's flat unless there are any stops you would like me to make along the way."

Avery opened her mouth to say that going straight to where they would be staying would be great, but before she got any words out, Riley put a hand on her arm and said, "Maybe it would be good to have Jacques take us to a grocery store in case there isn't one close. We don't want to be loaded down with bags and walking for blocks."

That was a good point.

"If I could interrupt," Jacques said, "Nicolas has already taken care of that for you. There will be food waiting for you at the flat."

"Wow, that's so thoughtful!" And so unexpected. She definitely wasn't used to people doing things for her like that. She could just picture Nicolas at the grocery store, trying to find things he remembered her liking from when they were teens, and it made her smile. The mental image Avery had of the closet-sized room with the single cot suddenly expanded in her mind to include some shelves for a few packaged food items. Who knew? Maybe it was even as big as a hotel room and had a mini-fridge and a microwave.

As they drove through the streets of Brussels, Avery soaked in as much of the surroundings as she could take in. As they neared the center of the city, the buildings were a mix of steel and glass, stone, and concrete, mostly in shades of gray and brown. The buildings rose from very close to the street, too, making it feel almost like they were driving down a tunnel. Then the streets widened more, and trees lined a big section of it. With as much as driving rules seemed to be relatively the same as back home, the street signs weren't so familiar.

There was such a mix of new and old buildings. *Very* old buildings, sometimes. Some were five, six, maybe even eight hundred years old. The oldest building in Lake Baldwin was probably the city center, and it was maybe

100 years old. The oldest in the entire state probably wasn't much more than 150 years old. This city felt like it had been around for ages. It was as though the whole place buzzed with a vast history that she struggled to comprehend.

It only took about twenty minutes to drive from the airport to the apartment building downtown that held the flat they'd be staying in. The building was sleek and curvy on the top floor, leaving room for a large balcony and making it stand out from all the buildings around it. Jacques turned down a narrow cobblestone road and dipped into an underground parking garage. On the first floor underground, he pulled into a numbered parking stall, then got out of the car and immediately opened their door for them before getting their luggage out of the trunk.

He led them to an elevator and pressed the button for the lobby. It only took a moment before the doors opened. "We don't need to get out here, but this is the lobby, in case you want to go exploring the city on foot or shop in the boutiques on the street level later. You would head right out those doors."

Jacques pulled a key card from his pocket and scanned it on a panel in the elevator, entered a code on the keypad, then pressed the button for the ninth floor, which was the top floor in the building. "You'll need a key card and password for the elevator to take you to the ninth floor—I have one waiting for each of you in your room."

Riley leaned in close to Avery and whispered, "Something tells me we aren't going to be staying in a closet-sized room."

Avery's eyes were still wide, taking everything in. The elevator alone was bigger and way more luxurious than the room she'd pictured them staying in.

When the elevator doors opened, it wasn't to a hallway —it was to an apartment. She took one step out of the elevator then saw that there were two people in there already, along with the smell of a delicious meal, so she took a step back, bumping into Jacques. He took a step back, too, and she turned to him and whispered, "Are we on the wrong floor? Or are other people staying in the same flat as us?" She hadn't mentally prepared for that.

He chuckled and stepped around her, a rolling suitcase in each hand. He stood them up to the side of the elevator, then held an arm out, welcoming the girls into the space with an amused smile. "They're the staff. I'll introduce you."

"Staff?"

He chuckled quietly before stopping himself. "To serve you."

"Serve us?" Avery knew she was just parroting everything Jacques said, but she was so baffled by not only the two women standing there, smiling and looking ready to greet them but by every single thing in the flat. She struggled to process it all. Was Nicolas's grandfather as wealthy as Avery's first impression of the scene suggested? She and Riley both took a few tentative steps into the living area as the two women in the apartment approached, stopping six feet in front of them.

"This is Delphine," he said, and a woman with light hair and high cheekbones gave a nod. "She's the chef and will be preparing all the meals you choose to eat here in the flat."

Someone was going to cook for them? As baffled as she was, she still managed to step forward and shake the woman's hand. She didn't know if that was the custom in Brussels, but Delphine didn't seem surprised by the gesture. Riley shook her hand, too.

"And this is the maid, Rania." He gestured to a woman who was almost as tall and every bit as stately, with olive skin and beautiful brown eyes, her loose curls pulled into a ponytail.

Rania held out her hand and said, "If you need anything laundered or cleaned or help with anything, please let me know." She spoke perfect English, but with a slight accent—Arabic, if Avery had to guess. Avery and Riley both shook Rania's as well, then the woman said, "I'll take care of these for you," and wheeled both of their suitcases away and down a hall to their left.

"And of course, myself," Jacques said. "I am happy to drive you anywhere you'd like, acquire tickets or reservations, suggest places to see, or anything else you might need. But, of course, Nicolas has left you a list of suggestions as well, and that's right over on the coffee table."

Avery glanced the direction he motioned, to where a seating area was inset one step below everything else, filled with pale golden couches and seats that looked rather comfy, positioned on a fluffy rug, all of it and the surrounding decorations in whites, golds, and tans. She took in the huge kitchen and dining area, then turned to Riley and jokingly said, "It seems we've been mistaken for celebrities again."

Riley lifted a shoulder in a shrug. "It happens."

Nicolas would've known that she and Riley wouldn't need a staff, so he wouldn't have set this up. Were these people simply the caretakers of the flat? And if so, how had Nicolas failed to mention that his grandfather was so wealthy?

"Seriously, though," Avery said, "It's just me and Riley. We aren't anyone special—we don't need to be served."

Jacques leaned in and put a cupped hand beside his mouth like he was telling them a great secret. "In my experience, everyone is special enough to be cared for by others."

"But—"

"We are happy to serve."

Riley's eyebrow rose in challenge. Truthfully, Avery felt the same.

"Master Servais only stays here one week a month. Delphine, Rania, and I enjoy the rare occasion when we get to serve guests."

"For real?" Riley asked.

"For real."

Riley grinned at Avery. Avery was just a bit uncomfortable with it, though. She always felt like she should be the one helping, not the one being helped. They hadn't expected anything beyond a small, possibly sketchy room to stay in. Being doted on by strangers in an unfamiliar city when they wouldn't be seeing the one person they knew very often was too much.

"Now, let me show you around while Delphine and Rania unpack your luggage."

Avery stepped forward, about to tell him no, that they could unpack themselves and that she wasn't entirely sure she was okay with someone else going through her stuff, but then it hit her that she'd never be in a situation where someone else would unpack her stuff while she toured a luxurious penthouse ever again. So why not just go with it?

Jacques showed them around the spacious living area, the kitchen and dining areas, and took them out onto the expansive curving balcony that they'd seen as they neared the building, which had the most incredible view of the city. Their building wasn't the tallest around, but it was still at a height that allowed them to see so much. Energy and excitement from the buzz of the city filled her as she gazed upon the city. It was so different from everything she knew.

"Jacques," she asked, "what's the population of Brussels?"

"About two million, Ms. Parks."

Avery pulled her phone out of her pocket, held down the side button, and asked, "What's the population of the state of South Dakota?"

It wasn't even a million. Her entire state had fewer than half the people this one city had.

Then a thought suddenly hit her. She'd had a picture in her head of what Nicolas's humble home was like for the past decade. Was it anything close to correct? It could be. It could be that it was exactly like she thought it was back when they were teens and she spent every day with him. His grandpa was clearly rather wealthy, but his parents might not be.

Or she could be very wrong and this place was what he considered normal. And if that was the case, what did he think of her hometown and the house she grew up in?

Once they were back inside, Jacques pointed to the right and said, "The staff quarters are down that way if you ever need us and we aren't in the main area. Let me show you to your rooms." He led them down a hallway to the left and stopped in front of an open door. "Riley, this will be your room for the duration of your stay."

Riley squealed and raced inside, and Jacques continued with Avery further down the hall. He stopped in front of the second doorway as both Delphine and Rania exited the room. "It's all set up for you," Rania said, and then they headed back toward the main living areas.

"Master Servais's personal quarters are those rooms further down the hallway," Jacques said as he motioned at a couple of doors. "I'll ask that you don't disturb his area. For now, I'll leave you both here to get settled and relax from your trip. Dinner should be ready in about twenty minutes."

Avery barely had time to marvel at the room that was at least twice as big as the bedroom she and Riley had shared growing up before Riley came running in and headed straight for a door that was open at the side of her room. Then she came back out. "We both have our own bathrooms and there are jetted tubs big enough to swim in. And look!" She motioned to the outer wall that was made entirely of windows, showing off the city. "We've got our own doors to the balcony!"

This was so much more than she had ever even dreamed of. She touched the silky cream-colored fabric of the bedding. "And it's all so beautiful." Her parents were practical people. She never went without while growing up, but she'd still never experienced things like this. All of her bedding, curtains, clothes, and everything was meant to be tough. To last through as many washings as needed. Even now, as an adult, Avery still kept things practical.

This room was anything but that. It was professionally decorated and everything from the gigantic four-poster bed to the side tables, dresser, padded chairs was either silky, ornate, or carved, and all of it was smooth. And even though she still had her shoes on, she could tell that the carpet was just as luxurious.

"And check this out," Riley said, opening the door to Avery's closet and motioning to all her neatly-hung clothes like she was showing off the prize in a game show. "I don't think I've ever hung my clothes up while on vacation. Isn't this the best?"

It was all so overwhelming. But she had to admit, she loved it. If Nicolas had asked her if she wanted all of this, she never would've said yes. But just having it dropped in her lap felt like a gift. Like a warm bubble bath at the end of a really hard week, only so much better.

"I'm going to FaceTime Mom and Dad to let them know we made it safely before Dad has to put his researching Belgium skills to work finding out how to report missing persons in another country."

As Riley talked with their parents, showing them all around the room and taking them out on the balcony, Avery looked around the room more. Everything was just so nice. And Delphine and Rania had put every single thing from her suitcase exactly where she would've put it if she had unpacked herself. She was a little afraid to touch anything, which she told herself was ridiculous. It had been a very long time since she'd been a farm girl with dirt under her fingernails. So she reached out and ran her fingers down the toffee-colored fabric of the curtains.

Yep. Every bit as soft as she had imagined.

There was just something about all of it that made her feel uncomfortable, and she tried to put her finger on why. It wasn't that it felt wrong, exactly. It just felt. . . weird. She was always the one who took care of others—never the one who got taken care of. Even if it meant that she often got more work piled on her than she could reasonably do.

But she never asked others for help. Ever.

So having a staff that was dedicated to helping her was strange. And new. And so luxurious. Did people manage to experience this without feeling guilty that they were the one being helped instead of the one helping? She wasn't sure she'd ever be able to. Why didn't Nicolas just keep this trip simple?

She told herself that one of the reasons why she'd decided to take a trip was to get more comfortable with stepping out of her comfort zone. Every new experience helped, and this was definitely something new.

When Riley came back into the room, Avery joined her at the phone, making sure her face was in the frame, smiling at her parents' faces.

"Avery," her mom said, "did you expect any of this? I don't remember Nicolas saying anything about having a grandpa who was loaded. Do you know what he does for a living?"

Avery shook her head. "I didn't expect it. Nicolas never really mentioned what his grandpa did—I assume he doesn't have anything to do with their chocolate shop, or he probably would have talked about him." She stepped away from Riley's phone when hers pinged, and she pulled it out of her pocket as Riley finished up the video call with her parents. It was a message from Nicolas.

NICOLAS: I got word that you both made it safely, even if it was a few hours later than you had planned. My 2:00 meeting tomorrow got canceled, so I figured it was a sign to blow off everything and canceled the rest of the afternoon. Can I come to get you and Riley around two-thirty and show you the city? I'm free until about seven.

Avery smiled down at the message before she typed her response. It had been a long time since she'd last seen her friend, and she was excited that she was going to get to see him again so quickly into their trip.

AVERY: I would love that! And thank you again for lining everything up for us here. Riley is eating it all up. But I have to say that you made this particular farm girl rather uncomfortable with all the pampering.

NICOLAS: You deserve nothing but the best.

Then he sent a grinning emoji. Avery shook her head. It was a good thing he'd always been such a sweet boy, or she might have been annoyed that he did so much for them without asking if it was okay. But he had worked with others so that he could take her home from junior prom in a limousine instead of her beat-up Corolla—she probably should've expected nothing less from this trip than him working with someone else to give her an amazing place to stay.

AVERY: I certainly didn't expect you to go all out for us, and I want you to know that we appreciate it.

As Avery put her phone back into her pocket, there was a lightness in her chest and a fluttering in her stomach as she thought about meeting Nicolas tomorrow after not seeing him for nearly a decade.

Then she reminded herself that she wasn't there for Nicolas—she was there to see Brussels. To be bold and try new things. To experience a country she'd heard so much about as a seventeen-year-old. To get out of her rut. To learn to take bigger risks. She didn't come all this way to "find a guy," as her dad would say.

No, do you know what? she said to herself. *It's okay to be excited to see Nicolas.* They had been good friends once, and she hadn't seen him for nearly ten years. She was excited to see him, and she wasn't going to try to talk herself out of being thrilled about that.

Even if she knew she absolutely could not fall for a guy who was not only unavailable but who lived in another country. But, with every message he sent, she worried more and more that she might be doing exactly that.

Chapter Eight

NICOLAS

*N*icolas pulled into the underground parking of his grandfather's downtown flat and parked on the first floor. He took off his jacket, folded it neatly, and placed it on the seat. Then he took off his tie and laid it on top of the jacket before shutting the door and heading to the elevator, unbuttoning the top two buttons of his shirt as he walked.

He got off the elevator in the lobby. A quick scan of the spacious area told him that Avery and Riley hadn't come down yet, which didn't surprise him—he was at least ten minutes early. He took a seat on an armchair in the sitting area just beyond the elevator and started going through emails on his phone.

A few minutes later, he saw two women step off the elevators and he immediately recognized them as Avery and Riley, even though it had been nearly a decade since he'd seen either of them in person. A longing to return to the time in his life when he lived with the Parks family washed over him.

Avery wore a pastel blue dress that reached the knees and a cardigan, her brown hair loose and just below her shoulders. A strap from a small bag crossed her body, the bag resting at her hip. Her posture was more confident now than when he'd last seen her, but she still had that same playfulness in her stride. Riley wore a light sweater and jeans, and they both looked ready to take on Brussels.

Both women glanced about, but neither turned around to see the area where he was seated. He stood, and as he walked toward them, he heard Riley say, "He's meeting us in the lobby, not outside, right?"

"Yes, in the lobby."

"Did he say what he would be wearing?"

He'd reached them before he got a chance to hear Avery's response and said hello. They both turned to greet him, and he saw immediate recognition cross their faces.

"Nicolas!" Avery said. "It's so good to see you!" She gave him a hug, squeezing him tightly, and he breathed in the scent of her shampoo, closing his eyes as he did, realizing how much he had missed her hugs over the years. And realizing how different they felt now caught him off guard.

Her eyes still held that same kindness and intelligence

that seemed to notice everything. All the things about everyone that most people missed. She was even more beautiful than he had remembered, and just like back in high school, she had an air about her that was intriguing and inviting. Even though he had been expecting that from her, he was still surprised at how instantly he was drawn to her.

Riley hugged him, too, but hers was quick, like it always was, before she pulled back and smiled at him.

As his attention went back to Avery, he caught the moment when he saw her eyes flick down to his whole body before going back to his face, and it made him smile.

Riley didn't try to hide her assessment of him. She motioned to his outfit from top to bottom. "Where do you work again?"

"Oma Servais. You knew that."

Avery cocked her head to the side. "Do you not make chocolates anymore?"

"Sometimes. I made the ones I left for you upstairs."

Riley grabbed his arm. "Oh my goodness, those were amazing! Avery and I were having a hard time not just gorging ourselves on them so we could spread them out throughout our visit."

Nicolas laughed. "I can bring you more anytime. But my position now is in marketing, so I don't spend much time in the kitchens."

"We saw that you have a store at the airport," Avery said. "It's so great that you're expanding."

"Yeah, it's pretty fun." He didn't mention that they had expanded long before he came to live with them as a teenager, or the extent of their expansion. They didn't need to know how many countries had Oma Servais shops in them. For this one moment, he just longed to be that teenager that they knew. He missed being the person he was back then. The kid who was carefree and didn't have so many worries and responsibilities on his shoulders. "Have you been able to get out and see any of the city yet?"

Riley immediately answered. "Yes. I dragged Avery to the Musical Instruments Museum this morning. It was amazing."

He turned to Avery. "Dragged you?"

She shrugged a shoulder and smiled. "It's seven hours earlier here, and I had a little jet lag—I don't know why Riley didn't. But she can be rather persuasive."

"Did you enjoy the museum?"

"I did. Just for different reasons from Riley."

Ahh. He'd forgotten how much Riley liked music, and how disinterested in it that Avery was. "Did you go to the room where they showed how the instruments were made?"

Avery's face lit up. "Yes! It was amazing. The architecture of the entire place was incredible." Of course, she loved that part. She always had been keenly aware of impressive craftsmanship.

She told of her favorite parts, and as she talked about it, he wished he could've been there with them.

"I want to take you to Notre Dame du Salon today. I think you'll find it even more extraordinary."

Avery nodded, so he looked to Riley, and she nodded, too.

"It's not a far distance, and it's a beautiful day outside." The spring weather had been fantastic lately— about the same temperature outside as inside, which didn't always happen at this time of year. Plus the sun was shining. "How do you feel about walking there?"

"This is exactly why I wore my walking shoes," Avery said while striking a pose, showing off her sneakers, that he found adorable. Everything about her was adorable.

"Great!" That meant he wouldn't have to take his car. If they thought he still worked in the factory, they might be expecting him to drive a run-down, beat-up car as Avery did as a teen, and his Bentley very much wasn't. And not driving them in the Bentley meant that he could enjoy being the person they were expecting him to be, even if it was just for a couple of hours.

"So," Riley said as they walked out of the lobby and onto the sidewalk, glancing at Avery quickly before looking back at Nicolas. "Could your girlfriend not make it today?"

His eyebrows drew together. "Sophie? Did I not tell you that we broke up? It was months ago."

Riley gave Avery a look like she thought Avery would be happy to hear that bit of news, but Avery's expression confused him. He couldn't quite interpret it before it was gone.

"I'm so sorry to hear that," Avery said. "Are you okay?"

"I am. I'm very relieved that I found out she isn't nearly as dedicated to monogamy as I am before we got married." Had he really forgotten to tell Avery? That might have been why she had always been so chatty when it was about random things but was so quick to keep things in the friend zone. Their worlds were still every bit as different as they were in high school and they still lived so far apart. The logical side of him had been grateful for her distance, even while his heart had been bemoaning the friend-zoning.

They chatted about things back on the farm as they walked, and the easy conversation made him realize how much he'd missed living with their family in South Dakota. How much he'd missed chatting with Avery in the chairs on her back porch under the stars, sometimes late into the night. And they chatted about what they'd seen so far in his country, and about staying in his grandfather's flat.

Seeing everything through their eyes as they witnessed all the things for the first time that he'd been taking for granted his entire life made him appreciate all the things around him more.

As they turned from the cobbled sidewalks to the street with the Roman Catholic cathedral, he kept his eyes on Avery's face to see the moment she took in the ornate building. She stopped walking as if taking in its beauty required every bit of her. "My goodness gosh golly," she breathed.

He'd forgotten that Avery used fake swears. He was surprised that he had—he'd always found it so odd yet endearing. It hadn't been until that first day in South Dakota that he'd heard anyone do that. He gave her a few minutes before he nudged her ahead. "Wait until you see it up close."

He led them both across the street as Avery shuffled forward, eyes wide, lips parted, as she looked up at the statues set in recesses in the many columns and arches of the ancient building. He hadn't come here nearly often enough in his life, but he felt that same sense of awe that he saw on her face every time he did.

Before going inside, they walked completely around the building, taking in all sides of it. Avery seemed to soak in every bit of the architecture, from the massive stained glass windows, to the ornate arches repeating throughout, to the columns of the nave with the twelve statues of apostles, to the majestic wooden carvings, the organ, and the murals in the choir area.

Nicolas found himself watching Avery take in the beauty more than he looked at the cathedral itself. Apparently, Riley noticed, because when Avery wandered away to study all the details of the dark wood carvings of the pulpit rising in the chapel, she stepped up to him and said, "You're attracted to Avery."

It wasn't a question, more a statement of fact. One he realized he couldn't deny. "I'm trying not to be."

She looked the same direction he was looking—to where Avery was engrossed in her appreciation of the craftsmanship of the room. "Why? Are you like her and swearing off dating right now?"

His brow crinkled. "Avery has sworn off dating?"

Riley waved a hand dismissively. "Something about figuring out life first. So, have you, too?

He shook his head. "No."

He was going to have to work on not showing how attracted to Avery he was. She lived half a world away. He'd lived in her world, and he rather liked it. It was nice. And she had a great family—he'd lived with them for nine months, so he'd gotten to see the best and the worst of them. And even their worst was pretty incredible. They were so different from his own family. He liked her world, and when he thought about his, it felt like so much was missing. He wouldn't ever want to drag her into his.

"Then why?"

He cleared his throat. "I don't think she'd like my world beyond visiting."

Riley's stomach growled just then. Nicolas didn't know if Avery had heard it, or if she'd just felt both his and Riley's eyes on her, but it seemed to pull her out of her reverie and she looked at them. "I'm sorry I got so caught up in this place. Would you two like to leave?"

Nicolas smiled and shook his head. Riley said, "No, this is good for you." But then her stomach growled again.

Avery's eyes were on her sister now, then on Nicolas, and he knew that they weren't going to get her to go back to looking at the cathedral. "No—it's okay. Maybe we should go get some food."

He nodded as Avery turned to start walking toward the exit. As they emerged into the sunlight, though, he saw Avery take one last longing glance at the cathedral. He vowed to bring her back another day.

The Sablon area was filled with places to eat and shop, and had many, many chocolate shops, including Oma Servais. He tried to steer their attention away from his family's store. He wasn't ready for them to ask more questions yet. "What are you two hungry for?"

Riley turned to Avery. "Oooh! Mussels and Frites. We *have* to, Avery."

Avery laughed. "Dad would be so proud." On the surface, she seemed happy with Riley's suggestion. There was something just underneath, though. Something he couldn't quite see that made him wonder if she wanted mussels and frites. But she turned to him and said, "Do you know of any good places around here?"

"I do. There's a great place just around the corner." He led them to one of his favorite little restaurants that had a *Moules et Frites* sign hanging from the building and then held the door open as they went inside.

Ten minutes later, the server set three enamel pots with handles down on the table, one in front of each of them, along with three cones of frites and sauce cups of mayonnaise. Nicolas took the lid off his pot and breathed in the smell of mussels and broth. Avery took her lid off and seemed unsure as she looked down at the black shells.

"Here," he said. "Let me show you how to eat them." He picked up a mussel. "Before they're cooked, they're closed. You know they're done when they're open like this. Just pull one apart, then you can pluck out the meat with your fingers or use your fork." He popped the meat in his mouth and smiled as he chewed. This was one of his favorites, and he loved the way this shop cooked them.

Riley did the same and looked like she loved it as much as he did. Avery, though, was still looking down at her pot with a look of disgust on her face that she was trying very hard to hide.

"I know that South Dakota isn't exactly known for its seafood," he said. "But Belgium is, and I'm determined to win you over."

"I don't know. These don't even look like food."

"Hey, you had me try *bison*. Remember? And pheasant. And what was that cubed venison called?"

"Chislic!" Riley said. "Mmm. I love chislic."

"Your dad even had me try Rocky Mountain Oysters, which isn't anything resembling an oyster, and if it's okay with you, we'll never talk about what they're actually made of ever again. I'm pretty sure you owe me after that one."

Avery laughed. "Okay, I was pretty impressed that you tried those."

"Then I'll even show you how to eat mussels like a Brussels native. You take your empty shell and see this part? It's basically a hinge." He clicked his mussel shell together like it was a pair of tongs. She still seemed hesitant, so he picked up one of her mussels, pulled it open, then used his empty shell to grab hold of the meat.

The look of repulsion on her face was less hidden as she studied it, but she still appeared fairly skeptical. She took the mussel shell and meat from him, brushing her fingers against his as she did, then held it up and took the bite of meat between her teeth.

As she chewed, the crinkled face softened and her eyebrows started to raise. Then she swallowed. "Oh, wow. It wasn't slimy like I had expected."

He grinned. And not just because he could still feel the tingle from her skin brushing his.

"And not as fishy-tasting as I thought it would be. Huh." She picked up the next one herself, opened it, then used her fork to pull out the meat and ate it. "They're actually pretty good."

"Which is more than I can say about Rocky Mountain Oysters." Avery liking mussels wasn't a personal victory, exactly, but the way his chest and shoulders lightened and he could feel his smile in his ears made it seem like one. He was happy he got to introduce her to something new that she liked. Well, two things new, if he counted the cathedral.

But the more she started liking his world, the more he could feel things in him shifting. Which was dangerous, because there was a lot more to his world than the touristy parts. He needed to remember that.

"We have to FaceTime dad. He's going to go nuts." Riley looked at her watch for a moment. "No, actually, they'll still be on the farm. We'll have to Marco Polo. Scoot in."

Riley opened the video messaging app and held her phone out in front of them. He scooted in close on Avery's left as Riley scooted in close on her right, and he tried not to focus on how amazing it felt to have Avery pushed up against him, side-to-side, seeing her brilliant smile on the screen as Riley narrated their experience to her parents.

"Nicolas," Avery said, "show them how it's done."

He picked up a mussel, opened it, then used another

shell to pull out the meat. "So, this is what it looks like," he said as he held it close to the camera, giving the folks who were his guardians for an entire school year a look at the meat. "Now I don't expect you to trust me that these taste good, since I've grown up with them, so I'll let you trust Avery."

He held the meat in front of her mouth, and this time, she smiled at him as she took the bite. She chewed it, swallowed, and then said, "*So* tasty!"

And then Riley dipped one of the frites in mayonnaise and held it in front of the camera before she stuck it in her mouth. "Whoa! How are these so much better than fries back home?"

They joked with Dalton and Jody—one-sided, of course, since they were just recording a video to send—and it gave him intense nostalgia. He wished he could be back in that place that had been such a refuge for him from family pressure and stress.

Of course, back when he lived with the Parks family, his attraction to Avery wasn't nearly as strong as it was today. How was it even possible for him to be so drawn to her now? Beyond knowing her well as a teenager, sending letters and messages occasionally over a ten-year time frame, and messaging each other frequently over the past six weeks, he had only been with her in person for all of about three hours.

After they finished eating, they made their way back to

his grandfather's building by a very meandering route, checking out antique and tourist shops along the way, smiling as they chatted about the stores by their building that they checked out earlier, and laughed when Avery told a story of Riley nearly passing out when she looked at the price tag on a pair of sunglasses. And since Riley was Riley, she was giving him knowing looks the entire time.

It was seven by the time they made it back to his grandfather's flat—the latest time he'd said he could stay. He'd given them that time frame because he had a lot of work to do to make up for leaving early that day, but right now, none of that seemed important. All he wanted to do was to stay with Avery.

As Riley walked over to push the button for the elevator, Nicolas's mind was churning over thoughts of how he could get free from work more often to be able to see Avery. He was always responsible. What would happen if he just showed a little irresponsibility and didn't go to work tomorrow? Or for the entire next week?

He shook his head at the ridiculousness of that thought. Avery must've sensed his reluctance to leave, though, because she said, "Do you know Jacques, Delphine, and Rania?"

"My grandfather's staff? A little. Not super well." He'd been the one to line things up with Jacques for Avery's and Riley's stay, but he only saw the staff once or twice a year.

"We are going up to play card games with them. Can you stay a little longer and join us?"

Play card games with the staff? He was always friendlier with his parents' staff than his parents thought was appropriate, but he'd never actually tried playing a game of cards with them. The fact that Avery set up games with them less than twenty-four hours after arriving at his grandfather's flat was impressive. His ex-fiancee Sophie would've died before ever setting up a game night with the staff. And his mother would probably die right along with her, knowing that he was about to say yes to doing exactly that.

Nicolas remembered playing card games with Avery and her family during his stay and smiled. Of course, she'd set up a game night with the staff. She had changed over the years, but she was the same in all the ways he loved most.

He nodded. "I'd like that." And he really liked the smile that spread across her face when he said he'd stay.

Oh, boy, was he in trouble.

Chapter Nine

AVERY

As the elevator took Avery, Riley, and Nicolas up to the ninth floor, Avery had an anxiety-filled emptiness in her stomach at inviting Nicolas to stick around after a day like today, because she knew she didn't want to get involved with anyone. Especially someone who lived so far away. And then her stomach would flip to a fluttery, happy, butterflies-in-sunshine feeling at having Nicolas stick around after a day like today when there seemed to be so much chemistry between them. Back and forth between the two.

And his accent! She had somehow forgotten just how much she loved that.

You are here for the experiences, not to "find a man," she reminded herself. It had been so much easier when she'd believed he had a girlfriend who was possibly also a fiancée.

Not that Sophie was the only reason that Avery wouldn't let herself fall for Nicolas. There was also the fact that he lived 4300 miles away. Oh, and the even bigger fact that she didn't want a relationship right now. Not before she learned whatever she needed to learn and figured out whatever she needed to figure out. She'd achieved her dream, career-wise, but there was more out there—she could feel it. A bigger dream she needed to shoot for. Nicolas had shown a lot of guts to go live in another country when he was seventeen. She'd never been brave enough to wander far from home before, but this was the first step in changing that. Of finding a bigger dream.

The moment the doors opened, Avery saw Jacques, Delphine, and Rania laughing and joking as they set out snacks on the big dining table. The moment they looked over, though, and saw that Nicolas was getting off the elevator with her and Riley, their demeanor instantly changed to that of professionalism.

"Jacques, Delphine, and Rania, you all know Nicolas, right?" she asked when they reached the table.

They nodded and Nicolas shook their hands, saying, "It's good to see you again."

"If it's okay with the three of you, we've invited Nicolas to stay and play."

They all nodded, but more in an "Of course—we're here to serve" way, not a "Sure! The more the merrier" kind of way. Not the way they had all been acting after they'd gotten to know each other between last night and when she and Riley had left to go exploring today. By the time breakfast was over this morning, they'd all seemed to be as comfortable with one another as if they'd been in a friend group for a while.

She seemed to be the only one who noticed the tenseness in the room, though. Riley said, "I'm going to head to my room and change into sweats."

"And I'm going to go wash up," Nicolas said, before heading back to one of the bathrooms.

Avery went over to where Jacques, Delphine, and Rania were giving each other looks while they straightened the bowls of sweet and salty snacks on the table that didn't need to be straightened.

"Was it bad that I invited Nicolas to join us?" she asked.

"Oh, no. It's fine," Delphine said.

"Totally fine," Rania added, her accent making the word "totally" sound almost out of place.

Avery raised an eyebrow at the three of them. Finally, Jacques let out a breath and said, "It is just not something we are used to. That's all. We've never dropped formality in front of guests before. Not until you and Riley. And most certainly not in front of the boss."

Avery pulled back in surprise. "He's not the boss." Jacques gave her a look in response, that she couldn't interpret. "I take it none of you know him very well?"

They all shook their heads.

"He isn't rich like his grandpa or pompous or anything. He's just a normal guy. He's just like me and Riley."

They gave each other looks again, then Delphine said, "Okay. Normal guy. Got it." But she said it like she was saying she would go along with Avery's fantasy if that was what she wanted. She was the guest, after all.

They really must not know him. "Listen. He lived with my family for nine months, so I got to know him pretty well. Trust me: you'll like him. I mean yeah, he was a teen back then, but he's a good guy. You'll see."

Nicolas came down the hall just then, rolling up the sleeves of his dress shirt as he did and holy heck specks if he wasn't the most beautiful man she'd ever known. And that smile he gave her pretty much melted her insides and fired up her outsides. It made his right eye crinkle more than his left and sugar-honey-iced-tea, she didn't even know what to do with the emotions it made her feel. Why? Why did he have to be so attractive? It was going to be tough to stay strong.

She took a deep breath as Riley came out of her room and Avery turned back to the others. "Ready?"

They all nodded and took their seats around the table,

Nicolas just to her left. "What are we playing?" Nicolas asked.

Jacques was going through the deck of cards he held, and it looked like he was pulling out all the twos through sixes and setting them aside. "We're going to start with Rammes. It's our favorite. Delphine, what do you want to use as counters?"

Delphine grabbed a bowl of chocolate almonds from the middle of the table. "Pick out five and set them on the table beside you. For any trick you lose, you eat a chocolate almond. If you eat all your almonds, you're out."

"Okay, okay," Riley said. "I can get behind this."

Jacques won the draw, so he dealt the first hand, passing five cards to each of them. They explained the game as they played, but there were aspects of it that Avery just didn't understand. She understood that each person played their highest card in the same suit as the card face-up in the middle, but other cards could be played, too, and she didn't get the trump card concept. Or what happened when someone called out "General Rammes."

It didn't help that on their playing cards, the ace card had the number 1 in the corners instead of the letter A, the King had an R instead of K, the Queen had a D, and the Jack had a V.

After eating three of her five chocolate almonds— which just happened to be way better than any she'd ever had before—she decided she needed Nicolas's help. She scooted her chair closer to him and aimed her cards so that he could see them, too. Through the next round, he would lean in close and whisper strategies and advice as they played, tickling her ear.

But she wasn't going to lie—it was nice being close to Nicolas. And sweet goodness, he smelled amazing. Even after spending hours outside. There was no way she could've named the scent, but it was manly and amazing and nothing at all like the city. The thought made her suddenly self-conscious that she probably smelled exactly like the city.

Nicolas whispered into her ear, "I think this one is your best bet," and reached out to touch a card she held in her hand. His hand brushed across hers, which sent ripples of goosebumps up her arms and across her body. She didn't think she was the only one affected by it, either, because Nicolas paused what he was saying the moment their skin touched, and his voice was just a little gruffer when he finished his sentence.

Through the first round of five tricks, the room felt stiff, like no one was quite themselves. Nicolas could sense the tension, too, she could tell. It was uncomfortable for a bit, and she knew he had other things he needed to do tonight. She kept expecting him to excuse himself and say that he needed to go, but he never did. He just kept working hard to help ease the tension in the room, and she loved that he would do that. She didn't know why, but it mattered to her that Jacques, Delphine, and Rania saw him the way she did.

By the second round, everyone started to lighten up. Delphine smack-talked every time anyone laid down cards, Rania started telling jokes that she snuck into the conversation, all ninja-like, and Jacques— well, he still stayed fairly proper, but his competitive side emerged.

After eating her tenth chocolate almond, and officially becoming the least hungry person at the table, Avery was ready for anything new. So when Riley nudged her and said, "You should teach them Nertz," Avery turned to Jacques.

"How many decks of cards do you have?"

Jacques perked up. "How many would you like, Ms. Parks?"

"Do you have six?"

Jacques ducked out of the room toward the staff wing and emerged a minute later with a grin and six decks of cards. So Avery explained Nertz, a game that was basically group solitaire, where everyone played off their own cards in front of them as well as off any cards placed in the middle by anyone else—a game won by speed, not strategy.

It took a bit for everyone to catch on, but by the second round, everyone was really getting into it. Jacques stood up partway into the game so he could reach to the middle better, and before long, all six of them were standing, being more vigorous with the placing of cards. There was so much smack-talking, cheers, frustrated grunts, and various unintelligible sounds made that probably livened up the room more than it had ever seen.

"Nertz!" Jacques shouted as he cleared the deck in front of him. He pumped his fist. "Yes!" He seemed to realize just how big his reaction was, and he cleared his throat, straightening his cardigan. In a much more professional tone, he said, "I enjoyed that game immensely, Ms. Parks. Thank you for suggesting it."

Avery smiled as everyone around the table stood, a little more out of breath than what playing a card game would normally elicit, cheeks flushed, grins on their faces. Having everyone around her enjoying themselves so much was such a great feeling.

As they separated the decks of cards, Nicolas said, "So, when are you two free for me to show you Ghent?"

"For you," Riley said, still pumped up from the game, "anytime."

Nicolas's eyebrows rose. "Even tomorrow?"

"Even tomorrow," Avery said.

Avery didn't miss the way a pleased smile crossed his face. "If you'll excuse me for a moment, I'd like to call my assistant and see if I can manage to take some time off."

As they all got up and stretched or took bathroom breaks, Nicolas walked over to the door leading out to the wrap-around balcony, slipped outside, and closed the door behind him. The balcony lights were on, but the lights nearest the full-length windows weren't, so Avery had a perfect view of him. She watched as he put his phone to his ear, then leaned forward, resting his arms on the railing as he looked out over the city. He looked like he belonged in a magazine. Sure, he'd been cute as a seventeen-year-old, but the last ten years had done amazing things for him.

And not just to his body. He'd gained a confidence that he hadn't had before. He seemed to have refined that sense he had of the people around him that had always helped him to include everyone back in high school. And just like before, he brought fun and happiness to everything and made people feel good about themselves. It was as if all the things she'd liked about him before were intensified now.

She hadn't even heard Jacques come up behind her until he said, "It seems Master Nicolas is very smitten with you."

Avery shook her head and gave a shaky laugh. "We're just old friends."

Jacques paused for a long moment before he nodded. "Whatever you say, Ms. Parks."

Nicolas was out on the patio for quite a while before he came back in, looking victorious. "We have managed to clear my schedule from lunch on. Can I stop by to pick you both up in the early afternoon to show you my city?"

———

AT AROUND ELEVEN, when Nicolas left, Avery flopped down on her big fluffy bed with a happy sigh. Everyone seemed to have enjoyed themselves quite a bit, and by the time the evening ended, Jacques, Delphine, and Rania seemed as comfortable with Nicolas as they were with her and Riley.

And she was finding herself *very* comfortable with Nicolas. And right now, she didn't even care.

A moment later, Riley plopped down on the bed beside her, laptop in hand. "Sit up. We have some Googling to do."

Oooh. Intriguing. Avery sat up and the two of them moved to the top of the bed so they could sit with their backs against the pillows at the headboard.

"When we were out wandering around, looking at shops, I saw another Oma Servais."

"Are you sure it was theirs? There were quite a few chocolate shops around."

"I'm sure. And not only did Nicolas not point it out, but I think he was trying to keep us from noticing it." Riley was already connecting to the flat's Wi-Fi and bringing up Google.

"Why would he do that?" He hadn't seemed to want to talk a lot about his work. She had never seen him as the type of person to lie or hide information, but he was the kind of guy who would downplay his accomplishments. Maybe it was something like that?

Riley shrugged. "I don't know. But taking into consideration that we know of at least three of their stores, the fact that he wears a suit to work—a very nice one, I might add—and, well, this place. . . I think there's more to the story."

Riley typed in the name of their chocolate shop and pressed enter. The first two results were both for their shop—an ad first, and then their regular listing. Right below that was a Google Map with locations nearby pinned. Avery reached out a finger that trembled ever so slightly and pointed at the second entry. "Click on that."

It brought up a website with the most beautiful, delicious-looking chocolates ever. A super professional-looking site. With award badge after award badge splayed just underneath the chocolates. Riley only stayed on the main page for a moment before she moved the mouse to the menu and clicked on *Locations*.

Avery's eyes widened as she looked at the extremely long list of locations. There had to be hundreds in Belgium alone, with at least that many spread all across Europe.

"Are those all his family's?"

Riley moved her head in a motion that was neither a

shake nor a nod but somehow both. "They don't own a chocolate shop—they own an entire chocolate empire! How did we not know this?"

Avery just stared at the screen as Riley clicked on the *About Us* page and started reading out loud about how it was a family-owned business. Then Avery looked around the room with different eyes.

"I don't know," she breathed. "I guess because Nicolas has always been so humble, it just never occurred to me. I thought they only had a single mom-and-pop store."

Then they went down a research rabbit hole and found out that Nicolas's mother was the CEO, his grandfather was the Chairman of the Board now and was the CEO preceding Nicolas's mom, and both Nicolas and his dad were part of the executive staff. When Nicolas had said that he worked in marketing, he'd meant that he was *the Marketing Director*.

Avery was still stunned speechless when her phone started buzzing and she picked it up, answering the FaceTime from her parents.

"Oh my goodness," her mom said, "you ate the mussels. I don't know if I'd have dared."

Her dad nodded. "If I had a gold star, I'd put it right on your forehead." He reached a finger out to the camera like he was trying to stick it on her forehead anyway.

Her mom's eyes went back and forth between Avery

and Riley. "Why do you two have those looks on your faces? Is everything okay?"

Avery opened her mouth to say something, but instead flipped the camera on the phone and aimed it at Riley's laptop screen. Riley clicked on the tab with the company website. Both parents squinted at their little screen.

"Those are all their locations," Riley said, scrolling as their mom's hand flew to her mouth. "Hundreds of them. We've been Googling and are finding a lot of repeating things—awards that they've won. International renown. A top place to work. Stuff about sustainability practices and improving labor conditions in the cocoa farms they work with. Oh, and get this—they're an official chocolatier to the Royal Court of Belgium *and* the Belgian Royal household."

"And, you're not going to believe this part," Avery added, "but not only is his family running the business, but Nicolas is on the executive staff. He's listed as Director of Marketing for the entire company."

Avery's mom's hand dropped from her mouth and her face went pale. And then, in a horrified voice, said, "I asked that boy to clean our bathroom!"

"We're right there with you, Mom," Riley said. Then she nodded and turned to Avery. "This explains the shopkeeper's unimpressed response when we went to their store in the airport and said how cool it was that they opened one there."

But Avery was in the middle of her own realization. "Son of a sea cook, he's paying for the staff while we're here."

Riley's attention flew to her. "Are you sure?"

She nodded, realizing how sure she was as she did. "I know they're his grandpa's staff, but I think Nicolas lined up their services. That explains why they were all so tense when we brought him over for game night. Jacques said they've never dropped professionalism before *in front of the boss.*"

"And what did you say to that?" her dad asked.

"I told them that he *wasn't* the boss. That he was just a normal guy. He was just like me and Riley."

Her mom clapped her hands once. "And do you know what? He is. He's still the same boy who would sleep in until fifteen minutes before the bus came, stumbling down the stairs with a backpack over his shoulder, wearing one shoe and trying to put on the other as he went, grabbing a bagel from the kitchen and barely taking a bite before he raced out the door."

"You're right," Avery said, closing the screen of Riley's laptop. "We just spent all day with him, and he's still the same person we knew back then."

Just better in every way.

"Oh, and," Riley said, dragging out the word, "we found out today that he's single."

As soon as her mom's hooting quieted, Avery threw

Riley a glare before saying, "And I would just like to take this moment to remind you that I'm not here looking for a man. I am here to gain experience only."

"That's my girl," her dad said, attempting to give her a fist bump through the phone's camera. "You stay strong and don't let him woo you and don't let yourself fall for him."

After spending the entire afternoon and evening with Nicolas, that was quickly becoming her number one goal.

Chapter Ten

NICOLAS

*N*icolas got back to his office after a budget meeting that, for once, didn't go long, feeling like he was floating through his day. Which was weird, because it wasn't like he and Avery had gone on a date last night. And there definitely hadn't been any time spent one-on-one. Yet he still had an excitement running through his veins today. He hadn't felt like that in a very long time.

He glanced at the clock on his wall as he walked over to his desk. An hour and a half, and he'd be able to leave and see Avery again, which meant two things: Avery was going to be on his mind more and more the closer to noon he got, and that he needed to be more focused than ever if he wanted to finish all he needed to finish before leaving.

He could do this. He sat down and pulled up the

images that the designers had sent over that they were going to be using in magazine ads if Oma Servais won the competition in a couple of weeks, as well as the ones they'd send in their place if they didn't win. He didn't normally check every image the design team made, but these were premium spots, and the Chocolatier Awards were a big deal.

The ads were close to perfect—there were only minor tweaks needed now. He pulled the touch screen forward and made a few notations right on the digital images, then typed up an explanation of the changes needed for both sets of ads. That part of his job had always been the easy part for him—it wasn't difficult at all to see what could improve ads. Which meant that his mind had time to wander.

As soon as he realized that he was thinking about Avery again, he forced himself to focus and sent the images and notes back. Then he opened the reports on individual products sold at each of their stores as a whole and by region. That part took a lot more focus, and he soon found himself buried deep in the data.

"Finn?" he called out as he jotted down some notes on a notepad, keeping his eyes on the screen.

Finn walked into his office a moment later, tablet in his hands, looking ready to take notes. He looked at Nicolas very curiously.

Nicolas ignored the look and said, "Will you contact

Louis in operations and see if he's free for a meeting early next week? Maybe loop in Elodie, too. Tell them I need to talk about some of the products that aren't selling as well. In my notes for the meeting, remind me that I wanted to see if we should try different packaging for the sesame nougats or some in-store ad placements to see if we can highlight the ones that are lagging before we decide if they should just be pulled."

Finn nodded. "Will do."

Nicolas stood up and started pacing his office as all the things he needed to do kept piling into his brain, rapid-fire. "Will you also invite the folks in Brand Management to the meeting with Advertising on Friday? And then put in my notes that I want to talk with them about tweaking our ad copy to make it better align with our brand."

Another nod from Finn as he tapped on his screen.

"But before that meeting," he said, twisting his watch around his wrist, "I need to meet with Cyriel, in the next thirty minutes, if possible. If not, then as early tomorrow morning as he can get free. I need to talk to him about a change in the advertising euros over what we had earmarked if we win the IRC Awards."

Finn tapped on his screen but hadn't gotten to the nodding part before he stopped and pulled his cell phone out of his pocket. In a rush, he said, "I have it on good authority that your mother is on her way here right now."

"She is? I thought she took the morning off."

"She must be back. So maybe you should stop looking so. . ." Finn waved his cell phone around in the general direction of Nicolas. . . "excited about leaving early, or whatever this is, or she'll get suspicious."

Nicolas stopped his pacing and chuckled. "Let her get suspicious."

Finn's eyes widened, so he knew his assistant thought it was a bad idea. But that was probably mostly because Margaux Servais terrified Finn. She walked into Nicolas's office just then, unannounced, and Finn quickly ducked out.

"Good morning, Mother. To what do I owe this pleasure?"

Her heels clacked as she crossed his floor, then were muffled for a moment as she crossed over the rug in his sitting area before coming to a stop in front of his desk. "I heard you're leaving early again today."

"You heard right." He'd learned long ago that the fewer details he gave his mother, the better.

"You're taking time off this close to the IRC Awards? You know how much this competition can affect our bottom line."

He didn't bring up the fact that she had taken several half days off over the past couple of weeks. "Believe me, I do. That's why we've been working on the marketing plan for it for months."

"Yet you're stumbling at the finish line."

He was on way too much of a high just knowing that he would see Avery in—he stealthily glanced at the clock—forty-seven minutes to let his mother's words affect him. "I'm not stumbling, Mother. You know how rarely I take time off and you know I never do without making sure all aspects of my job are covered. Everything is good. You just need to trust me."

She narrowed her eyes at him, studying him. "For what are you leaving early?"

He was about to say that it was personal business that didn't concern her, but much to his surprise, "I'm working on getting that date for next Friday's event" came out instead. It made him realize how much he wanted his date for that night to be Avery. Was that even possible?

"Well, she better be a good one," his mother said. "This is important. I heard that the marketing director at Alexandre's hired a beloved actress as his date for the evening with the express purpose of charming the judges, thereby giving them a leg up in the competition."

That made him chuckle. Who would've thought that Basil had it in him to try something like that? "That just means they're more worried about their prospects than we thought they were."

"Maybe, but I don't want to take any chances. I need that folder on your date by Friday."

"Don't worry," he said. "You'll have it."

———

SINCE HE'D PLANNED AHEAD of time to take off early to show Avery and Riley Ghent, he'd known to bring jeans and a t-shirt to change into before he left work. He blasted music during the ten-minute drive to his grandfather's flat, singing at the top of his lungs as he drove. When was the last time he'd felt this joyful?

He pulled into the curved drive in front of the apartment building and parked. He'd barely stepped out of the car when he saw Avery and Riley come through the front doors of the building. He felt his smile with his whole face. They were both wearing jeans this time, and Avery wore a grayish-green V-neck shirt that brought out the slightly reddish tint to her brown hair. She looked beautiful. And the smile on her face made him think that maybe she was just as happy to see him as he was to see her.

It wasn't until he saw Riley's eyes flick to his car that he realized that at least part of his cover was blown. Not that he'd planned to keep that cover beyond yesterday. He walked around to greet them and open the passenger door. Riley immediately climbed into the back seat, which gave him a flashback to when he lived with the Parks and both sisters used to call "shotgun" to get the front seat—a custom he still didn't quite understand.

He went around to his side of the car and got in. "Are you guys ready to go see the best city in all of Europe?"

"*The* best?" Avery asked as she put on her seatbelt.

He nodded, showing his most serious face. "*The. Best.* If you don't agree by the end of today, then that means I've done something terribly wrong." And he hoped they did agree. He wanted them to love it as he loved it.

They had barely pulled onto the motorway before Riley, who was sitting in the middle of the back seat, leaned as far forward as she could while wearing a seatbelt, one hand on each of the front seats. "We Googled you."

He closed his eyes for the briefest of seconds, then glanced at her in the rearview mirror. Based on the grin she was wearing, they had gotten the whole story. Which he'd known was going to happen—if they hadn't gotten it on their own, he would've told them today. It just also meant the end of playing a part he'd enjoyed and was back to reality.

"I guess the cat's out of the bag."

"Nicolas," Avery said, "why didn't you ever tell us when we were kids that your parents' company was more than a mom-and-pop shop?"

He shrugged. "Because it just hadn't seemed like important information." After a pause, he added, "And I loved just being a normal teenager in Lake Baldwin."

He glanced at Avery, who nodded as if she

understood, for which he felt immense gratitude. He wished he wasn't driving so he could study her face for longer. She may have understood his reasons, but that didn't mean that the knowledge of him and his family hadn't changed the way she thought of him. Had what she and Riley found out scared her?

"When you said you worked in marketing," Riley accused, "you failed to mention that you are *the* marketing director. Like, executive staff, marketing director."

He glanced in his rearview mirror and changed lanes. "Yeah, that's a temporary position."

"Temporary?" Avery asked.

"Well, at least that's the plan. My mother is the CEO, and she wants me to take over that position in six weeks when she leaves to run a nonprofit. Of course, the board has to approve it first."

"Your grandpa is the Chairman of the Board," Riley said, not as if it were a question.

"Yes, but that doesn't mean it's guaranteed. The others have a vote, too."

"Your grandpa is your dad's dad?"

He shook his head. People made that assumption often since they had the same last name. "He's my *mother's* father. My mother is a little attached to the family business and wasn't willing to give up the Servais name, so my father took her last name when they got married."

"How do you feel about becoming CEO?" Avery

asked, and he glanced at her in surprise. He'd gotten good at stating it without his emotions coloring it at all. No one ever asked how he felt about it.

"It's not the position I'd take if I could choose one myself, but I've been trained nearly my whole life for it."

For most of the thirty-five-minute drive, both Avery and Riley asked questions about working at Oma Servais and what parts he liked the most and what his plans there were, and even more about what his dreams there were. He kept trying to turn the conversation to them, but they kept asking questions that turned it back. It shocked him how good it felt to talk with them about the company. Nearly everyone in his life had something to do with Oma Servais, so there wasn't a soul he could open up to about how he truly felt.

"Okay, enough about work," he said as they pulled into downtown Ghent. "I have a city to show you." He noticed that Avery was already mesmerized by all the gothic buildings, street art, and cafes they were driving past. He started looking at his beloved city with fresh eyes. It still immediately had his heart.

He pulled into a parking spot in the general area he was hoping for, grateful he didn't have to drive out any further. They were at the very beginning of tourist season, so things weren't too crowded yet.

Once they were all out of the car, he said, "There are more things in this city that I want to show you than I'd ever be able to show in a single day, so we're going with what'll show you the most in the shortest amount of time. Starting with that." He was standing next to Avery, so he put his hands on her shoulders and turned her slightly so that she was facing the direction of the tallest of the three medieval towers that overlooked the city. He watched her face as it lit up.

"What is that?"

"The Belfry of Ghent. They started building it in thirteen-thirteen, and it was used as a watchtower. See that dragon up there on top of the spire? It keeps an eye on the city. On special occasions, he'll even breathe fire."

Her eyes whipped to his. "Really?" She was taking in the city like he had when he'd first decided that it would be his home, and he loved seeing that reaction in her.

"Really. And we're going inside."

They had almost reached the tower when the bells started ringing, marking the top of the hour. Riley stopped in her tracks and stared up at the marvel. By the way Avery's eyes widened just looking at the building and the way Riley stood with her head cocked for optimal listening to the bells, he knew he'd chosen the perfect landmark to introduce them to his city with.

He hadn't been inside the belfry for a long time, but the moment they stepped into the slightly musty building, everything came back to him. He showed them the stone statues guarding the underground chamber where they used to keep records many hundreds of years ago, then they walked up the narrow cement stairs that twisted in a spiral as they climbed. The red bricks and gray stones of the walls looked every bit as old as they were, a slight chill emanating from them.

He showed the women the fiery dragon on the first floor, the symbol of the city of Ghent. Then they went up to the second floor, which had bells of many different sizes, along with a video showing how the bells were made. Riley was mesmerized, so he told her about how the primary bell at the top of the tower was used in ancient times to warn of approaching enemies and to celebrate victories.

His favorite, though, was when they reached the top floor and he got to show Avery the city. Without thinking, he slipped his hand in hers to direct her toward the side of the tower that he wanted her to see first. She immediately looked down at their hands, as if to confirm that they were, in fact, holding hands. He nearly let go, thinking he'd overstepped, but then she smiled up at him and all he could do was soak in that glorious smile. Just past Avery, he caught Riley's amused grin.

He led her through the opening to the small balcony-like space on one side of the tower, Riley right behind them, and walked up to the waist-high stone barrier. Avery gasped as she took in the view, and he looked out, trying to see everything through her eyes.

The most eye-catching thing in their view was St. Nicholas' Church. It was built at about the same time as the belfry, and its bluish-gray stone and gothic architecture were impressive. The base of the back side was roundish and had tall windows ending in spires. Four thin turrets flanked the main section, its tower rising from the middle.

"It's incredible," Avery breathed.

Nicolas smiled out at his city. It really was.

"There are stairs leading up to the bell at the top," Riley said. "I'm going to go check it out."

"More stairs?" Avery asked.

Riley smiled. "Someone said there were three hundred sixty-six steps in here, and I want my feet on every one of them."

Still holding Avery's hand, Nicolas led her to another of the four sides of the belfry, so she could see more of Ghent. They both stood between the stone pillars situated every meter or so on the lookouts, gazing out at the mostly reddish-brown and gray buildings and roofs spread out across his city. He pointed out a row of buildings, all touching each other, that curved around and followed the curve of the street.

And then he pointed in the direction of his place. "My apartment is right over there."

"Oh, I think I see it." There was a sparkle in her eyes that he recognized from when she teased him as a teenager. He hadn't realized how much he missed that.

He chuckled and bumped his shoulder into hers.

"It's amazing," she said, gesturing to some tall cranes off in the distance. "To see new construction going on in the same city as buildings that were constructed so many centuries ago. And buildings of all ages everywhere in between. It's mind-blowing to think of the history. It makes me wish I could spend weeks here, learning the stories behind all of them."

He wished she could, too. "You'd find a lot of stories. From the eleventh to the sixteenth centuries, Ghent was considered one of the most important cities in all of Europe."

"Oh, yeah?"

"Some people say that it's still *the* most important city in Europe." He could tell by her smile that she had caught the teasing note in his voice.

"And are these people who believe it's the most important city here in this tower?"

"At least one of them is."

She looked out over the buildings and spires of cathedrals and trees and roads and people, then looked back up to meet his eyes. "I think maybe two of them are."

By the way she was looking at him, he was fairly certain that she was referring to herself. He kept gazing into her eyes to see if he could tell for sure. He could look into those eyes forever.

"That bell is huge!" Riley said as she came through the opening to the lookout. "Seriously amazing."

The moment was lost—or at least put on hold—so he showed them the views of the city from the remaining two sides of the belfry. Then he said, "Come on. I have more to show you."

As they exited the belfry and walked a few blocks to the Groentenmarkt, he took them down as many colorful alleys as possible. Street art was legal in Ghent, so artists brought their best to the giant canvases, even knowing it was temporary. They spent quite a while admiring all the different art styles before he looked down at his watch and saw that it was almost time for the canal cruise he had lined up.

When they crossed the paved pedestrian walks between the buildings and the river, he spotted the waiting boat. He'd met the captain before and knew he made an excellent tour guide. He was grateful that the guy was willing to book a private tour for them with less than twenty-four hours' notice.

Riley hurried ahead of them and looked down over the cement edge leading to the river, and then across the river to where the buildings on the other side went right down into the water, all the buildings touching each other. "You've got canals here? Like Venice?"

He smiled. "What do you say to seeing some of the sites while on a boat?"

Avery looked at him in a way that made his heart beat louder. "I would have to say that your 'Best city in Europe' is living up to its name."

He led them down the stone steps to the boat, gave the driver a thank-you nod, and sat down on one of the middle seats. Riley sat on one side and Avery the other, but much further away than he guessed she would. They'd had so many moments throughout the day when they brushed hands, bumped shoulders, and scooted in close for one reason or another. Every time, she had appeared to enjoy the closeness as much as he did.

So her distance now must mean that she was feeling conflicted about him. He understood—there were a myriad of things standing in the way of a possible relationship between the two of them. Not only did they come from two very different worlds socially, but they both lived in very different parts of the world physically. A part of him was reminded that keeping distance from Avery was a very smart choice.

And another part of him wanted to go to war with those obstacles in their way and tear every one of them down, impossible or not.

As they floated along the canal, the tour guide pointing out the buildings that were created in the twelfth century and explaining how the harbor had been the second biggest during medieval times, he watched Avery's and Riley's reactions.

He wished he could show them even more. He knew he was already trying to show them way too much for a single day, but their time in Belgium was so short, and he liked being the one introducing them to all of it.

He pointed out a few of his favorite places as they went under stone bridges and by waterfront cafes and weeping willows at the water's edge whose arching branches dipped right down into the water. And, of course, the apartments just beyond those willow trees that had a mix of houses from every single century from the 15th until now.

A mix of excitement built in his stomach as they came closer to the Gravensteen. As soon as they made the turn in the river that brought it into view, Avery's hand grabbed his arm. "You have a castle? A real live castle? Right here in the middle of the city? And the water goes right up to it! Is that its moat?"

He'd known she would love it.

The captain was even smiling at her reaction. "What you're seeing is the Castle of the Counts. It was finished in the year eleven eighty."

As their tour guide gave them more information about the castle, Avery must've noticed that she was still holding his arm and let go.

He wondered if she was conflicted about the two of them because they lived so far away from each other, or if it was because he was introducing her to his world—a world that was so different from hers—and she couldn't see herself there. She obviously liked visiting the touristy parts of his world, but he wondered if she would like *all* of his world.

As the tour guide turned the boat and headed back along the river, he decided to push things a little more. Introduce her to a bit more of his world outside of the tourist sites and see how she reacted. He hoped she wouldn't just run the other way.

On most nights, Nicolas didn't eat at fancy restaurants. But there were plenty of times when it was pretty much a requirement. And he just thought of the perfect restaurant that was not only fancy but would give her a great taste of the local cuisine.

He got the captain's attention. "Will you please drop us off just past the Grasbrug Bridge?"

As they went under the bridge and the tour guide maneuvered the boat up alongside the cement at the river's edge, Nicolas decided that he was all in with Avery. He would show her as much of his world as he could while she was in Belgium and see what she thought of it all.

He stepped out of the boat and onto the walkway, then turned and offered Riley and then Avery a hand up. Then he led them up the stairs and onto the cobbled pedestrian walk and just down the way to one of his favorite restaurants.

Chapter Eleven

AVERY

"This place looks fancy," Riley said, leaning in close to Avery as they both glanced around at the restaurant. Or at least what they could see of it from just inside the door.

Avery took the moment while Nicolas was speaking with the hostess to really look at him. She'd loved seeing him in slacks and a dress shirt—he had just looked so at home, comfortable, and confident in dress clothes that she hadn't been able to picture him as an adult so fully inhabiting the more casual clothing he'd worn as a teen. But here he was, dressed in jeans and a fitted t-shirt, looking every bit as comfortable and confident. If she was being honest with herself, she found it intoxicating.

The hostess looked at him with recognition. Not as if

she knew him personally, but that she was familiar with him. Like maybe he came here often.

After a moment, Nicolas walked back over to Avery and Riley and said, "Okay, they'll have a table for us in just over an hour, but first, we need to dress for the occasion."

"Um," Avery said, glancing at her sister, "we didn't bring other clothes, and we can't make it to Brussels and back in that amount of time."

"I know." He put his hand on the small of her back to direct her out of the restaurant and back onto the cobbled walk. "But don't worry—I know someone not far from here who will get us taken care of."

He led them about five shops down in the same row of buildings that touched each other, then held the front door of a boutique dress shop open as they both walked in. The inside wasn't large, but mannequins wore elegant dresses, the walls were filled with racks of even more gowns, padded seating areas were arranged in several places, and a beautiful chandelier hung from the ceiling in the middle of it all. The mere thought of what the price tags might show in a place like this made Avery's stomach clench.

"Nicolas," she leaned in and whispered, "I can't afford this."

He looked at her in shock. "You thought I would bully you into buying something you hadn't planned to buy? Avery, this all was my idea. Something *I* want to do. Of course, I'll pay for it."

She knew Nicolas well enough to know that he wasn't someone who would expect anything from his generosity. But it still made her uncomfortable to have someone offering so much. It wasn't something that she'd experienced often, so accepting help—no matter how freely or generously given—felt awkward.

A woman who looked like she was in her late thirties or early forties walked straight up to them, wearing a very nice yet understated dress and heels. Her dark hair was swept up into a bun. From what Avery could tell, she was the only shopkeeper in the boutique. She asked a question in Dutch that Avery didn't understand, but guessed it was probably some version of "Can I help you?"

Nicolas answered her question in Dutch as well, and Avery was mesmerized by the sound of it. She had heard him say a few words in Dutch before, but only a short sentence here and there. Nothing like what she was hearing now. Both he and the woman glanced over at Avery and Riley a few times as Nicolas talked.

Nicolas handed the woman a black credit card and she gave him a curt nod before going behind the counter with the cash register and locking it in the drawer.

Nicolas turned to Avery and Riley. "Okay, she knows what you need. My apartment isn't far from here, so I'm going to run home and change. Are you both okay with me leaving you in Eline's capable hands for a bit?" At their nods, he said, "I'll meet you back here in an hour."

As soon as the door closed behind Nicolas, Eline turned to them and clapped her hands once. "We have work to do. Let's get to it."

Avery exhaled in relief that so many people in Belgium spoke English, and was especially grateful that Eline did. The only other language Avery knew was French. And although she'd heard French spoken quite a bit since she'd arrived in Belgium, she only remembered enough French to barely order off a menu and ask for directions to the restroom.

Eline walked around her and Riley slowly, looking at them with a critical eye, which made Avery incredibly self-conscious about what she was wearing. The dresses here probably cost as much as a month of her rent did—or more—and the shirt she was wearing she had bought at Target for twenty bucks.

After Eline finished her assessment of them, she led them around the shop, pulling things off the racks, holding each one up to Avery or Riley. She would either make a displeased grunting *tsk* of a sound, or she would cock her head to the side a bit and add it to a rolling rack nearby.

Once there were three dresses for each of them on the rack, Eline led them to the back to try them on, pushing the cart with her. Avery expected to see a row of dressing rooms, each with its own door, but instead, Eline led them into a big room with mirrors covering two full walls on opposite sides of the room and parked the cart toward the back.

"Would you like me to dress you?"

"What?" Avery said. "No! I mean, no thank you. We've, um. We've got it." She shot Riley a look to see if she seemed as horrified as Avery was.

"This side is for you," Eline said to Avery, motioning to one side of the rack, then said to Riley, "and that side for you. I want to see you in all three of them, so don't change out of one before I get back. I'll be finding shoes."

As Avery and Riley stood side-by-side, looking at the dresses on the rack. Riley pulled one out, eyeing it. "Can you believe how much we've seen today, and it's not even dinnertime yet?"

"And Nicolas didn't even pick us up until after lunch." She felt the buttery-smooth fabric of each of the three dresses.

"So, do you feel like you've been properly pulled out of your boring life?"

"My life isn't boring." Avery wasn't willing to admit that it was. There was too much about it that she liked. "It's just predictable."

"Oh, my mistake. Do you feel like you've been properly pulled out of your *predictable* life?"

Avery laughed as she pulled a deep blue lacy dress off the rack that looked like it would go to her knees, with the thick straps resting just off her shoulders. "You could definitely say that I have. I just feel bad that he's doing stuff like this—spending lots of money on us."

Riley took a black and white print wraparound dress off the rack and held it up in front of her, looking into the mirrors before laying it on a padded bench and kicking off her sneakers. "I don't know—it looked to me like it was something he wanted to do. He's looked happy the whole time he's been with us. Who knows? Maybe we're pulling him out of his own boring life."

Avery doubted that. He lived in one of the most incredible cities she'd ever seen. Okay, she hadn't been to a bunch of different cities, but she watched TV and movies. None of the cities there were as captivating as what she'd seen today.

"I take that back," Riley said as she slid off her jeans. "Maybe he wasn't happy the *whole* time he's been with us. He seemed a little less happy when you chose to sit so far away from him on the boat that the tour guide could've easily sat between you two."

Avery had just pulled off her shirt, so she wadded it into a ball and threw it at her sister's stomach right as Riley was sliding her own shirt off. Riley laughed. "I'm just saying that I think he likes you. Is the feeling mutual?"

"Of course it is. I mean, he's Nicolas." Avery shimmied into the blue lace dress, then turned and moved her hair out of the way so Riley could zip it up for her. "He was amazing way back in high school, and he's only gotten better since then. That's not the issue. The issue is that he lives so far away. And what we've experienced of his life so far is . . ." She had to work to figure out what word she was looking for. "Intimidating."

She turned to look at herself in the mirror. Wow! The first thing she tried on looked this good? What were the chances? Something this well-fitting probably wouldn't come until the tenth try if she was shopping at home. And how had Eline even known what her dress size was?

"Ooo, pretty!" Riley said, and then spun in her dress to show it off. Her black and white dress looked amazing, too.

"Coming in," Eline said as she was already coming through the door, not before, carrying a stack of shoeboxes that she set down on another bench.

She turned and looked at Avery, a pleasant smile on her face. "You look beautiful."

"Thank you," Avery said with a little curtsy.

"That is not the dress for you. Take it off and try the next one."

Avery pulled her head back in surprise at the shopkeeper's change in tone. "Oh. Um, okay."

Eline turned to Riley and studied her, a finger tapping her lips. "It's good and shows off your curves. But I'm not sure it's the one. You change, too. We'll try on shoes once we've found the dress. I'll look for bags while you're changing."

"Bags?" Riley asked.

Eline looked at her like she was a slow thinker. "Purses. You can't exactly wear one of those," she said, pointing at the rack of dresses, "and have *that* or *that*," she motioned to where each of them had dropped their purses, "hanging on your shoulder."

When the woman turned to leave again, Riley giggled. "Silly me." As she unzipped Avery's dress for her, she added, "So do you think you couldn't handle being in Nicolas's life?"

"I think that what we're seeing is vacation life. Real life is nothing like vacation life."

She pulled the second dress off the rack—a light blue dress without sleeves that had a straight skirt and was cinched in ever so slightly at the waist. She stepped into it and pulled it up as Riley slipped into a dress that looked like various bright watercolors were used to make a design resembling flowers.

They took turns zipping each other up as Riley said, "But you enjoy his company."

"Very much."

"Then why do you keep pulling away from him?"

"Because how could we ever have a relationship? I'm not ready for a relationship—I need to figure out my new career goals and where I want to head—and he lives forever away. And that's not even counting whether or not I would be any good at being in his life. I mean, that might be the biggest issue right there. All of this—this dress shop, his grandfather's penthouse, Nicolas's car, the fancy dinner—is further away from the life of a farm girl than the ocean between Lake Baldwin and here."

Riley turned and put her hands on Avery's shoulders. "Avery. Who says this has to be a long-term relationship decision that you're making right now? Can't it just be something between the two of you until we leave a week from Monday? A vacation relationship. You came here looking for new experiences and new perspectives. Don't you think it falls into that category?"

Avery absently played with the fabric of the skirt at her thigh. Was she just thinking too far ahead and not enough about right now? "But what if that's not what he's looking for? Wouldn't that be rude, or be, I don't know, using him?"

"What I think is that you both know you're leaving in about eleven days. You both know there's an expiration date. Yet he still seems to like you and wants to spend time with you while you're here. And not just 'regular' time, but 'sit close to me on the boat' time." She wagged her eyebrows. "And, hey, here's a novel idea—you could *ask* him how he feels about all of it."

True. Why was she staying in her own head so much instead of talking with Nicolas about it?

Eline walked in just then, holding an obscene number of purses and clutches, and set them on a big round bench. With her eyes on Avery, she made a guttural sound resembling *Ick.* "That dress takes away your figure. You look like a light blue fudgesicle. Positively not the one."

Avery had apparently put all her focus on her conversation with Riley because she hadn't looked into the mirror. Yeah, the dress was not flattering on her. She didn't know if she would've called herself a fudgesicle, but it kind of fit.

Then Eline looked at Riley. "No. Just no. That one hides everything you've got, like a rainbow threw up on a chameleon. No, take them off. They look so bad, I can't even stay in the room with you two while you do."

Riley gave Avery a look as the woman left the changing room, waving a hand behind her like she was trying to erase everything as she went. Avery barely kept a laugh from bursting out of her before Eline was out of earshot.

They each put on their final dress, and Eline must've heard Riley pull up her zipper because she practically materialized into the room the moment it was up.

"Oh praise everything holy *that* is the dress," she said as her eyes landed on Avery.

Avery turned to look in the mirror. The soft fabric of the sage green dress was fairly fitted. The dress scooped up into a strap that went over one shoulder, leaving the other shoulder bare. The dress was slightly cinched at the waist on the side with the bare shoulder, making it look like she had more of a waist than she did.

A ruffle started at her hip and went down until it split at her thigh, the ruffle continuing along the fabric to where it fell just below her knees. The hue seemed to go perfectly with her skin tone and hair color and made her eyes look like they were the same green as the dress. She felt beautiful. And most surprising of all, comfortable.

"And you," Eline said, clapping her hands once in delight as she looked at Riley. You both look perfect."

Riley's dress was chocolate brown and looked very silky. It wasn't as fitted as Avery's—the bodice was flowing to where a belt of the same fabric tied around her waist, and then the dress flared out to her knees. The full sleeves reached her wrists, the neck soared above her collarbone, and the fabric opened to expose the middle of her back.

"Right?" Riley said, giving a little twirl. "We are going to stun everyone at the restaurant."

"Meneer Servais said you're going to dine at Trattenuto Andante." She studied the two of them, obviously trying to act like she wasn't as curious as she appeared. "Reservations take months to get—such a treat that he managed to get a table for exactly when you'd be here."

Months? He hadn't seemed to have reservations, and that he'd just decided while on the boat to go there. How had he gotten the hostess to get them a table for that same evening?

When the two of them didn't give any further

information other than the looks of surprise that were probably very evident on their faces, the woman said, "Now let's get you shoes and bags!"

At almost exactly an hour after they'd first stepped into the boutique, they were wearing their dresses and heels, purses on their shoulders, bags of the clothes they'd been wearing in hand, and walking out of the shop. The moment they stepped through the door, Avery saw Nicolas, leaning against the railing at the edge of the pedestrian walk. The sun was just setting behind him, and a brilliant cascade of colors spread across the city skyline, mirrored in the water of the river below.

He wore the nicest suit Avery had ever seen. Or maybe it only looked that nice because of who was wearing it. Whatever it was, the man took her breath away and she couldn't seem to form words. She looked him up and down, trying to take in everything.

Especially that smile and the way his eyes fixed on her like she was the most beautiful person he'd ever seen.

"Wow," Riley breathed beside her.

"Yeah," she managed to agree.

Nicolas stepped around a group coming down the walk and came over to them. "You two look exquisite. How did shopping go?"

"She knew what our sizes were without even asking," Riley said. "Shoes included."

Nicolas smiled. He had the greatest smile—it made his

right eye crinkle just more than his left. Probably because his lips lifted just slightly more on that side. It made it feel like it was a smile he completely owned. Nothing borrowed or fake about it, and it was uniquely his.

Nicolas glanced down at their shoes when Riley mentioned them, so Avery showed hers off. They were pumps in the same color as her skin, with a cute strap that started near her pinky toe and crossed her foot to near her ankle. She'd never felt like she had particularly long legs, but she felt like she did in those shoes. They were so cute, she could stare at them all day. The bottom part of the heels was a striking red, which she couldn't see right now, but just knowing it was there made them feel even cuter.

"These shoes are even more comfortable than my sneakers were," Avery said. "Eline wouldn't tell me the price, so I'm thinking that means they were probably somewhere around the same cost as my first car."

Nicolas tried to cover a smile. "That matte gray Toyota Corolla with the foil-colored duct tape holding up the muffler?"

"Hey, don't knock the duct tape. It was the shiniest part of the car." She looked back down at her shoes. "But seriously, though, we should stop by here after the restaurant and see if we can return them because you're not going to want to see that credit card bill come in."

He chuckled lightly and looked down at the ground, smiling, before meeting her eyes again. "You came across an ocean to see my country. Getting you shoes that make you smile like that is the least I could do."

"Does that mean I don't have to return mine either?" Riley asked while lifting a foot clad in a red heel with an ankle strap. "Because I love these so much I want to marry them."

That smile on Nicolas that Avery was beginning to love so much returned. "You too, of course."

As they headed toward the restaurant, the sun dipped lower behind the skyline, and more and more lights came on along the river. They lit up the buildings lining the river in golden hues, with strands of lights turning every waterfront café into a social event that felt magical. Music played from one of the buildings as the entire atmosphere around the canal changed. She could live out here. All she needed was a cot pushed to the side of the cobbled walkway.

If she thought the evening had made the outside more magical, it was nothing compared to what it did for the inside of Trattenuto Andante. Golden lights from ornate chandeliers and wall sconces lit up each of the dining areas, giving a soft glow to all the neutral colors. The atmosphere was calm and inviting, and every detail from the table linens and textured wallpaper to the clothes the wait staff wore spoke to the great care and attention they wanted to give their guests.

The hostess seated them at a candlelit table in a quiet,

secluded area. Their waiter came by soon after and said that tonight, they were serving their tasting menu.

"That's exactly what we were hoping for," Nicolas said. Once the server left to get their first course, he said, "I can't wait for you to taste the gourmet dishes here."

As they ate some of the most delicious and beautifully plated food Avery had ever seen—smoked sea bass amuse-bouche, barberie duck with beetroot, and haddock with pommes pont-neuf and wild turbot—the three of them talked.

"If you came from all this," Avery said, motioning to the opulent restaurant, "how did you end up in South Dakota when you were an exchange student? Did they not let you pick where you would be going?"

He smiled, but with a different emotion behind it than normal. Guilt, maybe? He dabbed at his mouth with his napkin, then placed it back in his lap. "Oh, that wasn't by chance. My parents one hundred percent wanted me to go to a school in New York because they thought that was what would most help me in my career. It wasn't that I was against going to New York at all—it was more that my parents had been controlling every aspect of my life and I needed to rebel.

"There were parts of the application that they had to fill out and parts I had to fill out, and by the time it was ready to submit, everything was to my mother's satisfaction. Then, after my parents went to bed, I brought it back up and changed the area we were requesting. I looked through the options, and I don't know. South Dakota just felt. . . *right*. And it also happened to be about the furthest thing from what my parents hoped for. So, I clicked on it and submitted the application."

"You did not," Riley said.

Nicolas nodded. "I did. And it was at the moment that I made the change that I truly understood why my brother, Maxim, decided to go into carpentry instead of the family business. I guess we both needed to feel like we were in control of our destinies, even if it was just a bit."

"What happened when your mom found out you changed it?" Avery asked.

He chuckled. "Well, let's just say that she didn't find out for weeks, that she was anything but happy about it, and that it was too late to do anything to change it."

They reminisced about all the things they used to do back when they all lived on her parents' farm in South Dakota. A place that felt so removed from where she currently was that it made her laugh.

But still, as she listened to Nicolas talk and saw his reactions to the stories that she or Riley told, she couldn't help but wonder how she'd lasted nine months in the same house with Nicolas back then without falling for him. How had they been able to remain just friends? Because every time he looked at her with those warm dark eyes and that perfectly curving up smile, it did things to her stomach and made her resolve to stay away from dating begin to waver.

And so did every accidental touch. Every brush of their fingers, every bump of their knees, every time she responded to something funny by putting her hand on his arm without even realizing she'd chosen to do it until she found her hand there. All of it made her crave those touches even more. Those smiles. Those soft eyes on hers. It all made her wonder why she'd been so against a relationship.

As much as she didn't want it to happen, eventually, the night came to an end. She hadn't even remembered that they had left his car back in a parking lot near the Belfry of Ghent earlier in the day until he walked them to the lot closest to the restaurant and there it was. He must've gone back for it while they'd been in the dress shop.

When they were almost back to his grandfather's flat, Riley said from the back seat, "Thanks for today, Nicolas. Today alone made this entire trip worth it."

Avery looked over at him to see the smile that crossed his face. He did seem happy to show them around. As he pulled into the curved drive in front of the building, she added, "Your city is amazing, Nicolas. I think I can now call it the best city in Europe, too."

He laughed. "But in all fairness, you've only been to two cities in Europe—Brussels and Ghent." He turned the car off, got out, and came around to open their doors. When they exited, he said, "How about tomorrow after work, I show you all of Europe? Then when you say that Ghent is the best, the words will have some power behind them."

"*All* of Europe?" Avery smiled up at him, noticing the way his hair was perfectly trimmed around his ears, the way his very slight scruff beautifully framed his jaw, the way his lips looked so soft and so kissable. "You're talking about the Mini Europe park, aren't you?"

He ran a single finger down her forearm, which sent shivers up her arm and neck. "Yep. It's not far from here. Can I pick you two up at six?"

"Sure thing," Riley said.

All Avery could do was try to remember to keep breathing as she watched Nicolas walk around to his side of the car, her arm still tingling from his touch. He gave her one last wink before getting inside.

"Do you really think it's okay if I stop fighting my attraction to him?" Avery asked.

Riley laughed as she turned to walk in the front doors. "Ave, let's be honest. You stopped fighting it hours ago."

Huh. Maybe she had.

Chapter Twelve

NICOLAS

$\mathcal{N}$icolas walked through the opening into the Mini Europe park with Avery and Riley at his side. The Atomium, the giant silver landmark in the shape of an iron crystal cell magnified 165 billion times—the monument that was even taller than the Belfry of Ghent—stood just beyond the park, serving as its backdrop.

He'd been in primary school the last time he'd visited Mini Europe. It was still an impressive sight. There were hundreds of monuments from all over Europe that were all replicated at one twenty-fifth of their actual size, complete with probably thousands of little people.

Many of the re-creations were animated. Waterways and grasses and real dwarf trees and bushes were planted everywhere, too. A cobbled pathway wound its way along the outer border of the park before entering in to see all of it, with lots of other people walking around, looking at the miniatures. Some weren't more than waist-high. Some were taller than him by quite a bit.

They'd added new things since he'd been here last. A long flag-lined walkway, displaying the flags of all twenty-seven countries represented led along one side before really getting up close to any of the monuments. They had mostly made it to the end, all three of them trying to get glimpses of everything they were about to see, when Riley yawned.

The walk turned, and the entrance into the area where they could walk right up to each of the monuments was in sight when Riley stretched. Nicolas looked over at her. "Are you okay?"

"I'm just *so* tired. I guess the jet lag is finally catching up with me."

Avery looked at her sister curiously.

"It's just been a long day. What I really want to do is go back to the flat and chill for a while."

"Oh," Nicolas said. "Okay, I can drive you back."

"No," Riley said, a little more forceful than needed. "You two stay here. Enjoy. I already texted Jacques and asked him to come pick me up." She pulled her phone out of her pocket and glanced at the screen, but from where Nicolas stood, he could see there weren't any notifications. "Oh, look—he's already here. And it sounds like Delphine and Rania are just hanging out at the flat, bored as could be. It'll be good if I head back and keep them company."

Avery folded her arms and narrowed her eyes at Riley. In response, Riley blew her a kiss and said, "Goodbye. You two have a great night!" And then she headed back the way they had come.

Nicolas turned to Avery. "What was that all about?"

Her gaze followed her retreating sister, eyebrows slightly drawn together. "I think that was probably her very strange way of getting us to go on a date."

His heart pounded. "Is that what this is then? A date?"

"Do we want it to be? I mean, I leave a week from Monday. And we live so far apart, so it's not like a relationship could last beyond then. Are we okay with there being. . . something more between us just until I leave?"

The distance was an obstacle. He hadn't seen it as being quite so unsurmountable, but he hadn't known how Avery might feel about it. Now he did. But the fact that she was asking if there could be something more while she was in his country confirmed that he hadn't been wrong when he'd guessed that she had feelings for him, too—feelings that went beyond their friendship that started a decade ago.

He smiled and took a step closer to her, noticing the way she held her breath whenever she waited for an answer, biting her lower lip just slightly. And the way her hazel eyes had gold just around the pupils. The way one lock of hair always came forward, brushing her left cheek. A week and a half wasn't nearly enough time with her. A lifetime might not be enough. But if a week and a half was all he was going to get, it was better than none. "I'm okay with it."

She smiled at him for a long moment. Then she slipped her hand into his, and they stepped onto the winding pathways that would take them through the park. He could only think of the warmth of her soft hand in his. How right it felt to be connected to her in that small way.

Avery stopped at the Børsen—the seventeenth-century stock exchange building in Denmark. "It's so intricate. And look at the little cars! And people! And boats! Is someone making them move by remote control? Or is there something under the water?" If she was that excited about boats moving in the water, he couldn't wait for her to see figurines moving, and trains and cranes and busses and garbage trucks with horns that honked.

As he watched her look at all of it in wonder, it made him want to show her everything. Not just in Brussels or Belgium, but in all of Europe. He wanted to see that sense of awe on her face as she experienced each of these monuments in person.

Avery glanced at him as they walked from Denmark to Sweden. "Tell me something I don't know about you that happened after you moved back here at the end of our junior year."

"Anything in particular?"

She squinched her face up as she gazed out at the groups of people nearest them in the park. "Um . . . how about something you did that was hard. Something you didn't think you could do, but then surprised yourself."

He paused for a minute, trying to think of what he wanted to share. "Okay, I graduated with a master's degree in International Business, and my focus was in marketing. But ever since I first started working at Oma Servais when I was fourteen, my parents wanted me to spend time working in all major departments so that when I become the CEO, I will know the company inside and out. I worked part-time all through college and full-time during any school breaks."

He stopped when they took a moment to see St. Olaf's Castle in Finland, but she looked up at him like she was waiting for him to continue, so as they admired the details of the castle, he said, "My first full-time position after graduation, though, was with my father in the legal department. What you need to know about me and department-hopping was that I had to do a lot of pretending that I knew more than I did and that I had to make friends quickly to survive in each one. Friends have been vital. It was how I found out all the things about a department that I didn't know.

"But when I got to the legal department, there was just a different vibe there. I haven't ever really figured out if it was just the type of people my father hired, or if it was a lawyer thing, but no one wanted to be friends at work, and no one wanted to share information. Which was too bad, because out of all the departments, the legal department was the one I had the least aptitude for."

"But you figured it out and succeeded?"

"Yeah. Well, I wouldn't use the term 'succeeded.' But I did survive, and I didn't accidentally get the company into any legal battles by my ineptitude, and that's the best I can say about that. But you asked what I didn't think I could do but surprised myself by doing, and that was to gain a new kind of respect for my father.

"My mother is a little . . . overbearing. My father backs my mother one hundred percent in everything. And because of that, for my whole life, I saw my parents as a single entity. When I worked in my father's department, I got to see him as an individual. As someone who made his own decisions and had the ability to lead.

"I might not have learned nearly as much about running Oma Servais during my time in the legal department as I did in every other department, but my time there was invaluable simply because of what it taught me about my father."

"Wow," she said as they walked along the path. "That's kind of beautiful. I'm glad you got that experience." They were nearing Belgium, but he was pretty sure she hadn't noticed yet.

Then she gasped as they walked up to a knee-high brick wall with a miniature hedge and the entire majestic Grand Place in miniature behind it. The buildings that formed three sides of the square were replicated with the most minute details, including the decorative archways, statues carved into the stone of the buildings, spires and turrets, pillars, and every delicate detail about the ancient buildings.

She pointed. "That's where Riley and I went today!"

"What did you think of it?"

"I think a day wasn't enough to take it all in." She was clearly trying to take more of it in by looking at the whole area from a giant's perspective. Maybe if he could show her enough wonders in Belgium, she'd want to return over and over.

As they moved on to look at the next monuments, he asked, "So, what about you? What was something hard you did that made you proud?"

She thought for a long moment as they walked and stopped to look at monuments, but then she glanced around at the other people nearby and shook her head. "It's stupid."

He squeezed her hand. "If it made you proud, it's anything but stupid."

She shook her head. "I don't share this about me with

many people, because they always look at me like I must not have the mental faculties needed to place importance on things and have that guide my decisions. But it isn't about that at all."

"I won't judge you."

She studied him for a long time, then must've decided that she believed him and took a slow breath. "Okay, I really wanted the job I have in the admissions department at LBSU. I worked in the department as a student employee my last two years of college, saw the work there that my boss did, and decided that was my dream job. It wasn't available when I graduated, so I worked at a job in retail that I hated until the position opened.

"It got down to just two candidates for the job, and they brought me back in for a final interview. They told me that the other person *really* wanted the job and to tell them why they should pick me.

"Here's the stupid part," she said, her cheeks reddening like she was embarrassed. "I—" she paused. "I feel the emotions of others. Even if they're just another applicant that I've never met before and I only know what they were feeling because someone else told me. And those feelings of others *do* feel like they have a great weight, so they *do* affect my decisions. So when they told me that this other person really wanted the job, my first instinct was to pull myself out of the running so they could have it."

She brushed a hand across a cheek like she was trying to brush away the feeling that made them red. Like she was trying to brush away the feeling of being embarrassed for who she was.

"I know that I don't stand up for what I want often enough. And *I* really wanted that job, too. Maybe even more than the other applicant. So, I decided right then that I was going to stand up for what I wanted. So I fought for it.

"I let my passion for it shine through and somehow convinced them to hire me instead of the other candidate. It might seem stupid, but it had been a huge obstacle for me, so I was pretty proud of myself. It's something that I still struggle with, actually, and I've been working on overcoming it."

He stopped walking in the United Kingdom, in the shadow of Big Ben, and just looked at Avery's beautiful face. He felt like she'd just opened a door to her mind to let him look inside and see how things worked. The memory of every reaction he'd ever seen from her started to shift as if the motivation behind everything she did moved ever so slightly, clicking into its actual place.

And then he realized that all the times when they were teens when he thought she was indecisive about where they should go or what they should do was probably only because she wanted others to be able to choose what mattered most to them. Which was possibly the biggest difference between Avery and Sophie. It was refreshing. But he wondered how often Avery overlooked what she wanted and instead chose what others wanted. He vowed to make sure to find out her wishes and to never overlook them.

"That's not stupid at all. You should never feel like something that is quintessentially you is something wrong with you. Those are the things that make you your best, most authentic self. Being able to feel the feelings of others is pretty incredible, actually, and the world needs that.

"And"—he paused a moment to figure out what he was feeling—"it also sounds a little exhausting."

She let out a breathy laugh that seemed to have relief woven into it, too. Maybe relief that he understood or that he didn't judge her harshly for it. "It can be."

Her eyes shifted just past him. "Is that the Eiffel Tower?" She hurried around the bend in the cobbled path to France, and he got the message that she wanted a change of subject, so he followed behind her. And it was an incredible monument to get distracted by. She gazed up at it for a long moment, then looked at everything else around them. "These are all built to scale, right? Is the Eiffel Tower that much bigger than everything else?"

"It really is." He added that to his very long mental list of things he wanted to show her in person.

By the time they had made their way around the park, the sun was setting, the outdoor lighting had come on, and everyone else had already exited. Avery was so entranced with so many of the monuments that she seemed not to have noticed the crowds thinning until she looked up from the red, gold, and white of Melk Abbey in Austria.

"Oh! Did they close? Are we supposed to be out of here already?"

"No," he said, shaking his head. "Not yet. I have something to show you." He took her hand in his and led her back down the pathway in the direction they had come from. The park was indeed closed, but he'd worked things out with the park's management beforehand to keep it open for them just a little longer. The evening still would've been fun with Riley present, but right now, he was profoundly grateful that it was just him and Avery.

The temperature had dropped since the sun went down. He noticed that Avery started to shiver, so he took off his suit coat and held it while she slid her arms into it.

When they got back to the area with Belgium, he could see that the staff had gotten everything they'd discussed set up. In the small grassy area that sat right next to Graslei Street and the Rabot in Ghent that wasn't part of any monument, they had laid out a blanket with the picnic basket that Nicolas had dropped off before picking Avery up. Little electric lanterns flickered like candlelight, casting all of it in a soft glow.

Avery's eyes widened at seeing it. "You set all this up?"

"Yeah. Are you hungry? I figured we'd eat in Ghent."

He motioned to the replica of the line of buildings, each one touching the next, right at the edge of the canal. "We traveled down that section of the river. Remember when we walked out of the restaurant last night and saw all the lights just across the river? We were looking at those buildings."

Avery let out an audible gasp before her eyes flew to his. "This is so perfect. *So* perfect."

He knelt on the blanket and started pulling fruits and cheeses out of the basket as she sat down beside him. "So, now that you've seen all of Europe, can you say that Belgium is the best?"

She shrugged. "I don't know. There are some pretty great things here. I mean, the Houses of Parliament building in the United Kingdom was pretty impressive."

"But we have the Grand Place. And you've got to admit after going there earlier today that it was also pretty impressive." He sat on the blanket and stretched out his legs in front of him.

"True. But Paris has the Eiffel Tower."

"We have the Atomium. They were each built for the World's Fair. And the Atomium is shinier. And based on the duct tape you chose for your Corolla's exhaust pipe, you like shiny."

Avery laughed. "You got me there. Okay, what else?"

"We've seen quite a few countries with castles and medieval cathedrals, but ours are better." He twisted his watch around his wrist as he glanced about the park, looking for things. "Oh, and London has a Ferris wheel, but Brussels and Ghent both have one, too. I'll have to take you on the one in Ghent sometime—you can see everything from it."

"Oh, but we saw ruins. Does Belgium have any ruins?"

He bit his lip, looking up like he was thinking. "They just tore down a building a few blocks from here. We could drive by on the way home if you'd like."

She laughed again, and he decided he wanted to make her do that every single day. "Are you comparing a torn-down building to the Acropolis?"

"Okay, maybe not, but we do have ruins—the Coudenberg Underground Palace. You can even go tour them by going to the BELvue Museum of Belgian history."

"Okay, okay," Avery said, "I'll admit that Belgium is the best." She paused for a long moment, absently running her fingers along the handle of the picnic basket. Then her eyes met his. "Although I can't guarantee how much of my opinion is swayed by the fact that Belgium is where you are."

He noticed the moment that her eyes flicked to his lips before going back up to his eyes. The motion made his eyes go to her lips, too. They looked so soft and so perfect and still so very kissable. He pushed the picnic basket and the food he'd started pulling out of it to the side, and Avery scooted into the space it vacated.

Her nearness brought warmth to the cool evening. A yearning to be even closer to her. A feeling of knocking down the rusty old fence that served as the only barrier between a friendship that started a decade ago washed over him, and something more. A thrumming buzz of possibility. The entire world—or at least all of Europe—felt like it held its breath as they gazed into each other's eyes as thoughts intensified and decisions were made.

And then Avery leaned forward, closing the distance between them, and pressed her lips so softly and tentatively to his. A question. He cupped her face with his hands and answered by kissing her with all the longing he'd been feeling. She scooted even closer, the calf of her bent leg pressing against his thigh, and he dropped a hand to wrap it around her waist.

She let out the softest moan, and his heart rate kicked up. He deepened the kiss, and her hand went to his neck, her fingers tickling the skin near his ear and he let out his own soft moan. He would kiss her thoroughly for as long as she wanted him to.

Eventually, she pulled back slightly and gave him that smile that he loved, her fingers slowly running along the inside of the collar of his shirt. "I think it's a good thing that we never thought about dating back when we were seventeen. Because if you had kissed me like that back then, I don't think I would've ever been okay with you going back home."

He chuckled. "In all fairness, I probably wasn't nearly as good of a kisser back then."

"But you were still you, so it probably would've had the same effect." Something intense flared in his chest as her soft eyes searched his face.

"I hope it's okay to ask this, because I'm genuinely curious, now that I know that you sense the emotions of others. Did you kiss me because you could sense how badly I wanted to kiss you? Or did you kiss me because of how badly you wanted to kiss me?"

She playfully smacked his arm with the back of her hand.

"No, I'm serious. I really want to know."

She must've sensed his earnestness, because she said, "I kissed you because I think I've wanted to kiss you since the moment you responded to my note with a handwritten one of your own, even though you were responding over Messenger and didn't need to."

He felt a smile spread across his face. She had wanted this as much as he had. He cleared his throat and tried to make his words come out less gravelly than he feared they would. "I have a work event coming up next Friday. It's a reception that's kind of the opening event for a week-long international chocolatier competition, and I need a date. Will you go with me?"

Her eyebrows rose, her expression intrigued.

He rubbed his fingertips on the small of her back,

where his hand still rested. "I feel the need to warn you, though, that it's a very formal event and my mother will be there."

She chuckled. "I would love to meet your mother. Yes, I'll go with you." And then she leaned forward and gave him another kiss.

Chapter Thirteen

AVERY

*A*very and Riley stood on the back part of the L-shaped rooftop terrace of the Royal Library of Belgium, holding umbrellas in an attempt to stay somewhat dry. From where they leaned against the square stone eco-garden planters, they could see the beautifully-shaped gardens of the Mont des Arts that they had spent the morning exploring.

She and Riley probably should've chosen something entirely indoors for such a rainy day, but the city just looked so beautiful in the rain, and they wanted to be out in it. All of its colors just seemed more vibrant and alive. And from their vantage point, they could see even more of the city. This terrace was a gem of a place they only knew about because it was on the list that Nicolas had left for them.

Avery's phone rang, so she pulled it out and looked at the screen. "Oh! It's Summer from work." She'd planned to check in with work friends often, but with the time difference and the fact that she'd been with Nicolas most of the time when her friends back home had been awake, she just hadn't.

"Take it," Riley said. "I'm going to go post some pictures to Instagram."

As Avery pressed to answer the call, her sister walked over to the other side of the L-shaped area and sat down on one of the colorful chairs shielded from the rain by a giant umbrella over the table, pulling out her phone.

Avery turned away. "Summer! Hi!"

"You sound like you're enjoying your trip," her friend said.

"I am. Right now, I'm standing on the rooftop terrace of the Royal Library of Belgium, in the rain, looking out at one of the most beautiful cities I've ever seen."

"Oh, yeah? Is it simply the city that's so beautiful, or is it something else, too?"

"What do you mean?" She shook her head as she peeked out from her umbrella to glance at the sky. Summer was perceptive, but she couldn't have guessed that something was going on with her and Nicolas.

"I don't know. There's just an extra something to your voice." Summer paused a moment. "Oh my goodness, you fell for your friend Nicolas, didn't you?"

Avery laughed. "There's no way you could've known that by hearing me say one sentence about the city."

"Oh, so you're saying I am right! I want to hear all the details. Wait. Didn't you say he has a girlfriend?"

"*Had* a girlfriend. They broke up five months ago. But nothing is happening between us." She had told Summer that she was swearing off dating, after all, so she didn't want to tell all the details. Besides, her agreement to see Nicolas was only until she left Belgium, so it wasn't a big deal. Even if she had opened up to him in ways she never opened up to people. And even if he maybe did, too.

"Okay," Summer said, dragging out the word like she didn't believe Avery at all.

"A long-distance thing wouldn't work for us," Avery said, trying to get Summer to understand as she wandered further from earshot of a small group who were waiting out the rain from under one of the big umbrellas. "It's not like the other person lives an hour away or even in another state. He lives across the ocean. This is an amazing country, but I also really love Lake Baldwin. I couldn't just leave."

"I get that," Summer said.

"Oh, and I forgot to mention—his family is super-rich, so there are so many parts of his life that I wouldn't have a clue how to navigate."

"I don't know. I bet you could figure it out."

"Hopefully I can a little bit, at least. Because I agreed

to be his date at the International Royal Chocolatier reception on Friday before some big week-long competition."

"Oooh, a date! I knew it. And you're going to do great."

"I'm getting nervous just talking about it. Tell me about what's going on there."

"Oh, we have news in the office! But it's not my secret to tell." Summer seemed to hold the phone away from her mouth and call out "Pavani!" Then, to Avery, she said, "Okay, I've got you on speakerphone now. Pavani, it's Avery. She wants to hear your news."

Avery glanced at her sister. She still seemed content to keep scrolling through pictures to post to Instagram.

"Oh, hi! Okay, remember how I was telling you that I wasn't feeling great when we were walking into work together that one time? I found out why. I'm expecting! It hadn't occurred to me that it might be the reason because Zain and I hadn't even decided that we were ready to start trying for a family yet. But we'll have to get ourselves ready because we're going to be parents!"

"That's the most incredible reason to be sick, Pavani! Congratulations!" As much as she was loving every moment in Belgium, hearing Pavani's news made her homesick for the office. Avery tilted her umbrella so she could see over to where Riley was still looking at her phone, tapping on the screen.

They chatted for a bit about the baby and how Pavani was feeling, then Avery asked Summer how the wedding planning was going.

"Really well. We're getting lots done since we're pretty much pros at planning big events together now." Summer laughed. "Brock is the cutest. He wants everything to be perfect, and I just keep reminding him that it's not going to be perfect no matter how hard we try, and that's okay. The only thing that matters is us getting married, not that we have a perfect wedding."

Hearing Summer talk about getting married just made Avery want to move her life in that direction even more. While being on this trip, she'd experienced new things, for certain, and that had helped her perspective. She'd even tried things out of her comfort zone. But she hadn't been challenged as much as she needed to be. She was far from having everything figured out.

"And let's see," Pavani said. "The school magazine asked Elle to start a project of interviewing alumni that went on to do incredible things and then writing articles about them. Did she tell you? And Everett is going on dates with someone new again, like always."

Avery wanted to tell them that she'd gone on a date, too, with Nicolas last night. But since it was a Belgium-only thing, it felt wrong to bring it up with friends from work. Like saying it to someone in South Dakota would make it true there, when it was only true in Belgium.

After they ended the call, Avery walked over to Riley, brushed the rain off the seat next to her, and sat down. Riley finished whatever she was doing on her phone and slipped it back into her bag.

"Okay," Riley said, "so we are now five days into our trip."

Had it only been that long? It felt like so much longer.

"You came here with goals. Let's do a goal check."

Avery looked up to make sure that the umbrella over the table was covering her, then closed her own umbrella, thinking about it. "As far as my goal to stand up for what I believe in, I can't say I've done too much of that. But we've done so much here that it feels like I've been making progress on my goals to do bigger things in life, take risks and try new things, and get more comfortable stepping out of my comfort zone. I know I'm going to have to do a lot more to be ready to take the next step in my career, but it feels good. It feels like progress."

Riley grinned at her.

"What about your goals for this trip?"

Riley held her hand flat, palm up, like it was a pad of paper, and held the other hand like it held an invisible pen. "Hmm. See many great sites . . . *check.* Try new foods . . . *check.* Have an amazing time . . . *check.*"

"Play matchmaker for your sister . . ." Avery said.

"Also check," Riley said with a flourish of her fake pen.

"Why were you so sneaky about leaving Mini Europe

last night? You know you could've just said that you wanted us to go by ourselves."

Riley chuckled. "No, I couldn't have, because you wouldn't have still gone. You would've felt bad that you were leaving me alone and you would've stayed behind. I didn't want you worrying about my feelings—I wanted you to go have fun! Besides, I had fun back at the flat with Jacques, Delphine, and Rania. *Plus*, Mom is going to award me the 'favorite daughter' title for being your wingman. She loves Nicolas."

Avery laughed. "And Dad is going to award me the 'favorite daughter' title by default just because he'll be mad that you're trying to get his daughter involved with someone from another country."

Riley shrugged. "Eh, you win some, you lose some."

"But seriously, though. Thank you for last night."

"You can thank me by letting me borrow the heels you got a couple of nights ago when we get back home."

"Deal."

Chapter Fourteen

*N*icolas tried to force back a yawn. He was tired from staying up so late with Avery and Riley each night, then making the long drive back to his home in Ghent afterward. Plus, he'd been coming in very early every morning, trying to make up for the missed hours of work that week, especially because it was such a busy time with the competition coming up.

But it was all worth it because it was great to see them both again after all these years. Every minute he got to spend with Avery was worth it. Especially last night. The whole evening had been perfect.

He was working on prepping for the executive staff meeting when his mother walked into his office unannounced, which meant she wanted to catch him unprepared. He looked up from his desk just as she slapped the file folder down on his desk about his date for the reception that he'd had Finn deliver to her earlier that morning.

In Nicolas's report on Avery, he'd been careful not to point out that she was a member of the host family he'd stayed with while he was in America. He'd painted it in a way that he'd hoped his mother wouldn't notice. It wasn't like she'd ever called to chat with his host family while he'd been living there or wanted to hear stories about them. She'd been so upset that he had gone to South Dakota, of all places, that she'd wanted nothing to do with them. He hadn't thought she would've even remembered their names.

But since he'd given his mother a folder about a woman with a name she wouldn't have recognized, she would've researched to know if they were "someone worthy." She'd have dug pretty deep to find out all she could about Avery. By the furious look on her face, he knew she'd figured it out. Not that it would've been hard. She and Riley were currently staying at his grandfather's flat, after all.

"This is a hugely important event, Nicolas. This is my last IRC Awards as CEO of this company, and I want us to be successful at it. And not only that, but you know the difference it makes in our sales for the whole year. We have a lot of people depending on this company for their livelihood."

"I know."

"And not only that but who you bring matters. Remember when Mon Paradis sent an inexperienced fool to the reception and they made an off-color joke to one of the judges and the entire company was disqualified from competing? Or six years ago when Ihre Schokolade's CEO got drunk and confronted one of the judges and their company got blacklisted? *Six years* and they still haven't recovered."

"It's not like—"

"So you are *not* bringing a hillbilly from South Dakota as your date."

"Mother—"

"No." She pointed a finger at him. "You do not get to defend her. We agreed to send you to the United States because we thought you'd be going to one of the business capitals of the world. Somewhere you could make connections that would help you throughout your life here.

"We did not agree to send you to farm country." She said the last two words like they were something foul stuck to the bottom of her shoe. "I knew we shouldn't have let you go through with it. But I never imagined that it would still be coming back to cause problems for us this many years later."

Her breathing was fast and her nostrils flared. It was rare to see this much emotion from his mother.

He'd known back when he was a teen and made the switch that his mother would never get over being upset about it. And he'd known that announcing that he was bringing Avery would reignite her anger about it.

Nicolas didn't even stand up from his desk to even out the height advantage his mother had. He didn't need it. In a very firm yet calm voice, he said, "Avery will surprise you. And she's who I'm bringing, end of story."

Many thoughts and emotions crossed his mother's face. Before she'd been able to form them into words, though, her assistant, Elias, stepped into the room. "Excuse me, Ms. Servais. You are needed for an emergency call with our operations manager in Antwerp and then you have that appointment off-campus soon."

She kept her eyes on Nicolas for a long moment, still furious. But instead of saying anything more, she turned and walked out of his office.

He knew that she wouldn't just drop the subject and that she'd have more to say about it very soon. Yet he was still taking it as a win.

Chapter Fifteen

*A*very and Riley stood from their seats on the terrace of the Royal Library of Belgium to head down to the ground level to meet Jacques and go back to the flat, excited to get into dry clothes again and warm up. Before they exited the terrace, though, Riley got a call from her business partner.

"Hi, Sara!" Riley's eyebrows drew together. "Oh. Hi, David." She listened for a moment, then a shocked look covered her face. She mouthed to Avery, *Sara got into a car accident.*

Avery was shocked at first, too. But then she wondered if this was all part of Riley's plan to give Avery and Nicolas more time alone together, just like she had last night. But there was no way she would let Riley cut her vacation short on her account.

"Is she going to be okay?" Riley shot Avery a worried look—one genuine enough that Avery suddenly wondered if maybe Riley wasn't faking the situation. Then Riley said, "Hang on. I've got Avery here with me—I'm going to put you on speakerphone."

Riley pressed the speaker icon and held the phone between the two of them. Avery scooted in close enough that their umbrellas were overlapping.

"They think she'll be in the hospital for several days," David said. "Maybe even a week."

Avery could tell by the worry in Sara's husband's voice that he was definitely not part of a ploy with Riley. This was real.

"I know you two are doing the flowers for that big wedding next week, so I don't know what to do. Sara's either in a ton of pain or on a ton of pain medicine, so I can't ask her. And even if she could answer coherently, I don't want to stress her out by asking. But she won't be out of the hospital before the wedding, so there's no way she can do it. Should I cancel the wedding?"

Riley glanced at Avery. "No. You absolutely cannot cancel. You can't do that to the bride—that would stress her out unimaginably, and there's no way she could get someone else to cover in that short of a time frame."

Riley started pacing on the wet cement, so Avery paced right along with her, keeping their umbrellas close.

"And you can't do that to our business. Not only is our

reputation on the line, but we've put so much work into it already. And so much expense. If we don't get paid for this wedding, it'll sink our business. Canceling isn't even a little bit of an option."

"Do the temp employees know what they're doing enough to pull it off on their own?"

Riley paused her pacing. "No. They don't. I'll come home on the next flight. But hopefully, they know enough to keep working without supervision for a bit. Regardless, I'll take care of it. If Sara brings it up, tell her not to worry about it. Don't you worry, either. Focus on her recovery. Tell her that I was jealous of her being the one to gain all the superpowers, so I decided I wanted to gain some, too."

David gave a weak laugh. "Okay, I will."

"And David? Tell her she already has superpowers, and she's going to come through this just fine."

After they hung up, Avery asked, "Is she okay?"

Riley nodded and put her phone into her bag. "It sounds like she's pretty banged up. She'll have to stay in the hospital for a while because she's got a punctured lung and some bleeding around her spleen and possibly a concussion. It'll take some time to see how her body's responding, but they don't think she'll need surgery."

They heard a ding, so Riley pulled her phone back out to look at the text. "Oh. It's Jacques. He's here to pick us up."

Avery nodded and started walking toward the door

that would lead them down to the ground level. "I guess we better hurry back and get packed." Her chest and throat ached at the thought of leaving when things were going so well and she was enjoying it there so much. She didn't feel done here yet. No part of her was ready to leave.

Riley stopped walking and grabbed Avery's arm. "*I* need to go home. Not you. You should stay."

But the whole way back down to the street and during the trip back to the flat, she thought about how she didn't want Riley to have to make that long trip home by herself.

And she thought about how it would be to stay in Brussels by herself. That would definitely be stepping out of her comfort zone. She wanted to stretch and grow, but she hadn't planned on doing it like that. And if she was in Belgium without Riley, that would probably mean spending a lot more time with Nicolas. As much as she would love that, could she do it and still keep from falling for him? Because going home with a broken heart wasn't really what she was looking for.

But she'd just told Nicolas that she would be his date at that event next Friday. How could she skip out on him?

As they walked off the elevator into the flat, Avery still felt like her insides were torn between all the awfulness of leaving and all the awfulness of staying. Right along with it was all the concern she felt about Sara's health and all the work and stress Riley would be facing as she headed back home. She should go along to support Riley in all she was about to do. She still had work off, so she could be one of Riley's temp employees and help with that, too.

As they walked into Riley's room, Riley turned and put her hands on Avery's shoulders. "You're not coming with me."

"I'm not letting you travel alone and face all of this at home without help."

Riley rolled her eyes. "I won't be traveling alone—there will be like three hundred of us on the plane. And Shelly's probably bored out of her mind by now without us at the apartment, so she'll be glad to have me back home. Besides," she said, her voice sounding somewhat teasing, "I want that *Favorite Child* title Mom is going to bestow upon me—and the *Favorite Sister* title, too—because now you're going to have tons of time to fall in love with Nicolas."

Avery wiped a tear that threatened to spill over her eyelid and let out a breathy laugh. "You're my only sister."

"Yes, but right now I hold both the *Favorite Sister* title and the *Least Favorite Sister* title, also because I'm your only sister. I want to ditch the second one."

"You could never be my least favorite sister."

"Aww, I ditched it already."

But Avery still wasn't sure that staying by herself was the right choice.

Riley FaceTimed their parents to update them on the

change of plans. It was still early morning in Lake Baldwin and her parents were already out on the farm, but they just happened to be in the same area, so they both came to the phone.

After Riley explained everything to them, Avery said, "So do you think I should come home, too, or do you think I should stay?"

"I think you should stay," her mom said pretty quickly. But of course, she would say that—she was Team Nicolas all the way.

But her dad would feel differently. He'd be concerned about her safety, especially being across an ocean and by herself. "Dad?"

He paused for a good long minute, thinking, his lips pursed. Then he took off his wide-brimmed hat, ran his hand over the top of his head, and put the hat back on. "I think you should stay."

Avery's eyebrows shot up. "Really?"

"What was your whole point in going to Belgium?" he asked.

She shrugged. "To figure out where I want to go with my career next. To step out of my comfort zone. Take risks. Experience new things." She let out a breath of a laugh. "And to have more interesting things to put on any bio I'm ever asked to write."

"And is staying going to help you accomplish that goal?"

"Yes."

He nodded. "Probably even more so, since you'll be forced to figure all those things out without your sister at your side. It's going to take a heck ton of bravery, though. And do you know what rhymes with bravery?"

She laughed because she'd known that was coming. "Avery."

"As scary as it is to be somewhere on your own, I think you can do it. And I think you'll be glad that you did."

"Besides, you won't be all the way alone," her mom said with a sly smile and a wink. "You'll have Nicolas."

"Plus," Riley said, "you'll have Jacques, Delphine, and Rania."

True. She wouldn't exactly be alone. She took a really deep breath to calm her nerves, then blew it out slowly. "Okay, I'll stay."

After Riley hung up the phone, she turned to Avery. "You can thank me for this by one day being just as excellent of a wingman for me as I've been for you, right when I need it the most."

Avery hugged her sister. "You've got it."

Chapter Sixteen

NICOLAS

Nicolas was gathering the things he needed for the executive staff meeting he was about to head into when a text from Avery came in.

AVERY: Riley's business partner, Sara, got in a bad car accident, so Riley has to head back home tonight.

He immediately called Avery. As soon as she answered, he said, "Is Sara okay?"

"She will be. But she'll be in the hospital for probably a week, and they are doing the flowers for a big wedding, so Riley has to go back to take care of everything."

"And are you staying?" He held his breath as he waited for her answer.

The moment she said "Yes," he felt massive relief. He couldn't handle having her leave yet—there was still so much he wanted to show her. So much time he wanted to spend with her.

"How does Riley feel about leaving?"

"She's sad, of course. But her business means a lot to her, so she needs to go back. And thanks in large part to you, she got to see an entire vacation's worth of sights in the time we've been here."

"Are you okay staying without her?"

"I'm trying to be."

He glanced up at the clock, then grabbed his iPad and pencil and headed out of his office. "Do you have plans for tomorrow?" He had too much on his plate today to get away, and she was probably going to be busy getting Riley off to the airport. But he wanted to see her in person soon to make sure she really was okay. And since tomorrow was Saturday, he had the day off.

"Not anymore, no."

"How do you feel about going on a shopping trip with me and my friend, Fleur, to find you a dress for the reception? She is an excellent shopper who has been to more than enough of these kinds of events to know what to shop for, and she says she's happy to help." He stopped in front of the glass conference room door. He held up a finger letting them know he needed just a minute.

"Another dress? Nicolas, I can wear the dress I got when we went to Trattenuto Andante."

"That dress was semi-formal, and this event is black tie."

"There's a difference?"

He chuckled. "There is. So is tomorrow a yes?"

"Yes."

"Great. I've got to head into this meeting, but I'll talk to you tomorrow. Tell Riley I said goodbye and safe travels?"

He ended the call and headed into the meeting, taking the last chair. His mother sat in her place at the head of the table and gave him a look that told him she wasn't too pleased that he was not only late, but the last person to arrive. He wasn't helping ease her anger toward him.

His mother ran these meetings tight, never letting them veer off track or address agenda items out of order. Ten minutes into the meeting, she asked their Chief Operating Officer, Christophe Mertens, for an update on manufacturing. He said that they'd discovered some of the international suppliers they'd been working with weren't strictly following Oma Servais's no-child-labor rules. "Asking for changes hasn't gotten results. I suggest that we cancel their contract with us for defaulting on the agreed-upon terms because that's what will promote change."

Christophe was so much better about looking out for the entire company as a whole than Nicolas imagined he would be himself. Nicolas was great at looking out for the people at their corporate offices and even the workers in their shops throughout the country, the people he interacted with most. He was good at coming up with new ideas for marketing and products. He was good at all of that. He just never thought as globally as Christophe did.

Nicolas's mother pressed her lips together in a tight line, then asked, "How bad is it?"

"Not as bad as it was years ago. They've got workers a year or two below the minimum age."

"Will we still have the cocoa we need to keep up with demand?"

Christophe shook his head. "Not entirely. We get fourteen percent of our cocoa from them. We can make up for roughly ten percent of the difference by increasing our orders with our other current suppliers. But we'll be short the other four percent until either that country or that company changes their practices or until we get some contracts signed with some other suppliers, which could take upwards of eight weeks."

"Then no, we aren't canceling their contracts."

Christophe glanced to the side, at all of them sitting on one side of the table. "With all due respect, Margaux, we have the influence needed to help their entire country to better enforce the laws that protect their children. We should use that influence."

"No. Find another way."

Nicolas's mother wasn't that cold. In fact, she'd been behind the initial discovery that many companies were using underage workers and had pushed for change. She was probably just extra irritable because of Nicolas's date choice and his refusal to bend.

"Wait," Nicolas said. "I think Christophe has a good idea. We should hear more about his plan."

Jean-Pierre held up his pen. "I agree with Nicolas that it's a good idea." Then Jean-Pierre gave Nicolas a glance that said *I've got your back on this.*

Nicolas's mother let out a long, slow breath. "I'm not saying it's a bad idea. But if we win the IRCAs, we're going to need those supply chains intact."

Nicolas knew how important it was to his mother that she stepped out of her position as CEO with Oma Servais in great shape, so he knew he needed to speak her language. "But we've also got to protect our brand image through it all. It can make us look great if we cancel the contract, and very *very* bad if the press realizes that we turned a blind eye to a big issue affecting the well-being of children that we had the power to change."

His mother rubbed her forehead with her forefinger and thumb. Then she turned to Nicolas's father. "Renaud, what are your thoughts on this?"

Nodding, his father said, "We have the law on our side and will be able to cancel the contract over them using underage workers."

"Christophe, meet with Renaud after we finish here and work up a plan. Get back to me with the details and other options for suppliers. Jean-Pierre, an update on the competition, if you will."

Jean-Pierre sat up straighter. "The chocolatiers are ready. They've gone through everything many times and have plans in place for any obstacles that could crop up. I think we have a really strong chance this year."

And then, much to Nicolas's surprise, he added, "Nicolas created an exquisite bonbon about six weeks ago. We've added it as a product to Servais First and demand for it has been high. We should consider swapping it for the praline we're going to make in the competition in the 'Upcoming Product' category. It fits the requirements since it hasn't gone out to all the stores. I think it has a chance to be a very strong competitor."

Nicolas's chest filled with Jean-Pierre's words. He'd been proud of his creation. Hearing that customers were responding to it and that the Chief of Product Development thought it was good enough to be a strong competitor at the IRC Awards thrilled him.

"Is this the one that Finn brought to my office?" his mother asked.

Jean-Pierre glanced at Nicolas, and Nicolas nodded. "Yes."

Nicolas let himself dream for a moment about what it would be like to move into Jean-Pierre's position instead of his mother's. Being the CPD would allow him to have so much more flexibility with his time in the office and with travel. Being the CEO would take all his time, and his travel would be almost exclusively limited to business, so a relationship with Avery would be pretty impossible.

Not that Avery planned on their relationship going past a week from Monday. But she could change her mind, and if she did, being over product development would open it up as a possibility.

But then his mother said, "No," and it felt like she was giving a solid *no* to his dream, too. Like she'd known exactly what he'd been thinking.

"We already made the decision on which chocolates to compete with," she said, "and we aren't going to change things this late in the game."

The meeting went on for another twenty minutes, during which time, Nicolas felt more and more deflated. As soon as the meeting ended, his mother walked right up to him, leaned in close, and hissed, "Get your head out of the clouds. You were raised for greater things."

Chapter Seventeen

AVERY

very finished applying lipstick and had just begun to put in her earrings, walking out of her bathroom, when Jacques's presence in her doorway startled her. "Son of a Sea Cook!"

"I apologize for startling you, Ms. Parks. I just wanted to let you know that Mr. Servais is here to pick you up for your outing."

"Oh. Tell him I'll be right out." She looked at her watch as she grabbed her bag. She wasn't late—he was just early. It was so strange not having a doorbell to the place here.

As soon as she rounded the corner to the main living area, she saw Nicolas leaning against the counter in the kitchen, chatting with Delphine and Rania. Her heart jumped. When was she going to stop being surprised at how good-looking he was? Or how happy it seemed to make her entire soul to see him?

He gave her that smile that made his right eye crinkle more than his left, and it hit her how much that smile was for her—smiles he gave others didn't have that eye crinkle. Her breath caught and her stomach gave a *whooshing* feeling like she was suddenly floating.

"Hi," he said, and that single word melted her. "Are you ready to go?"

She nodded and said goodbye to Jacques, Delphine, and Rania.

As soon as they stepped onto the elevator and the doors closed, he said, "I missed seeing you yesterday."

She stepped closer to him, only a breath of air between their bodies, her face turned toward his. "Was that as long as I went without seeing you? A single day? It felt much longer."

He breathed out a chuckle. "I know what you mean." His lips were so close to hers that she could almost feel the movement of his words in the tickle of air that touched her lips. "It was awful."

"Terrible. Let's not do that again."

He put his hands on her hips, gently tugging her in closer until their bodies touched, and her lips ached with the need to be pressed against his. Instead, he left a trail of the softest kisses—barely skimming her skin—along her jaw and right next to her ear. Then he said, his words a husky whisper, "Mini Europe wasn't the first time I wanted to kiss you."

It wasn't the first time she'd wanted to kiss him, either. "Oh, yeah?"

He left a few more kisses down her neck to the hollow between her neck and shoulder before whispering again, "Well, it definitely wasn't the first time since you arrived in Belgium, but I meant before this trip."

"Before? When?" She could think of a few times while they'd been messaging back and forth in the five weeks before she arrived when the thought of kissing him had invaded her dreams. Her hand was on his chest, but she slid it up to his shoulder, feeling the strength of his muscles just under the fabric of his shirt.

His mouth was next to her ear again, and she longed for it to be on her lips. "The night of junior prom."

She pushed back from him, needing to see his face. "Junior prom?" How could that even be?

He shrugged one shoulder, tipping his head in the most vulnerable, adorable, nearly embarrassed way. Almost apologetic.

"For real? *Junior prom?* Like when we were seventeen. You wanted to kiss me then?" How had she not known? What would've happened if he had? Her mind buzzed with the revelation.

"I think I had a crush on you from about the first day I came to South Dakota."

"On *me?*" She was baffled. It couldn't be true.

He nodded. "I knew a relationship with you back then would've been a very bad idea. I mean, I was living in your family's home, so it felt as if liking you would be a betrayal to your family. Plus, I was heading back to Belgium at the end of the school year. And my life was so different from yours. Luckily, you had a boyfriend, so that helped keep me from thinking about it too much. And I'd kept it a secret almost to the end of the school year.

"The entire evening of prom, though, I was so afraid that I'd let my feelings for you be known. Because you no longer had a boyfriend, and we were each other's date, and it just became so much more difficult to keep those feelings hidden. And I knew if I drove you home and it was just the two of us, the chances of me having a moment of weakness and blurting out something about being in love with you were way too high."

"So that's why you talked the other group into letting us ride home in their limo?"

He nodded. "I didn't want to ruin everything between us."

She turned and collapsed against the elevator wall. "For real? You liked *me?*"

He leaned against the wall, too, facing her. He reached

out and tucked a lock of hair behind her ear. "Why do you sound so shocked by this?"

"I just don't really believe it. I was just a farm girl. I kind of still am. I'm just. . . me."

"See, but that's where I think you're wrong. You're smart, always willing to help everyone, and you care about what's going on in people's lives. You bring people together and you make them feel important and loved and safe. Plus, you've got the cutest little dimple right here that only appears when you're looking skeptical. And I know that if I put one of those moveable basketball standards in my grandfather's flat, I could get you to play with me any time of day."

She laughed. "That's true."

"And it doesn't matter how many fears I share or how much I question anything, you'll never judge and always leave me feeling like everything's going to be okay. You did that for me back when we were teens, when we messaged back and forth for the five weeks before you arrived, and you've done it for me here even more than you know. And it's my mission while you're here to help you realize how incredible 'just' you are."

She was pretty sure that he was 100 percent the incredible one. She gazed into his eyes, then she realized something that made no sense. "Why are we not already down in the—" She cut off her sentence as she realized that she'd never pressed the elevator button for the lobby. Her cheeks flushed as she reached out and stabbed it.

Nicolas gave her an amused smile and then a quick kiss on the lips. "I'm really glad that I get you for the whole day today."

———

THE SHOP NICOLAS led her to was much bigger than the boutique they had visited in Ghent. This one had clothes for men and women and everything from what she now knew was semi-formal to black tie to wedding attire—all spread across two floors. They took the escalators to the second floor and turned right toward the women's formalwear.

They walked up to a tall woman with long, wavy, light brown tresses with golden highlights who was waiting for them. She looked fashionable and strong and absolutely intimidating. Which made Avery feel absolutely out of her element.

Smiling broadly, Nicolas said, "Fleur, I'd like you to meet Avery, my date for the IRCA reception. Avery, this is my friend, Fleur."

Avery didn't know what kind of greeting to give Fleur. A handshake? A hug? Air kisses? She looked like she could be royalty, and they did have royalty in Belgium. Should she bow or curtsy? Nicolas would've told her if Fleur was royalty, right? She waited to see what Fleur did.

Fleur smiled and slowly nodded, almost like a bow using just her head, and said, "It is lovely to meet the person Nicolas regards highly enough to take as his date to that event."

Avery smiled much bigger—she'd just been called "highly regarded," after all—and said, "It's so great to meet you, too."

Fleur strode through the department with the movements of a pro. Whenever a salesperson approached and asked if they needed help, Fleur waved them off and said, "Just a dressing room when we're ready."

Fleur asked Avery about her preferences, then studied Avery and Nicolas side-by-side, to decide which colors were going to complement both of their skin tones the most. And Nicolas told stories about how he and Fleur grew up together and about their families being friends. And he told Fleur stories about living in South Dakota with Avery's family.

Fleur had draped four or five dresses over Avery's arm when Nicolas pulled his phone out and frowned at it. He typed in something, slid the phone back into his pocket, and turned to Avery. "I know I said that I had the entire day free, but there is a work issue with a digital campaign in an online magazine that they're saying isn't scheduled to air when it's supposed to. And since it's related to the

IRC Awards, it's not something I can put off until Monday. Would you mind if I left? My office isn't far from here, and it shouldn't take long."

Okay, Fleur seemed nice. And still very intimidating. But Avery could handle this fine. She smiled at Nicolas and said, "No problem at all. I'll see you soon."

Fleur had been looking through some dresses on a rack and kept doing it, casually watching Nicolas heading toward the escalator.

She placed another dress across Avery's arm and walked to a display a few feet away. Then, as soon as Nicolas was out of sight, she said, "Nicolas tells me that you two are an item, but only until you leave in nine days."

Avery nodded. "Yeah. That's when I head back home."

Fleur glanced at Avery, and then her eyes went back to the display before looking at the dresses next to it. "Then you should know that Nicolas isn't a casual dater. He never has been. At least since the end of secondary school. So whatever you think the two of you have going on—this end of vacation thing—that's not likely how he's hoping it'll end."

"But we talked about it. That's what we —"

"I know. But I'm his friend, and I don't want to see him get hurt. His heart is likely tied up in your relationship more than he's letting on." Fleur stopped looking at the dresses and turned the full force of her very intimidating gaze on Avery. "So if you're planning to end things a week from Monday, you be careful with his heart before then."

Avery bit her lip and nodded. "I will."

Fleur nodded and went back to looking at dresses. Avery had told Nicolas that she wasn't interested in anything long-term with him, and on the surface, she still very much felt the same way. But it seemed that her heart had other ideas and kept planting images of their relationship continuing past the end of her vacation.

But even if she was willing to stop her ban on dating, they still lived so far apart. She knew Nicolas loved his job and his life here, and she loved South Dakota. They couldn't be together and both stay where they were. And they still came from such different backgrounds, too, regardless of how she felt. Was she doing them both a disservice by letting this relationship continue for the next nine days? Or was her heart already in too deep?

"Did the two of you ever date?" It was probably too personal of a question to ask Fleur. But Fleur said they'd been friends for a very long time, and Avery suddenly needed to know if this insight into his heart had been from firsthand experience.

Fleur let out a light chuckle. "No. Our interests do not align. The reason we can always see each other as a 'safe date' is that we know nothing will ever happen between us."

She was quiet for a moment, then added, "The problem is, my parents are not okay with the kind of person I'm drawn to. So in ten years, I'll probably be just as single as I am now. At least as far as they know."

Avery gave her a sad smile. "Do you think that will ever change?"

Fleur pulled a dress off the rack and held it up. "Miracles happen. It just doesn't seem like one will happen with my parents." She put the dress back on the rack and held up a hand to signal a salesperson.

"Another thing you'll want to know is that Margaux, Nicolas's mother, loves him very much. Fiercely." She turned to the saleswoman as she walked up. "A dressing room, please."

The woman nodded, lifted the dresses from Avery's arm, and headed toward the dressing rooms.

"Now you might think that's a good thing," Fleur said. "Margaux loves Nicolas, Nicolas loves you, so that means Margaux will love you. But she also has an unshakable belief that she knows what's best for Nicolas. So if she doesn't think you're what's best for him, she won't ever stop fighting against you."

Avery swallowed hard. She was doomed. How would Nicolas's mother ever think Avery was what was best for him? Both Nicolas and Fleur made it sound like Nicolas's mom approved of Fleur just fine. Now that she was here, with Fleur, seeing how regal and confident and commanding she was, Avery knew how much she didn't have a chance with Margaux.

Her best bet would be to go the next nine days without ever meeting the woman. And then ending things with Nicolas, just like they'd planned.

The dressing rooms did have separate changing stalls, as she'd expected in the boutique, but they were huge. Big enough to fit the fluffiest of ball gowns, the person trying it on, the person helping her get into the fluffy monstrosity, and half a dozen more dresses just like it.

Fleur didn't ask to help Avery in her dressing room, for which she was grateful. Having Fleur help wasn't exactly the same as having Riley help when they'd both been in the dressing room in Ghent. As she tried on different dresses, emerging to show them to Fleur and to see it in the big mirrors that also showed it from the back, Fleur explained what they were looking for. "Black tie gowns can't be too extravagant or out there. The simpler the better—the focus needs to be on the quality of the fabric and the fit."

She was glad she had Fleur to guide her through finding a dress. If she'd had to find one all by herself, she was pretty sure she would fail the test.

The fifth dress she pulled off its hanger was the color of her favorite dark blue blouse but turned into a jewel tone. It was a deep, rich, gorgeous color with the most luxurious fabric Avery had ever touched. She unzipped the back and stepped into the dress, the fabric giving her skin the silkiest caress she'd ever felt as she pulled it up.

Fleur had asked her to bring the shoes she planned to wear in a bag, so Avery slipped her feet into the ones she'd gotten at the dress boutique earlier in the week. Then she stepped out of the dressing room and let Fleur zip it up for her.

She turned and looked into the full-length mirrors. Her hands flew to her face. "Oh, I want to cry—it's so beautiful!" The dress had a very high neck and no sleeves, and somehow made her shoulders look incredible and her torso long and lean. It was fitted and sleek down to just below her hips, then flared out just enough to make ripples as it fell to the ground. She turned slightly to see the back —it dipped just below mid-back. Even that part looked good on her.

"That is one perfect dress," Fleur said as she walked around Avery, checking the fit at the sides and shoulders. "I don't think it needs any alterations up here at all. That's so unusual. And that cut accentuates your form so well." She took several steps back and studied Avery in the dress. "So elegant, too. I think this is the one. What do you think?"

"I think I'm in love with it."

Fleur gave her a very pleased smile.

Avery bit her lip. "It's so long, though." Several inches

of fabric pooled on the floor, even wearing her heels. "I think I'm going to trip and fall wearing this."

"Nonsense. I'll get the tailor in here right now to mark where alterations need to be made."

When Fleur left, Avery looked herself over in the mirror again, reaching a hand up to hold her hair as if it were pulled up, to see how it would look. She just couldn't get over how pretty the dress was! Right now, she was kind of glad that Nicolas wasn't present. She wanted to wait to see his reaction when he saw her wearing it on Friday, with her hair and makeup all done.

Fleur stepped back into the open area a minute later and said that the tailor would be in shortly. "Are you still liking it just as much?"

Avery nodded. "I feel powerful. Like I can take on the world." Then a terrible thought occurred to her, and the smile dropped from her face. "Do you think Margaux will be at the reception on Friday?"

"She most definitely will."

Avery was going to be sick.

Fleur stepped up close to her, her height still intimidating even though Avery was wearing four-inch heels now, and lifted Avery's chin with a beautifully manicured finger. "You," she said with so much force behind the word that it felt like a physical thing, "are going to do great on Friday night. You feel powerful? That's because you *are* powerful. Don't let her make you think otherwise. If you can travel to a new country without speaking the language and capture the heart of a man like Nicolas, you can take on Margaux Servais."

Avery gulped and nodded. She didn't know if she believed Fleur, but Fleur seemed terrifying enough at that moment that she didn't dare *not* believe her, either.

Chapter Eighteen

*L*ate Sunday night, Nicolas plopped down on his bed, smiling up at the ceiling after having spent the entire weekend with Avery.

Shopping had seemed to go well Saturday morning. He'd missed nearly an hour of it, but based on how excited Avery was about her dress, it was easy to assume it had been a success. And she and Fleur seemed to have gotten along well, too.

He and Avery had spent the morning meandering their way through the Italian Renaissance-inspired Galleries Royales Saint-Hubert, admiring the architecture and the impressive window displays and the grandeur of the glass-roofed shops. They had taken a seat for a few moments on a bench, and he'd just sat there, admiring the way that the sun shone on her face. Then they had dined one hundred meters above ground in the restaurant at the top of the Atomium, with its panoramic views of all of Brussels.

They ended the evening by watching a movie back at his grandfather's flat, along with all the staff, which had thrilled Avery. It had thrilled him, too, because she had leaned against him through the movie, her head cradled against his chest. But one by one, Jacques, Delphine, and Rania had excused themselves to go to bed during the second half of the movie, leaving Nicolas and Avery alone for the ending, which made him wonder if they all were trying to do a bit of matchmaking. He wasn't going to complain, though—it had left plenty of time for Avery and him to kiss.

And then today, he'd been able to spend the day with her in his own city. He'd shown her St. Bavo's Cathedral, which made him happy because Avery loved it every bit as much as he'd thought she would. They got to see the fifteenth-century architecture; all the artwork, including a manuscript from the ninth century; a pulpit of marble and gilded wood; and the famous altarpiece with all its history of wars, fire, and theft. He'd told her that they could stay to look at everything for as long as she wanted, and he loved seeing how entranced she was by it all. He especially loved all the flirty banter that had gone back and forth between them the entire weekend. He wasn't sure he'd ever laughed so much.

As they had wandered the city, looking at whatever seemed to catch Avery's attention, they'd both opened up about a lot of things that Nicolas had never told anyone before. When they exited a tourist shop where she had bought some gifts for her family and coworkers, she'd asked, "So what is your greatest fear?"

He'd chuckled. "Oh, so we're going into the heavy-hitting topics now, huh?" It took him a bit to think about how to put it into words, but he was strangely not hesitant about sharing. "I guess it's being alone. Not in an 'I'm alone in this room' kind of way. More in an 'alone in life' way."

"When do you think that became your biggest fear?"

"Good question. Probably when my grandma passed away. I was seven, and we'd been buddies—I'd spent much more time with her up until that point than I'd spent with my own parents. She taught me so much and was always there for me. Her death was sudden and unexpected, and it had been hard."

Eventually, he'd talked about the other things that probably led to his fear of being alone. The big one, of course, was everything that happened with Maxim when Nicolas had been thirteen. That had probably had the largest impact on him of everything. Looking back on it, he'd realized how traumatic it had been for him.

He'd said, "When my grandmother passed, I was devastated, but I knew that a part of her was still with me and always would be. But when everything happened with Maxim, not only had my family been pulled apart, but it felt like my future was threatened. And it definitely *changed* my future."

Avery had given support without judgment and calmly listened as he worked through everything, which was exactly what he'd needed but hadn't even realized he'd needed.

He'd even told her about how Sophie cheating on him had fed his fears of being alone. "I think I'm always kind of worried that something would unravel and I'd lose everything. So whenever I'm feeling anxious, I work lots of extra hours, hoping that it'll somehow help me to hold onto everything."

She'd bitten her lower lip while she was thinking—something he noticed that she did often—and then asked, "So, do you feel like you're always trying to please your parents?"

He'd stopped right there on the sidewalk in front of a flower shop and considered it for a moment. "I don't think so. I mean, that relationship matters to me, so I put effort into it. But the reason why I work hard at Oma Servais is because I love the company, enjoy what I do, and want to see it succeed." She'd stayed quiet, giving him space to think and analyze it as they walked. Eventually, he'd said, "I think it's more that I'm trying not to *dis*please my parents."

She'd nodded and said, "That makes sense. So what do you think would happen if you displeased your parents? I'm talking worst-case scenario here."

"Worst case? Being disowned and losing everything. Not just my family, but my job at Oma Servais, including all friends and acquaintances."

"Okay," she'd said, "and if that happened, what would you do?"

It had been painful to think about, but he pushed through the pain and came to a conclusion. "I guess I'd start over at a new company. I do have skills and experience. And I would still have Maxim." It had been amazing to think past the fear to what he'd actually do. Liberating, really. Because now that he'd thought all the way through to a plan of action, he knew he could do it. It'd be very difficult and he wouldn't want it to happen, but he'd survive if it did.

"And now let's talk about *likely* scenarios," she'd said as she slipped her hand into his and started walking again. "Do you think your parents would actually disown you?"

"I don't know."

"Okay, let's look at the evidence. They have you over for dinner weekly, right?" He'd nodded. "That shows that a relationship with you matters to them. And they want you to take over as CEO soon, so that shows they have a lot of trust in you."

"True," he'd said. "Family dinners happened

infrequently before Maxim left, and now they happen religiously. So maybe they're trying harder to hold our family together, too."

"I think that is a good indicator. Now let's look at you. You *did* stand up to them and you did displease them when you chose to go to South Dakota instead of New York during high school, which took loads of bravery, by the way. So you have a history of standing up for what you want. You made a life choice they didn't agree with, and the consequences *weren't* the worst-case scenario."

Realizing all that caused a huge shift in his mindset. Those fears had been so deep down that he'd never admitted them to anyone before. Not even to Sophie after dating her for nearly two years. Just like Avery always did when they were teens, sitting on her family's patio, looking up at the stars, and sharing their deepest thoughts, she helped him to dig deeper to see the truth behind his fears.

It had been exactly what he'd needed. Someone to talk him through everything rationally. They were all things he normally didn't think too much about because fears would enter in, which made his mind always go to the most tragic outcome. And he didn't want to spend time fearing the worst, so he brushed too many things under the rug.

But she had helped him to see the truth without fear clouding everything. And she helped to remind him of his successes in the past. No wonder he always felt more fortified to face life after he talked with her. She seemed to always know just what to do to build him up in the exact way he needed.

He rubbed the side of his finger over his eyebrow, chuckling as he thought back to how she'd noticed that he twisted his watch when he was nervous—something he hadn't even known he did.

And she'd talked about how she believed that people were good enough as they were at any given moment and that they didn't have to earn people's love. "And I believe that," she'd said. "I do. But deep down, I think I only believe that is true for other people. Not for me." It took him a while to get her to really open up about it, but it seemed that she felt that when she was being helpful to others, then she was worthy of love. And that if she wasn't helping, then she hadn't earned it.

It was baffling to him that she felt so much of her worth was tied up in her ability to be productive and do things for others, all while ignoring what she needed. She didn't seem to realize how much she was loved for her heart and her mind. He'd tried to help her to see just how important she was. He didn't think he had helped her nearly as much as she'd helped him, so he would continue to help her to see her worth for as long as she would let him.

As tough as those things had been to talk about, he loved that they'd connected so deeply. It had been freeing in a way. And strangely, it hadn't brought either of them down in the end—they had somehow gotten more energy by releasing those fears and had been ready to take on all of Ghent.

When they were meandering around Groentenmarkt, he'd taken her to one of the carts selling cuberdon—a deep purple cone-shaped candy with filling. It was something that Ghent, in particular, was known for. As soon as she bit into one, her face scrunched up.

He'd asked her if she didn't like it, and she'd said, "It tastes like medicine." It wasn't uncommon—many people from outside of Belgium thought the same. But then she'd looked around and asked, "Are we being pranked? This isn't really candy, is it."

He'd laughed so hard. He'd eaten one, said that he thought they were great and that they reminded him of his childhood. And she'd said, "Why? Did you have to take medicine a lot as a child?" and he'd laughed even more.

He'd taken her to one of his favorite fine dining restaurants last time they'd been in Ghent. Today, he'd taken her to a street vendor with the best meatball, pineapple, and vegetable burger with frites, and he'd thought to ask the vendor to make Avery's well done. His lungs swelled at the look on Avery's face that he'd remembered to make the request. When they were teens, they'd gone to a burger joint, and her "well-done" burger came out a little more medium-rare. She'd had a bite in her mouth before she saw the pink meat and had to run off to the restroom, trying not to vomit on the way. They'd even joked about that as they ate the Belgian specialty on a bench in the park.

And then they rode the giant Ferris wheel after the sun went down, so they got to see the city lights from a height where they could see everything.

The day had been amazing, and if he was being realistic, he knew he was going to stay lying on his messy bed, staring up at the ceiling, replaying everything for quite a while.

But then his phone rang. It was his mother, so he answered. He knew she was calling about Avery being his date for the IRCA reception—he was rather surprised that she'd managed to go two and a half days without bringing it up or trying to get him to change his mind.

"Hello, Mother."

"Nicolas." She started by reiterating what a hugely important thing the reception was—which he already knew—and that it was only five days away and that the competition started in eight days. And that they needed to make an impression. Which he also already knew.

"So if you're going to insist on bringing Avery as your date, we want to meet her first."

He was so shocked he dropped the phone on his bed and had to pick it up again. She was requesting a meeting? Not demanding that he cancel and bring an approved date? He sat up.

"After all, you lived with her and her family for nine months. Nine months, and we've never even talked to her before."

The "not talking" hadn't been his or Avery's fault. He didn't bring that up, though.

"Your father and I would love it if you brought her to family dinner tomorrow night so that we can meet her. Especially if she's someone special to you, which, by your actions, I'm assuming is true."

"She is." Wow. His mother seemed to care about meeting Avery. Maybe she'd had time to calm herself during the past two-and-a-half days about the event and about Nicolas taking Avery as his date. He was impressed. His mother wasn't usually like that with the women he dated.

"Okay, I'll ask her and let you know."

After he hung up with his mom, he called Avery.

"Miss me already?"

He smiled just hearing her voice. "Yes."

She chuckled softly.

"My mother just called—she asked if you would be willing to come with me to family dinner tomorrow night. They want to meet you."

"Oh."

It was the tiniest word, but he tried to guess the emotions that were behind it. Was that worry? Excitement? Surprise? Dread? He couldn't tell. Based on what Avery knew of his mother, he was guessing it was probably more along the lines of worry and dread. "How do you feel about that? Because you can say no."

"I would love to meet your parents."

"Really? You're not nervous?"

"You never said not being nervous is a requirement. You just asked about willingness."

"True. If I swear to stay by your side the whole time, will that make you less nervous?"

"It will." He could hear the smile in her voice.

"Okay, I'll pick you up right after work tomorrow."

He hung up the phone feeling equal parts excited and nervous. He'd lived with Avery's family for nine months. He got to experience her home life and her family as extensively as anyone could. But as glad as he was that he'd be able to see her tomorrow when he thought he wouldn't be able to, he was nervous to show her what his own home was like. Because he was pretty sure that she wouldn't leave his parents' house being as enamored with his family as he'd been with hers.

Chapter Nineteen

The drive from Nicolas's grandfather's flat to his parents' home in the southeastern part of Brussels was only about fifteen minutes long, but Avery was surprised by how many nervous vibes she got from Nicolas during that time. Which, of course, made her nervous. Meeting his parents was kind of a big deal.

She was wearing her fancy new heels and her favorite skirt and blouse. She ran her hands across the skirt, smoothing out the fabric, and it made her realize that it was showing some signs of its age. She looked over at Nicolas in the driver's seat. "So what about tonight is making you so nervous?"

He glanced over. "I worry that you aren't going to like my parents. And that my mother might be getting subtle jabs in all night. Please don't take it personally, though. That's just what she does."

Great.

"But, listen. I don't want you to feel like you have to be here. If, at any time tonight you want to leave, just take my hand and give it two squeezes. I'll make up an excuse to get us out of there right away."

Nicolas's parents' home was at the edge of the Sonian Forest, which gave the entire area such a peaceful feel for it being so close to a big city. He pulled onto a cobbled road that she suddenly realized was a long driveway leading only to their house. The yard was massive, with big open grassy areas and plenty of trees and shrubs and flowers everywhere.

Then Nicolas pulled the car into the circular drive right in front of a mansion much larger and more ornate than Avery had imagined, which was impressive, considering all the very large, very ornate buildings she'd been touring for the past week. It left her kind of speechless.

Nicolas opened her car door for her and placed his hand gently on her back as they walked to the door, and she was grateful for the comfort it brought. Just as they reached the front door, an older man opened it for them and welcomed them in. Nicolas shook the man's hand and introduced him to Avery as Philippe, the butler, then he asked about the man's granddaughter and said something about a student council.

Nicolas's parents came into the foyer just then and stopped on the marble floors at the base of a large, curving staircase with an ornate metal balustrade. His dad wore a full suit and his mom a business suit with a skirt, and suddenly Avery felt under-dressed in her skirt and blouse. She probably should've worn the dress Nicolas got for her last week instead.

"Avery, I would like you to meet my parents, Margaux and Renaud. Mother, Father, this is Avery."

Margaux put a hand on each of Avery's shoulders and leaned in, giving her an air kiss on each cheek. "Lovely to meet you, dear." Her accent was similar to Nicolas's but sounded slightly more French. And a lot more haughty. Her eyes were keen and sharp like they took in everything and dissected and judged it.

Renaud held out a hand to shake hers, and as he did, she noticed that Margaux subtly wiped her hands on her skirt, like the feel of the fabric of Avery's shirt was offensive to her skin.

Avery took a deep breath to brace herself. She was determined to see this through and stay strong against Margaux.

They led them through a very high-ceilinged, ornate hallway into a sitting room that was even more opulent. Avery suddenly felt very small.

Renaud took them on a short tour of their very large house, showing her mostly the rooms she could see from the sitting room. They didn't chat for long before Margaux suggested that Grégoire was ready to serve them dinner so they should probably take a seat.

A woman dressed in something that might be a maid's uniform came around the table, pouring red wine into Renaud's and Margaux's wine glasses. Then she placed it in ice on a side table and poured a pitcher of some kind of clear liquid into Avery's and Nicolas's glasses. Nicolas looked at his mom, eyebrow raised, and she said, mostly to Avery, "We respect that Nicolas doesn't like to drink here, so we're extending that same courtesy to you by giving you both club soda."

Avery gave Margaux a tight smile. She wasn't a drinker, but if there was ever a time when she felt like she probably needed one, she sensed it was going to be here. She sipped her club soda.

The maid then brought out a tray of what must've been an appetizer or salad course. Strangely, it was a tomato with the top cut off—the stem still on it—and stuffed with something that looked like a mixture of little brown shrimp and mayonnaise.

"It's called *tomates aux crevettes grises*, dear," Margaux said.

Avery was from South Dakota—a place where there wasn't a lot of seafood on the menus. Salmon and Tilapia and trout, sure, but what limited experience she had with seafood wasn't the best. But she tried mussels a few days ago—a dish she thought she'd hate but was delicious—and she could do this. Nicolas picked up his fork and knife and started cutting into the tomato, so she did the same.

She slipped a bite into her mouth and managed to chew it without cringing. The tomato was stuffed with something that reminded her a little bit of chicken salad, but with a vastly different texture and taste that she wasn't so fond of. But she did manage to swallow and take a second bite.

"So," Margaux said, "I understand you grew up on a farm. What is it that your parents grow?"

"They rotate, but oats, mostly. And my mom just started doing microgreens in their new greenhouse."

"Whew," Renaud said. "Farming sounds like a messy job, with all the dirt and farm equipment."

Margaux nodded. "I bet the maids hated that."

"Oh, we didn't have maids."

"My mistake," Margaux said. "*Farmhands.*"

Avery cocked her head, trying to figure out if Nicolas's mom was just attempting to be funny. "The farmhands work on the farm, not on cleaning our house."

"So there was no one to clean the house?"

"Well, we were pretty good at doing it ourselves." Avery debated whether she should act like she enjoyed the tomato thing and take a third bite, or if she would get asked another question the moment she put it in her mouth. Luckily, she didn't, because the next question from his mom came quickly.

"Where did you get your education?"

"I got my degree at Lake Baldwin State University. It's the same school I work at."

"Oh, right. That's your cute little hometown school, isn't it?"

"Yes." She kept a smile on her face. She deserved a gold star.

"Did you graduate with honors?"

"No. I mostly graduated with student debt." That answer wasn't going to earn her any brownie points with the woman. She didn't know why she said it, other than the fact that it made her chuckle inside, which helped. It also made the maid, who was just walking in to collect their dishes, fight not to smile. Honestly, that helped, too.

So did imagining how Riley would be reacting to Margaux's interrogation if she were still in Brussels. And picturing her parents in this room—and how her mom might respond to Margaux—nearly made a laugh escape from Avery's mouth.

Seeing Nicolas twist his watch around his wrist didn't. "Mother," Nicolas said, the word coming out as a warning.

"What? I'm just trying to get to know our guest a little better. Avery, you said you work there—I didn't know you were a professor. What do you teach?"

Avery leaned to the side a bit so the maid could collect her tomato dish. At least she wouldn't have to fake enjoying it anymore. "I'm not a professor. I work in the admissions department."

"Oh, so you get to decide who is admitted into the school?"

"No. As long as applicants meet the GPA and ACT or SAT scores needed, they're automatically accepted."

"Oh," Margaux said with as much judgy-ness as Avery could imagine a single syllable holding. "Automatic acceptance."

"Mother," Nicolas said as the maid set a very vibrant green dish down in front of each of them, "you don't even like eel in green sauce."

"Nonsense. I love *paling in 't groen*."

Nicolas let out a quiet growl, then said to Avery, "The sauce is quite good. It's just made from fresh herbs, like parsley, mint, spinach, sorrel, and watercress." Then he gave a glance to his mom before saying, "If you don't want to eat the eel, you don't have to."

Avery dipped the tines of her fork in the sauce and then tasted it. It actually was delicious. She wished she'd have grabbed the crusty roll off the plate with the tomato thing. Maybe she could've dipped it in the sauce, and that would've counted as eating this dish.

She just smiled at Nicolas, grateful that he gave her an out yet also equally determined to eat it. She managed eighteen college students as employees during finals weeks. She could handle some strange foods that were unlike anything she'd been exposed to. No big deal. The eel pieces were a couple of inches long and maybe a half-inch in diameter. She cut one into a smaller piece, dipped in the sauce to cover it even more, hoping to douse whatever taste the eel had, and put it in her mouth.

But it wasn't the taste that got her—it was the texture. *Just don't think about what it is. Just don't think about what it is.* She tried to get her mind on anything other than what she was eating, and chewed it enough to swallow. She nearly gagged on it but covered it by taking a sip of her club soda.

Margaux forked a piece of eel and cut into it with her knife. "What about your parents? Did they go to your local college, too?"

"Yes, they went to Lake Baldwin State University. It's where they met."

"How. . . quaint."

So the jabs weren't exactly going to be subtle. Got it.

"How much do they do on the farm?" Renaud asked. "Do they just oversee, or do they get their hands down in the soil?"

At least his questions seemed like they came from genuine curiosity, not from a desire for more ammunition.

"Both, actually."

The not-so-subtle jabs continued until the maid

cleared their green covered dishes, and then the chef wheeled in a tray that had on it a meat grinder, a glass bowl inside a bigger glass bowl with ice between the two of them, and an assortment of little containers filled with various things chopped fine and a couple of small liquid containers. And an iced bowl of very red, very raw meat that looked like it might be steak.

"And for our main course this evening," the man said in a thick French accent, "I'll be preparing my specialty, steak tartare, for you tableside."

Another growl came from Nicolas, and he said, "Did you purposely choose menu items you knew she'd be least familiar with?"

"I chose items that Grégoire is amazing at. You love Grégoire's steak tartare. And you heard him—this dish is his specialty." She nodded for Grégoire to continue.

Avery put a hand on Nicolas's leg to tell him that it was okay.

He talked through what he was doing, mixing together onions, capers, olive oil, raw egg yolks, mustard, tabasco, and Worcestershire sauce. She couldn't get over the raw egg. That was until he put the cold, raw steak into the grinder and added it to the other ingredients. Wait. Was he not going to cook it? She didn't see anything on his rolling tray that looked like a heat source. Maybe he would take it back into the kitchen to grill it or something after he finished.

As he was mixing it all, the maid brought in a tray with plates containing the other items in the main course, including something Grégoire called stoemp, which was apparently like mashed potatoes, but with a bunch of other vegetables mixed in, too. She was excited about eating that. But then he spooned the soft, somewhat liquidy raw meat onto the plates with it, without cooking it first, and she could feel bile rising in her throat. Would the FDA approve of this meal? She was pretty sure that they wouldn't.

Avery liked her meat well done. Or "burnt in the middle," as her dad always referred to her preferences, since she didn't like it even slightly pink.

Nicolas reached his hand out and held hers, but she didn't squeeze it twice. She didn't want Margaux to win. Avery just kept staring at the dish as he finished and as the maid brought one around to each of them, keeping her focus on not gagging. And talking herself into being able to eat it.

But then it was right in front of her, and she wasn't sure she was going to be able to. If she squinted, it kind of looked like it was fresh salsa. The red was tomatoes; the green was cilantro and peppers. Maybe she could fool herself long enough to down a bite. But she worried that the second it touched her tongue, the gag reflex would win.

The chef turned to leave, but Margaux said, "Stay so you can see what Avery thinks of your delicious dish."

So Grégoire stayed, and it was clear from the look on his face that he knew Avery was not going to be thinking his dish was delicious.

"No, mother," Nicolas said. "You are not going to bully her into eating this."

Margaux stared Nicolas down for a long moment like they were in a battle of wills. One that she didn't intend to lose. Then, head held high and clearly counting it as a win, she said, "Fine. I worried her palate wasn't refined enough for haute cuisine. I asked Grégoire to also prepare an American hamburger for her if that was the case. Amandine, will you please bring that in for our guest?"

Amandine reached out to take Avery's plate, but before she did, Avery grabbed her fork and jabbed it into the stoemp, getting a forkful, almost out of spite. She *did* appreciate good food. She'd have taken a bite of the steak tartare out of spite, too, if she wasn't so worried that she'd immediately throw it up. When Amandine lifted the plate, she'd never been so glad to see a dish of food taken from her before.

She savored the stoemp as she waited for her new food, even though it seemed impolite, somehow, to eat something when there was no plate in front of her. It really was delicious. A moment later, Amandine returned with a plate with a single hamburger in the middle, on a sad-looking bun. But she'd had plenty of burgers that looked less appetizing than this one in her life, so it wasn't a big deal at all.

When everyone started eating, she bit into her burger. She didn't even care that it had been a rude gesture—her stomach was growling, and the burger felt like home in a place where she felt as far from anything even resembling home as possible. Surprisingly, it was well-done. Margaux had probably requested Grégoire make it that way as an insult, not knowing it was how Avery preferred it.

Partway through her meal, Margaux set down her fork. "Nicolas, can I talk to you in my office for a moment?"

He shook his head. "I'm here with Avery, so I'm going to stay by her side."

Avery smiled, thrilled that he was keeping his promise. Margaux seemed to seethe, but picked up her fork and took another bite.

When they were mostly finished, the maid came back in to retrieve their plates, then returned with a tray containing a dessert of some kind that looked delicious from what Avery could see. Before she could serve it, though, Margaux said, "Will you just put the tray on the banquet, dear?"

Amandine hesitated for a brief moment, then set the tray on the side table.

"So, we have the International Royal Chocolatier

Awards reception coming up on Friday. Avery, have you ever been to anything like that before? I'm just wondering if you understand the intricacies of social hierarchy and the delicate nature of business receptions like this."

"No, but I've seen things like that in TV shows and movies and they always make it more dramatic than in real life, so I probably have a good idea." Avery dreaded even insignificant conflicts, like letting the worker at the drive-through know that she was handed the wrong order. When she'd made a goal to stand up for herself more, she hadn't pictured it happening with someone like Margaux.

But it wasn't like she could hide who she was behind a knowledge of Margaux's world, because she didn't have that knowledge. If Margaux was convicting her of not knowing what she needed to know, she might as well own it.

Margaux's lips drew to a thin line before she said, "Well. I'll get dessert then." She got up to grab the tray and tipped it, like it was too heavy or like she hadn't had a good grip on it, and said, "Help."

Nicolas was the closest, so he immediately jumped up to help right the tray. The moment his hands were on it, Margaux turned from looking helpless to fierce and hissed in a quiet voice that was still loud enough for Avery to hear, "You are not bringing her to the reception."

Was this seriously happening? Something like this wouldn't take place in a million years at Avery's parents' house, regardless of who Avery brought home as a date. Avery hated conflict. Still, though, she nearly leaped out of her seat to confront Margaux. The woman clearly disliked Avery, but she didn't need to make it such a problem for Nicolas.

The only thing that stopped her was a part of her that said, *But if you step in, will you be making more of a problem for Nicolas?*

Nicolas hissed something back at Margaux that Avery didn't hear, and she chanced a glance in Renaud's direction. He looked just as uncomfortable witnessing the situation as Avery felt being the star of it.

Avery didn't know the dynamic between Nicolas and Margaux, so she had no business stepping in to fight this fight when Nicolas was standing up for her already.

Nicolas's response must've been pretty firm because it seemed to frustrate his mom. Then he turned and placed the entire tray on the table and said, "Thank you so much for inviting us. I appreciate your attempt at hospitality, but we are leaving now."

He held a hand out to Avery, and she gratefully accepted it as he took big strides, leading them out of the house. As soon as they were outside and Philippe was shutting the door behind them, Nicolas wrapped his arms around her, holding her tight. She hadn't realized she'd been shaking until that moment. It wasn't that any one thing tonight had been too much. They were all small things, after all. It was more that there had been so many of them, coming at her, rapid-fire.

And the fact that she had made Nicolas look bad in the process.

"I am so sorry for subjecting you to that. I should've said that we were leaving the moment Grégoire rolled that cart out. No, the moment my mother started taking jabs at your school. No, I shouldn't have ever agreed to bring you tonight at all."

Avery shook her head. "It was important that I meet them."

Nicolas glanced out across the expansive lawn toward the main road. "Let's get back to the flat."

As they drove through the posh neighborhood on their way back to the highway, Avery started worrying about what kind of flack he was going to get from his parents once she wasn't around. Her going with him to the reception would make things tough between Nicolas and his mom. It was probably best if she didn't go.

Besides, what was she thinking, believing that she could fit into this world for even a minute? She was so out of her element. There was no way she could hold her own at the event.

She cleared her throat. "Fleur said that you and she fill in as each other's dates when you need one for an event."

"Yeah?" His voice sounded wary.

"You should ask her to be your date for the reception. I bet she'd go with you."

Nicolas breathed in a long, slow breath, then let it out as he pulled to the side of the road and came to a stop. He turned to look at her, his expressions visible in the light of a street lamp. "I don't want to go with Fleur. I want to go with you, Avery, regardless of how much my mother wishes I'd take someone on her 'acceptable' list."

"I don't want to make things tough for you."

"The toughest thing for me would not be having you by my side."

Her heart leaped at his words, at the same time a fear niggled in her belly. Had Fleur been right and he wasn't in this just until Monday? Was she okay with that?

Nicolas shook his head. "I do worry, though, about exposing you to more of my crazy world. You don't deserve any of this. As much as I want you there, if you want to back out right this minute, I will accept that answer."

She looked into his eyes and realized how much she wanted to be by his side, no matter how hard it was. "No. I'll go with you."

The smile that crossed his face was so glorious that she leaned across the center console and kissed it. And then hoped her choice wasn't a huge mistake.

Chapter Twenty

NICOLAS

During the drive with Avery to his brother Maxim's house in Mechelen, Nicolas was completely relaxed—unlike two days ago when he was driving Avery to meet his parents. But this time, Avery was the nervous one. Probably because she had now experienced some of his family and knew to worry. But for whatever reason, she was willing to go see more of them.

He reached across the center console and put a hand on her leg. "I swear Maxim and Léa are not like my parents."

"So, are you saying that there won't be any raw beef served?"

He gave her leg a squeeze. "No raw meat. But I can't guarantee that they won't make you give your opinions on baby names."

She chuckled. "That I can handle."

He could tell that she was still nervous. Once she met them, though, he knew her nervousness would go away.

Thoughts of work and to-do lists invaded his mind. It wasn't an unusual occurrence—before Avery came, it was normal. But since she'd arrived in Belgium, he'd been feeling increasingly pulled between her and work. The job needed his unwavering attention right now, but all he wanted to do was to spend every minute with Avery.

Why had he ever thought it was a good idea to invite her to come to Belgium over the same dates as the craziness leading up to the IRC competition? He'd known it was coming up and that he'd be busy.

But back when he had given her the dates that his grandfather's flat would be free, he hadn't expected to want to see her so much. She and Riley were just supposed to be old friends he'd want to get together with a few times outside of work.

"I picked up my dress for the reception today."

"Oh, yeah? How did it look?"

"I tried it on—the hem is perfect. I FaceTimed Riley while I was wearing it, and she said that you are going to 'lose your mind' when you see me in it. You'll find your mind, of course, but then you'll look at me a second time and lose it all over again."

He winked at her. "I've never wanted to lose my mind

more." He was losing his mind a bit right now, just thinking about it.

"And I realized why I loved the color so much—it reminds me of the dress I wore in the interview portion of the Little Miss Lake Baldwin pageant when I was eleven."

"Pageant? For real? Not that I knew what you were like back then, but I have a hard time imagining eleven-year-old you wanting to compete in a pageant."

"Yeah, looking back, I know pageants weren't my thing. I think I knew it at the time, too, but I still thought it sounded fun. But the talent portion worried me. I hadn't taken dance since I was six—long, embarrassing story there—and I didn't start playing the flute until the next year, and I was super uncomfortable with my singing voice.

"But I was obsessed with two things when I was eleven—basketball, and our dog, Bandit. So I came up with a routine that involved a lot of dribbling with some footwork I considered to be pretty fancy and tricks I had taught Bandit. I used a playground ball since they're softer, and we had a little hoop on stage. Bandit would bump the ball up with his nose to make a basket. When it worked out, it was pretty cool."

He cocked his head. "Does that mean it didn't work out?"

"Oh, it did. Until the ball went flying out into the audience and Bandit went chasing after it, taking out the judge's table."

Nicolas laughed. "And yet you still have fond memories of the dress from that night."

"Well, yeah, because it was beautiful. And since I already knew from the talent portion that I wasn't going to win, it took the pressure off the interview portion. So I got to just stand up there, all eyes on me in my beautiful dress, and not stress out. I had worried that I'd be too nervous, but it turned out that I loved the feeling of everyone listening to me, caring about what I said."

He wanted to give her that feeling of someone caring about what she said all the time. "Fleur told me that the two of you went out shopping and exploring the city together today. She has given you her official seal of approval, which she doesn't do often." He took his eyes off the road long enough to see the smile spread across Avery's face.

"You choose pretty great friends. We've had a lot of fun hanging out together. And she is coming over to help me get ready on Friday night." She paused for a moment. "On a scale of one to ten, how nervous should I be about seeing your mother there?"

"Just know that I'll have your back the whole time. And if at any time you want to cancel on me, I respect that."

"So, what I'm hearing is that I should be nervous to the amount of ten."

He shook his head, chuckling. "It's all going to be

great. She'll be distracted by all the people she needs to kiss up to and probably won't even notice you. And you will love so many things there that you probably won't even notice her."

He had thought of just letting her off the hook completely so she didn't have to be exposed to more of his mother. But there were also a lot of really great things about the reception that he thought she would like. All he needed to do was to keep a good distance from his mother, and he could introduce Avery to all the wonders of the event.

"And you've been having fun, even with Riley being gone?" He wished he could've taken work off the entire time she would be in town.

Avery nodded. "I don't know if you've noticed, but Riley is kind of the bossy sister. So most of the time, she was the one who chose where we were going and what we were doing. And for the first couple of days after she left, I actually kind of missed that. I even felt a little lost. But then I realized how great it was to choose everything myself."

Nicolas completely understood, even if his situation was different. Maxim wasn't exactly bossy, but his mother quite often was.

He smiled as he pulled into the cobbled driveway of Maxim's house because he could already guess how Avery felt about the place. His brother lived in a small, narrow two-story house with grayish-brown bricks and a small front yard filled with flowers and small shrubs. A cobbled walk led right up to a reddish wooden door with no porch.

The left side of the house had a driveway only big enough for a single car between the house and a small fence dividing it from the neighbor's property, and the right side of the house was attached to their neighbor's red brick house. Maxim's house was simple and unpretentious and always made him feel happy and calm.

He walked hand-in-hand with Avery up to the front door and knocked. Maxim and Léa both answered the door, all smiles, and welcomed them in. Nicolas introduced everyone and Léa hugged Avery—a hug that didn't look forced or awkward like they'd each instinctively known that the other person was kind and safe.

Maxim and Léa showed them around their place. It didn't take long, since the ground floor only had a living room, kitchen, small dining area, and bathroom. Then Léa grabbed Avery's hand and said, "Come upstairs with me. I want to show you what we're doing with the baby's room."

Avery threw him a grin before heading up the stairs, and he smiled back at her, so glad that she and Léa had seemed to hit it off so quickly. Maxim leaned against his kitchen counter, so Nicolas did, too. It was good to have Avery meet them. She'd be able to see that his family wasn't all so complicated and dramatic.

"Thanks for bringing Avery."

Maxim spoke to him in Dutch, since they were alone. Growing up, they'd spoken Dutch in school and English at home. It was laughable that they'd considered it such a rebellion to speak Dutch whenever it was just the two of them. They probably should've gotten a little more creative with their rebellions.

"Léa has already shown her friends the work that we've been doing in the baby's room, and she's been dying to show it to someone else." Maxim paused a moment, watching Nicolas's face, then said, "You really like this woman, don't you?"

"Yeah. I really, really do."

"And I bet Mother hates her."

"She really, really does."

"So what are you going to do about that?"

"I don't know yet. But I'm not willing to just let Avery go. I'm going to have to figure something out."

"You stayed with her family in America, right? And she still lives there?"

Nicolas nodded.

"And what are you going to do about *that*?"

"That's another thing I don't know."

Maxim clapped Nicolas on the shoulder. "Let me know if you want to talk through it all." He paused a moment, then added, "Because Léa's a good listener." When Nicolas gave him a shove, he laughed. "Just kidding, brother. I'll listen all you want. I'll even offer advice anytime. Or keep my mouth shut if you'd prefer. You've always given me your support, so whatever you need, just know you've got mine."

Nicolas could hear Avery and Léa chatting about Avery's friend who just unexpectedly found out she was pregnant recently as they walked down the stairs. He got the sense that if the two of them were left alone together, they could talk for hours.

Maxim clapped his hands once when the women joined them in the kitchen. "Is everyone ready for dinner? We just got this new air fryer," he said as he put his hands on the sides of the black appliance sitting on his kitchen counter, "and it makes the best frites anywhere. And I just finished making mussels. Léa made us a green salad—she wants to make sure that none of us die from a lack of vegetables."

As they sat down and started eating, Avery said, a mussel shell in her hand, "These taste different from the ones we had last week, but they are so *so* good! And these fries are to die for!" She dipped another one in the mayonnaise that Maxim had made and closed her eyes as she ate it. Nicolas glanced over at his brother to see him beaming at Avery's compliments.

They chatted about random things for the first part of dinner, but then Avery said to Maxim, "So did you ever work at Oma Servais?"

Maxim nodded, and it felt like the room quieted. "Until I was eighteen."

Avery knew a teeny part of Maxim's story from when she and Nicolas were teens—he'd told her that Maxim didn't get along with their parents. And he had told her while she'd been in town that his brother and his parents were estranged, but he hadn't told Maxim's story. That was his to tell.

"Why did you quit?"

"Because I wasn't okay with my entire life being planned out for me, especially when the path I was on led straight to being CEO—a job I never wanted."

"Oh. Is that why you and your parents don't get along?"

"We don't get along because instead of working to be okay with my decisions about my life, they cut me off completely."

Avery gasped.

Nicolas had known that Maxim would tell his story. He just hadn't expected Maxim to be so blunt.

"They cut you off just because you went against their wishes? They don't even talk to you now?"

"Not even a card at my birthday. Not that they'd know where to send it. They don't know about the baby, either."

Avery shot Nicolas a look that told him she was thinking about how she, herself, was against Nicolas's mother's wishes for him. He saw the worry lines in her face about causing the same thing to happen to Nicolas.

Honestly, he was worried about that, too.

Avery cracked open another mussel, obviously trying to keep the mood light. "You went into carpentry, right?"

"Nah. Carpentry was just my way of rebelling as efficiently as possible since I knew how strongly my mother would disapprove of it. Heaven forbid I have a job where I get all dusty and sweaty. I knew they'd freak out—I just hadn't guessed that they would freak out so fully."

"Yeah, that's kind of extreme," she said.

"I think that, more than the carpentry thing, it was that they realized that I was serious about not being cowed into doing exactly what they told me to do to get myself out of that 'mess.' I was proud of myself for standing strong, but I've got to tell you, it was tough, being an eighteen-year-old without parents. And really, without any extended family, once the rest of them found out. Most of them work at Oma Servais, so they kind of had to turn their backs on me." He smiled at Nicolas. "But not Nicolas. He never once turned his back on me."

"I was only thirteen at the time, though, so there wasn't much I could do."

Maxim shook his head. "It didn't matter. You were there for me from the beginning and every moment since, and that was all that mattered."

Maxim reached across the table and clasped arms with Nicolas like they always did.

"It wasn't an easy choice but, in the end, but it got me to where I wanted to be, which is right here." Maxim smiled at Léa, and she gave him the sweetest smile back. "But there were many tough years in between. I did want to go to university, so I finished my optional year in carpentry so I could. There were tough times. I was even homeless for a few weeks, showering at the university gym in the mornings and sleeping on benches at night."

Maxim's story brought back so many difficult memories. All Maxim went through had been so hard for Nicolas to watch, especially when Nicolas was younger and couldn't do much to help other than to listen and be there for his brother. He couldn't have made the same choices that his brother did. He and Maxim had different tolerances, different fears, and different goals. Maxim's biggest need had always been autonomy and the freedom to make his own decisions. Nicolas's biggest need was to have his support structure intact. But he was insanely proud of all his brother had accomplished to create the life he'd dreamed of.

"I became an emergency medical technician, as I'd wanted, and then a paramedic. Now I fly helicopters on search and rescue missions. It's how I met Léa."

Avery looked across the table to Léa. "Really?"

She nodded. "I'd had a terrible week and decided to go

on a hike through the forest in Florenville, alone—"

"—which you should never do," Maxim cut in.

"Which you should *definitely* never do," Léa agreed. She spoke English, too, just not as often as Nicolas and Maxim had growing up, so her accent was a little thicker. "I hiked to the top of La Roche à l'Appel, got to see the amazing summit, then promptly fell and broke my leg on the way back down. And then managed to get myself wedged between two boulders.

"I couldn't get a call to go through, but luckily I'd left my roommate a note, saying where I was going and when I'd be back. When I didn't come home, she called search and rescue. Several agonizing hours later, I heard a helicopter overhead. It shone a light down in the area where I was. And then, like a knight in a shining EMT uniform, Maxim helped get me to safety. The rest is history."

"Aww," Avery said, looking at Maxim, "that's so sweet."

"She forgot the part where I visited her in the hospital, then followed her around like a lovesick puppy until I could convince her to marry me."

"No, he properly wooed me like a gentleman until my heart was so entwined with his that I had no other choice."

The two of them looked at each other with such love that Nicolas yearned for the same thing.

"And then we got married," Maxim said. "Nicolas was

the only one in attendance from my side of the family, but that was okay. He was the only person I cared about having there. And now I have all I ever wanted—Léa, the baby, our home, a job that I love."

Nicolas didn't exactly want to be CEO at this point in his life. Later, maybe. Much further down the road. But he actually really liked working at Oma Servais. He liked the position he was in right now, and he was good at it. He had loved his job in product development years ago, and he was *really* good at that. He couldn't think of any position in the world he'd like more than Chief of Product Development at Oma Servais.

And he loved his support system. All of it. The people at work, all of his extended family, and even though his parents tried to control his life too often, he loved them, too. He could've never sacrificed them the way that Maxim did. Which was why it had always been so important to him to somewhat go along with his mother's wishes. Most of the time, it wasn't too big of a deal—sure, it meant he occasionally had a job that hadn't suited him, and it meant that he was headed for a job he didn't want, but it hadn't been *that* problematic.

Except now he was falling completely for Avery. Never had anything come into conflict with his most basic need of keeping his support system than falling for her did. And never had anything been so important or potentially life-altering to him.

Chapter Twenty-One

AVERY

On Friday morning, Avery slept in just because she could. No one was waiting for her and she didn't have to be anywhere at a certain time, so she didn't even set an alarm. She woke to the morning sun streaming into her bedroom through the wall of windows and patio door and stretched.

She realized that it had been a full week since Riley had flown back home. The week had not gone at all as she'd expected. She'd surprised herself by going to tourist sights by herself during the day. She'd also become much better friends with Jacques, Delphine, Rania, and Fleur, and had spent quite a bit of time enjoying the city with each of them, too. She'd been having experiences that made her feel more full, more alive. Like she'd been developing all of her instead of just one part of her like she'd been feeling back home.

She'd even gone to a restaurant alone and ordered in French. And found a meal that she loved that Nicolas hadn't introduced her to—*maigre sauvage, mousse d'artichaut, oignons grelots, galette de pommes de terre.* She had probably butchered the pronunciation when she ordered, but she was still proud of herself.

For some strange reason, she now noticed all the sounds and smells and colors and emotions that were everywhere in Brussels that she hadn't noticed before.

The way the wind blew the scent of waffles when she was on Rue de l'Etuve street, or flowers when she neared Floralia Brussels in the park of the castle of Grand Bigard. The warmth of the sun on her skin. And when she came back home at night and Jacques had turned on the fire in the main room and had hot chocolate waiting for her, she seemed to notice the way the fire crackled and the heat pricked at her skin more than she had before.

But most of all, she noticed the way it felt every evening when Nicolas got off work and took her out to see the city. The way it felt when his arm brushed against hers.

When he touched her back lightly to signal which way to go.

When he put an arm around her shoulder or her waist to pull her in close when they were in a crowd.

When he'd skim his knuckles against her cheek to brush a lock of hair away from her face.

When they sat so close that their knees or thighs would press against each other.

When he'd whisper in her ear, his lips so close they tickled. When he pressed his lips against hers, making every nerve hum with bliss when he came to pick her up in the evening or drop her off at night or anytime they were alone for a moment.

When they would talk about all the things going on in their lives and all their hopes and dreams. When they talked about things they never shared with anyone else.

She took her time showering and towel drying her hair before she meandered out into the main area of the flat. She could immediately tell that the feeling in the entire place had shifted. A tenseness that hadn't been there before was now present, and Jacques, Delphine, and Rania had the same professional air about them that they'd had the very first time she'd walked through the elevator and into the flat. Before they'd all become friends.

"Can I get you any breakfast, Ms. Parks?" Delphine asked.

Ms. Parks? "What's going on?"

Jacques was dusting while Rania hurried around, straightening things. He said, "We just got word that Master Servais's plans have changed, and he'll be coming into Brussels this evening to attend the reception tonight."

Nicolas's grandfather? "And he's staying here?"

"Yes. Of course."

"Will he want me to leave?"

"No," Jacques said. "He'll certainly be fine with you staying." But Avery didn't miss the quick look he shot Delphine's direction.

Avery grabbed a yogurt from the fridge and a spoon, afraid to even make herself toast, fearing it would leave crumbs, and headed back into her room to finish getting ready for the day. The longer she lingered, though, the more she worried about the reception tonight. She wanted to go talk with Delphine, Rania, and Jacques about it, but she didn't get the sense that they would be okay with getting personal right now.

And the more they were stressed, the more Avery got stressed about Nicolas's grandfather coming. Now that she'd met Nicolas's mother, her guess at what the grandfather could be like was scarier. Especially seeing how all the staff, who *did* know him, were reacting to him coming many hours from now. Maybe he'd be every bit as awful to her as Margaux was.

Once she was ready, she headed out into the city to escape. She already knew that Fleur wasn't free until four when she was arriving to help Avery. Jacques and Delphine and Rania were clearly busy. And Léa was at work. And so was Nicolas, and it would be a busy day for him.

So she walked in a direction she hadn't yet explored, trying to do anything but think about what was going to be happening later tonight.

———

AVERY SAT on a padded chair in the big open space of her room in front of the full-length, standing mirror as Fleur put the finishing touches on her makeup. She could see Delphine and Rania sitting on the edge of her bed from the corner of her eye, so she noticed when Delphine lifted her wrist to look at her watch.

Avery tried not to move her face at all while she asked, "How long until Nicolas's grandfather gets here?"

"A good forty minutes. Maybe forty-five."

Avery might even be gone before he arrived, then. That would be nice. If Riley was still in town, they'd both be in this room, getting ready together. The thought made her miss her sister. And it made Avery extra grateful that Fleur had been willing to lend her expertise.

"Okay, and done," Fleur said with a flourish of her brush. "Stand up. Let's see you."

Avery stood and looked at herself in the full mirror. If it was possible, she loved the dress even more now than she had back when she'd first tried it on. With the high neck, fitted bodice down to just below her hips, and the way the fabric flared out so gracefully, it made her look taller than she was. Sleek. Stately. The deep, rich, jewel-toned blue did amazing things for her skin and hair, making them look even more vibrant. Now, with her heels, the fabric just barely skimmed the floor.

Fleur grabbed a long strand of pearls from a case in her bag and put it around Avery's neck. The pearls rested on the fabric about two inches below the top of the high neck in front, but she turned to see that a single strand fell right down the middle of her bare back to just above her mid-back. Wow. That was something she'd have never tried on her own, but she loved it.

She couldn't wait for Nicolas to see her in this dress. She couldn't wait to see him in his tux. For as nervous as she was about the night, there still managed to be a lot of room left for excitement. She knew tonight was important, and she wanted to make sure she did well. Or at least looked good.

Her makeup was perfect. More perfect than she would've ever been able to manage alone. And her hair was pulled up all fancy and looked so shiny and amazing and had a jeweled clip that made it look even more elegant.

She looked like someone who mattered.

She blew out a deep breath as slowly as she could, shaking out her hands. She was only going to be able to fool everyone for so long before they found out that she wasn't. She was just a girl who worked in the admissions department at Lake Baldwin State University, had an average family, and lived in a small town where half the people farmed and the other half worked at the college.

"Your nerves are getting the best of you," Rania said.

They were. She could feel it in every cell of her body.

Fleur walked in front of Avery. She put her hands on her shoulders, looking deeply into her eyes. "Remember when we were trying on dresses and you told me that you felt powerful in this dress?"

"I do." Avery bit her lip and wiggled her fingers, then waved her hands back and forth, trying to make them not get sweaty. "I just don't think I'll feel that way in front of Margaux."

"Say it," Fleur said. "Say 'I am powerful.'"

"I am powerful."

"That was weak," Fleur said. She moved to her side, positioning Avery directly in front of the mirror. "Do it again."

Avery looked at herself in the mirror and tried to use a stronger voice. "I am powerful."

Fleur shook her head. "Not strong enough. I want to hear it louder."

"I feel silly."

"Then you haven't convinced yourself yet. Try to really feel it when you say it."

Avery took a breath, attempting to calm her nerves.

She looked at herself in the mirror. She did look powerful. She tried to channel all she was seeing. "I am powerful!"

"Okay, you're getting there," Fleur said. "Louder still."

"I am powerful!"

"Good! Okay, now I want you to *really* convince me. Convince Delphine and Rania. Convince the people who live on the floor below. Convince Jacques and Mr. Servais wherever they are on the road between Kapellen and here. I want you to shout it loud enough that no matter where you are that you'll still be convinced. Give it every single bit of energy and focus and strength that you've got."

Avery nodded and looked at herself. During this week alone in a foreign country, she'd made friends, and they were in the room with her now, supporting her. She'd survived the encounter with Nicolas's mother and it hadn't scared her off. She was pretty freaking proud of herself for that. She was becoming the person she wanted to be. And she looked amazing. She had what it took to make it through tonight.

She gave herself her most winning smile, then sucked in the hugest breath she possibly could. Then, at the top of her lungs, she shouted, "I. Am. *Powerful!*"

At the sound of an "Oh," behind her, her gaze flew to a reflection in the mirror and she spun around when she realized it was Jacques and Nicolas's grandfather. Delphine and Rania immediately shot to their feet, standing stiff and professional, as heat flew to Avery's cheeks. How had they arrived so early?

She grabbed fistfuls of her skirt so she wouldn't trip and hurried across the room to where the two men stood just inside the doorway. She let go of her skirt, smoothed it out a bit, and said, "I'm so sorry about that." Thrusting out her hand, she added, "Hello. It's very nice to meet you. I didn't think you'd be— I'm sorry for yelling in your— I didn't mean to—" She couldn't think straight she was so lightheaded. Was she breathing? Maybe she wasn't breathing. Okay, now she felt like she was breathing too fast. Was she going to pass out?

The man took her hand and gave it a shake, a somewhat amused smile on his wrinkled yet very dignified face. He turned his head slightly to Jacques. "This is the woman whose family my grandson stayed with in America?"

"Avery Parks, sir. Yes."

"Makes sense."

"Thank you for letting me stay at your place while I'm here," Avery managed to say. A complete sentence. That was something. But she should probably stop shaking his hand already. She managed to let go. "I swear I won't scream in here again."

"You're very welcome. And thank you for letting my grandson stay at your place for nine months all those years ago. Scream all you want."

She let out a chuckle that wasn't at all pretty or refined or even sounded human.

"I take it you're going to the reception tonight?" he asked.

"Yes." Simple answers were good. Less of a chance to trip through them.

"Very good. I am, too. Now if you'll excuse me, I need to retire to get ready as well. Fleur," he said, giving her a small nod, "nice to see you again."

"You, too, sir."

Then he turned and left the room. All five of them shared a look before Delphine, Rania, and Jacques hurried out to whatever duties awaited them, Delphine squeezing Avery's shoulder on her way out.

Once it was just Avery and Fleur in the room, Avery pressed her fingers lightly against her cheeks and then her forehead, trying to cool the burning skin while not doing anything to mess up her makeup. "That's the first impression I gave him? Shouting 'I am powerful' in his house at the top of my lungs?"

"It wasn't that bad. My guess? He thinks you're spirited."

"Whatever he thought, I don't think it was anything good. I should just be glad that he isn't kicking me out onto the street."

Chapter Twenty-Two

NICOLAS

When Nicolas stepped off the elevator into his grandfather's flat, Jacques, Delphine, and Rania were standing tall and stiff, wearing masks of professionalism except for the broad smiles on their faces. At first, he was confused—they hadn't acted that way since Avery had arrived. Then he said, "My grandfather's here?"

Jacques nodded. "He is. He'll be attending the reception tonight after all. And Ms. Parks is ready for you. I'll go let her know you've arrived."

Jacques returned a moment later, escorting Avery, Fleur right behind them. The moment Avery rounded the corner, Nicolas stopped breathing. Avery looked exquisite. He'd been to many black-tie events in his life, yet he'd never seen anyone as beautiful as Avery. Her auburn hair was up, the color of her dress fit not just her skin tone perfectly, but also her personality, and its design, while completely proper, skimmed all of her curves beautifully.

Avery let go of Jacques's arm and posed, then turned so he could see the back, looking over her shoulder and smiling as she did. A line of pearls skimmed her spine on her bare back, falling to just past her mid-back and now, not only could he not breathe, but he also couldn't speak. She turned back around and smiled at him and confidence radiated from her. She looked refined. Regal. Radiant.

She walked over to him and he knew that she was going to steal the attention of every person at the reception. He took both of her hands in both of his. "You— I don't even have words for how incredible you look. It's like—" He couldn't explain what he was feeling. It wasn't even really about the dress or the hair. It was about everything else. "I know how amazing you are on the inside. And right now, I think any stranger could look at you and guess at least a part of how amazing you are because so much of it is shining through. You are stunning."

She looked down, her cheeks reddening slightly, then her eyes met his again. "Thank you."

Fleur, Jacques, Delphine, and Rania all stood behind her, beaming. "Thank you all," he said.

And then he remembered what was in his pocket. They had stopped in a souvenir shop while out exploring the city one night, and they had some little figurines sculpted by a local artist that Avery had fallen in love with. He'd gone back later and hadn't found exactly what he'd been looking for, so he'd contacted the artist. Nicolas explained what he wanted, and the woman had created a design that was close to his vision.

He reached into his pocket and pulled out a little resin sculpture of a young girl who looked about the same age that he pictured Avery was in the story she'd told him about competing in the Little Miss pageant. The girl had both hands over her head, holding a big star, a posture of pride, a smile on her face.

"I want you to have this. It made me think of you, standing on that stage as a pre-teen, all eyes on you, shining for all the world to see. You shine, Avery. The world is a better place because of your light."

Avery waved her hands in front of her eyes. "You're not supposed to make me cry! Fleur is going to be mad."

Rania rushed forward and handed her a tissue, and Avery dabbed it right below her bottom eyelashes. Then she squeezed the figurine tight before reluctantly holding it out toward Rania. "Do you mind putting this on my pillow?"

Rania nodded and took the figurine.

"Shall we head out?" He held his arm bent at the elbow, and Avery placed her arm in his.

When they got downstairs and walked out to the car, her eyes flew to Nicolas's. "We are taking a limo?"

He shrugged. "I thought it would be fun, and it makes things easier when we get there." The driver opened the door for them and they both climbed inside. Since his grandfather's flat was downtown, it would only be about a seven-minute drive to the event center.

As they pulled away, Avery said, "Hey, if you talk to your grandfather while we are there, or anytime, really, tell him not to share any embarrassing stories about me, okay?"

He raised an eyebrow, suddenly curious.

"It's nothing. Just not the way I wanted our introduction to go."

It wasn't long before their limo entered the line of vehicles dropping people off for the reception, and Avery craned to see all the people lining the red carpet, filming, taking pictures, and standing with microphones. She turned back to him. "What's going on up there? Are there supposed to be celebrities here tonight?"

Nicolas chuckled and rubbed his knuckles against his jaw. He hadn't thought to tell her about this part because it had just seemed so normal for the International Royal Chocolatier Awards reception that he'd somehow thought she knew, even though now he realized she couldn't have. He didn't quite know how to tell her.

She grabbed his arm. "Are chocolatiers celebrities here?"

He nodded slowly. "Chocolate is pretty important here."

"Do we go in a different way then?"

"No, we're, um, considered celebrities, too, so we'll need to stop on the red carpet. It's not a big deal, though—you'll just stand by me, pose, and smile while they take pictures."

"But why?" she asked, looking baffled. "Who is the audience for this kind of thing?"

He shrugged. "All the people who read the websites and blogs, magazines and newspapers, YouTube channels, social media. Things like that. This is the biggest event of the year and Belgium only hosts it once every three years, so when it's here, people go all out for it."

"Wow," she said, looking out the window again. "Your mother wasn't exaggerating when she said this reception was a big deal."

When their limo reached the front of the line, their driver opened their door for them. Nicolas helped Avery out and didn't release her hand as they made their way down the red carpet. They stopped and talked with a few reporters, then eventually got to the spot where they were supposed to pose.

Avery seemed a tad nervous, but she handled it all like a pro. Maybe she was even a little excited by it. He thought back again to her story of being up on stage, loving that she had all eyes on her, and it made him happy to see that she was getting that here. He wanted her to soak in as much of it as she could.

He leaned in and whispered in her ear, "Stay here," then stepped away so she could have the spotlight all to herself. As she placed her hand on her hip and leveled her gaze at the cameras, showing off how incredible she looked tonight, Nicolas pulled out his cell phone and took a picture of her, too.

Then he led her inside to the gallery. All through the middle of the long, narrow area were all the chocolate creations the chocolatiers had made for this event. Ushers were stationed every dozen feet along the sides, making sure no one was touching the chocolate.

Nicolas motioned at the works of art. "Each company competing in the IRCAs next week sends a team of three people here early on the day of this event, and they have eight hours to make something out of chocolate. It isn't part of the competition—it's mostly to just show off and get some good exposure for your company before the creations are auctioned off for charity tomorrow."

"All of these are made out of chocolate? But there are so many colors!"

"They are airbrushed with colored cocoa butter."

She walked up to a working Ferris wheel right at the front. "This," she gestured to all of it, "is made *entirely* of chocolate?"

He smiled and nodded, loving the look of wonder on her face.

"What does Oma Servais usually make?"

"On years when the IRCAs aren't in Belgium, we usually do a re-creation of a historical site somewhere in Belgium but not in Brussels. A few years ago, they did Gravensteen—the castle of the Counts that we saw on our river tour in Ghent. In the years when it *is* here, we like to do something that the judges and all the people coming to this event will see on their way into Brussels. Like the Atomium, the Town Hall, or a cathedral or church. This year, we did the Royal Palace."

Avery was mesmerized as they gazed at all of the sculptures. They saw one that looked like a bouquet of delicate flowers, others of famous buildings, one motorcycle, a carousel, a train, a dragon, and even a grand piano. She had such an expression of awe on her face as they looked at them all that made him glad he brought her. She seemed to love it even more than he thought she would.

And *he* loved it more than he thought he would, too. He felt a bit taller every moment as she admired and respected what he'd spent his life working on. Last year and the year before, he'd come to this same event with Sophie. Nothing in the gallery had even garnered a look from her—she'd just wanted to stroll past everything and get to the reception where *she* could be seen and admired.

She didn't care about any of his work. Only the prestige it brought with it.

As Avery stopped to look at the chocolate air plane from the 1940s at the end of the gallery, he thought about how fun it would be to take Avery to this event next year in Paris. He could show her how big the Eiffel Tower was in real life.

And then he remembered that their relationship was ending Monday. There was no next year for them.

But by the time they reached the other side of the gallery and were almost to the doors leading into the reception, he was pretty sure they could both feel the tension of how much was riding on this event.

"Are you ready?" he asked her.

She nodded and slid her hand into his, giving it a squeeze.

They walked up the three steps that stretched wide in front of the double doors leading into the reception area and nodded to the two guards flanking the doorway.

Not everyone had arrived at the reception yet, of course, but the grand hall was already filled with dozens of people dressed in their finest, chatting in groups. He and Avery both took a deep breath, then stepped into the room to start making the rounds.

They chatted with several people, shaking hands, making small talk. After the first couple of groups, they came to one of the women who was an IRCA judge and had been for years. She was a Black woman with whitish-gray hair and a smile that Nicolas always thought was so much more genuine than the other judges. He said hello to her, shook her hand warmly, and told her how great it was to see her again.

"I would like you to meet my date, Avery Parks," he continued. "Avery, this is Madame Blanchet, one of the experts who will be judging the competition next week."

Madame Blanchet shook Avery's hand, and the two of them chatted for a few minutes. Just as he'd guessed, everyone seemed to be drawn to Avery. Then Madame Blanchet said, "It was wonderful to meet you," and went off to greet others.

It felt like a weight settled in Nicolas's stomach. "Oh, no."

Avery's eyes immediately flew to him. "What?"

He didn't want to point Sophie out to Avery. He didn't want them to ever meet. But now that she was here, Avery needed to know. He turned to face Avery, his body nearly touching hers, and leaned in close to her ear. "See that woman directly across the room from you? Wearing a red dress, standing next to my mother? That's Sophie."

Avery pulled back. "Your ex-fiancee Sophie?"

He nodded and tried to push down his dread.

"Oh, *ship*. What is she doing here?"

"She has to be here at my mother's request, which means my mother took matters into her own hands. She may have asked her to come because Sophie's good at schmoozing with people, judges especially." Or, he worried, she could be here for the worst-case scenario. His mother could've suggested that Sophie tell people that she and Nicolas were back together since that was what she wanted.

Sophie had her back to Nicolas and Avery, but someone she was talking to gestured in Nicolas's direction, and Sophie turned, saw him across the room, and smiled broadly.

Nicolas swallowed. "Oh, *ship*."

Chapter Twenty-Three

AVERY

Avery had barely gotten a chance to recover from finding out that Nicolas's ex-fiancee was in the same room as her *and* that she was cover-of-a-magazine gorgeous before the woman sauntered across the room toward them, long blonde curls bouncing, hips swaying.

"Darling!" she said to Nicolas as she reached him. "I'm so glad you made it." She hooked her arm in Nicolas's, pulling him away from Avery, not even acknowledging that Avery was there. And she was acting like she was Nicolas's date.

Avery was too stunned to even move.

Nicolas turned to get out of Sophie's grasp and reach back to Avery, but his mother stepped in between them and hissed something in his ear that, based on the facial expression she wore, was pretty intense.

Then Sophie said as she steered Nicolas away from Avery, "The De Smets were asking how we're doing. I told them I would bring you over to say hello the moment you arrived." She led him toward the middle of the reception hall.

Nicolas turned to look back at Avery, but she didn't even get to see the expression on his face before Margaux pulled her aside. She gave Avery the most insincere smile she'd ever witnessed firsthand, then said, "It's cute that you got all dressed up. It must be so 'cool' for you to be at an event like this. But you'll be gone on Monday. Sophie's going to be around for a while. She's the type of woman a man in Nicolas's position needs. So let him go. This is a work event—let him do his *job*."

Heat rushed through Avery's body as she ground her teeth. She couldn't believe that Margaux would do something like this, especially knowing exactly what Nicolas wanted.

But then a certain resignation washed over her. Margaux was right. It was true—she was going to be gone in just three days, and she didn't fit in here or know exactly what she needed to do to help Oma Servais and Nicolas. She suddenly felt very small, so she moved out of the way and found somewhere near the wall to stand. And the longer she stood there, feeling the effect of Margaux's words, the more invisible and insignificant she felt.

After a while, she told herself that she was the one

choosing to be there, all alone. She could go out into the middle of the room and socialize by herself, just like she had been doing with Nicolas. But she didn't move.

And the more she stayed there, the more it felt like all the other times in her life when she'd felt so insignificant. Invisible. Forgotten. So much of her life had been exactly that.

But since she'd been in Belgium, Nicolas had always made her feel so seen. Like she was important. She'd stepped into that feeling so easily that she hadn't quite realized it. But now, with those old feelings returning, it was clear how stark the difference was.

Every once in a while, she and Nicolas would make eye contact and he'd give her a pained look that told her how badly he wanted to be by her side.

She wasn't the least bit upset at Nicolas for what was going on. She understood the situation he was in and knew he didn't want to be in it. And after talking to Maxim and knowing what Margaux was capable of, and knowing how important family and a support system were to Nicolas, she knew he wasn't the kind of person who could defy Margaux's wishes and walk away from everyone as Maxim had. And she didn't expect him to.

Then, when Nicolas was in the middle of the room, he looked at her and held his arm out to her. She took two steps toward him but hadn't noticed his parents standing nearby until Margaux grabbed her arm and pulled her into a conversation they were having with another couple.

"Mila and Mathieu, I'd love you to meet Avery Parks. She's an underprivileged farm girl whom our family took in on a week-long exchange program. We are showing her the big city and how things work in the chocolate business. It's been so special that the timing worked out for her to experience an event like this before she heads back to the farm in her little town in the middle of nowhere."

The man put a hand on his chest. "Oh, the two of you are so kindhearted to open your home to those less fortunate. That's what the newspapers should be focused on—singing the praises of good people like yourselves." They were speaking English, but based on their accents, German was probably their native language.

Margaux smiled at Avery. "Oh, you're too kind. You know, our son Nicolas did an exchange program while he was in secondary school. We are just paying it forward."

Anger built in Avery with every lie that Margaux told. Before she could even consider what to say to the couple or to Nicolas's parents, the lights dimmed and an announcer stepped up to the microphone. He announced in English, which seemed to be the official language of the event, the beginning of the evening's dancing portion and the orchestra started playing more loudly. Everyone either shifted from the middle of the floor to the outer edge or more toward the middle to start dancing.

Avery's gaze immediately went to Nicolas and his eyes were on her as he and Sophie went out onto the dance floor. Sophie placed her wrists on Nicolas's shoulders, her hands wrapping around behind his neck, a movement that looked so practiced and comfortable. Probably because she'd done it a million times before.

At that moment, it became crystal clear to Avery exactly how much her heart was wrapped up in Nicolas. She'd been fooling herself for quite a while now that she'd be able to just say goodbye to him on Monday and go on with her life.

Nicolas's grandfather stepped up beside her, a drink in hand, and looked out at the dancing couples too. Avery stiffened, remembering their last exchange. As a waiter came by holding a tray, he took one last sip of his drink and then placed it on the tray before putting both hands in his pockets. "My wife, Nicolas's grandmother, passed away twenty years ago. I've stood here on the sidelines at many events since then, wishing I was out on the dance floor with her."

Avery looked over at him. "Oh, I'm so sorry for your loss."

He waved a hand. "I've had plenty of years to get accustomed to it. But what do you say we share a dance, so you don't have to be over here, looking at my grandson, wishing it was you dancing with him?"

She looked over and gave him a weak smile, then a nod.

He led her onto the dance floor and they began, she with one hand on his shoulder and the other holding his hand high, and he with one hand on her waist. Not only was he super respectful as they danced, but he was pretty good at leading her in a way that she didn't have to see Nicolas.

"I know this has to be hard," he said. "Are you doing okay?"

She nodded. "I only agreed to a relationship with him until Monday, because that's when I fly back home. I have no claim on him. This is something short-term, and I know that tonight's event has long-term consequences."

He had a thoughtful expression on his face as they danced, his eyes on her. "Is your heart planning on being done on Monday?"

She tried to keep her emotions in check, biting her lip. But then she gave her head a little shake. "No."

"I see."

He must've lost track of where Nicolas and Sophie had moved to on the dance floor, because as they spun a bit, she could suddenly see Nicolas again, or at least the back of him. Sophie slid in closer to Nicolas, laying her head on his shoulder, and a longing for Nicolas filled Avery so fully she could no longer contain it.

"I'm sorry. I can't," she said, pulling away from

Nicolas's grandfather. She hurried off to the hallway leading to the restrooms and went inside.

For the most part, she'd controlled her breathing and held her tears in, so she hadn't destroyed her makeup. She finished dabbing her lower eyelids with a tissue and tossed it into the trash. As soon as she turned around, she saw Margaux walk into the restroom. Her stomach dropped, and she suddenly felt itchy in her own skin. She just needed to leave as quickly as possible.

"You get that Nicolas understands how important today is, right? He was willing to step up and do what needed to be done because of how many people's livelihood depend on Oma Servais doing well in this competition."

Avery nodded. "I know." That was the only reason he was out there with Sophie right now. Otherwise, he'd have been by her side, no matter what. They both understood that more was at stake than just something between his mother and him and Avery.

Margaux gave her a pitying smile. "Do you want me to call you a cab? I know you don't want to stay here all by yourself, off on the sidelines, being an emotional wallflower. This has to be an uncomfortable place for you, and I don't want you to spend any more time here than you have to. We should get you back where you belong."

Avery was tired of seeing others living their lives, shining, while she acted more like a spectator. And she was very sick of Nicolas's mom trying to force her into that role. Of making her feel like she didn't matter. Margaux had seen Avery leaving the reception area, looking upset, and she followed her to the bathroom where she knew she'd likely be crying. To do what? Make her feel worse? What kind of person did that? And why?

And then the reason behind Margaux's actions suddenly hit her, and all the frustration that had been building in her all evening burst free. "I am sick of you going out of your way to make me feel less than I am. I figure the only reason you're doing that is because you're afraid of how powerful I actually am."

She was surprised that came out of her mouth. Maybe Fleur having her scream it earlier actually worked. It was helping her to finally stand up for herself, to the person who was most difficult for her to stand up to. Margaux seemed to be shocked enough by Avery's reaction that it had momentarily silenced her. And Avery had more to say, so she kept going.

"If you didn't think I had the power to make a difference in Nicolas's life, you wouldn't be afraid of me. You'd have ignored me, knowing I would be gone and out of his life in less than three days. You *know* I'm not insignificant, and that's exactly why you're trying to make me feel like I am. And you're afraid of losing some of your control.

"Well, maybe instead of trying to control everyone

else's life, you should try to control your own actions. Making your kids do what you want already lost you one son." She shook her head. "You don't even know what is going on with him, and you've missed so much. I'd think that would matter to you."

To Avery's surprise, Margaux just stood there, looking shocked, yet not saying a word, and Avery couldn't fathom why.

So Avery added, "And you might want to give your kids a chance to do the things they're good at. I think you'd find out that they're even more incredible than you knew."

She wanted to walk out of the bathroom right then before Margaux found her voice again. Just drop the mic and walk off stage. But before she even took a step, one of the bathroom stall doors opened—she hadn't realized they weren't alone in there—and out walked Madame Blanchet, the judge that Nicolas had introduced her to earlier.

Avery put her hands over her face. How could she let herself explode like that to Margaux, *in front of a judge?* In less than two minutes, she'd likely destroyed everything Nicolas had been working for. Everything their whole company had been working for.

Avery dropped her hands and faced the woman. "I am so sorry. I had no idea anyone else was in here. Please forget everything you just heard me say. I was frustrated, and I shouldn't have let it come out like that."

"Avery," Margaux said, "I think you've done enough."

Avery turned to look at Nicolas's mother and then hurried out of the restroom. She had to leave. *Right now.* She couldn't stay at this event where everyone was working so hard to make their company shine, and she'd just ruined everything by allowing herself to get angry. Her. An outsider. She'd known that she didn't belong in this world, yet she had selfishly stepped right into it, not even thinking of the consequences.

Once she made it through the reception center doors into the gallery and saw that there weren't many people around, she ran through it, pushed open the doors at the other end, and stepped out into the cool night air just as the bell from the Carillon du Mont des Arts rang on the hour.

Was there any public transportation this time of night in this part of the city? She had no idea. Maybe she could walk. It hadn't seemed that far by car.

But then Jacques stepped up to her. She hadn't even seen him out there. "I got a text from Master Servais, saying to watch for you because you might need a ride back to the flat soon. Are you ready to head back right now, Ms. Parks?"

"Yes, thank you, Jacques," she said as the tears began to fall in earnest.

On the drive home, she kept feeling worse and worse as the evening replayed in her mind. She'd ruined everything. And to top it off, she was leaving, just like Margaux had wanted her to.

As they stopped at the light nearest the flat, Jacques said, "I'll park and walk you up."

"No. Just pull up and let me out. You need to get back to the event, and I just want to be alone."

He looked at her through the rearview mirror for a moment and then nodded. "As you wish."

He pulled into the curved drive in front of the building, got out, then opened the door for her. She gathered up the skirt of her dress and stepped out. Jacques looked at her for a long moment, then dropped all professionalism and wrapped his arms around her in a hug. A good, tight squeeze that just made more tears fall on Avery's face.

Then he pulled back, straightened his jacket, gave her a nod, and then got back into the car.

Chapter Twenty-Four

NICOLAS

"It's so great to see you and Sophie together again," a counterpart from another chocolatier said, and Nicolas added it to the growing list of phrases that he was sick of hearing tonight and never in his entire lifetime wanted to hear again.

When the dancing began, Nicolas was relieved. It would give him a chance to talk to Sophie without another couple or group being part of the conversation. He could finally tell her how he felt about her part in everything tonight, tell her to stay away, and then go find Avery and salvage what he could of this terrible night.

She immediately put her arms on his shoulders, so he put his on her hips, mainly so they could have the appearance of dancing, yet he could force as much distance between them as possible.

The two of them had dated for two years. They'd been engaged. When she'd cheated on him, it had destroyed him. He hadn't seen her in five months—being with her tonight and not experiencing any of the feelings he'd had for her before helped him to realize how fully he had moved on. And after spending so much time with Avery and seeing her inner beauty shine like the sun, Sophie seemed like a dim candle in a dark room. He wondered how he could've ever seen so much in her.

When they were away enough from others, he said, "I cannot believe you did this tonight, without my permission. I can't believe you came at all."

Sophie shrugged, looking entirely unapologetic. "Your mom can be convincing."

"Even if she was convincing about getting you to come here to charm people, that's all you should've done. You should've stayed by her side while you were doing it if you had to, and left me out of it. You should've never made people believe we were back together." He could hear the tremor of barely-controlled anger in his tone, but he couldn't do anything to stop it. "And to come early so you could get around to as many people as possible before I even arrived, making me look like a liar if I said otherwise was low. What you did to Avery was especially low."

She seemed shocked by his tone at first, but she recovered quickly and settled back into her flirty ways.

She leaned in close. "Oh, come on, Nicolas. You know we were good together. We should give us another chance."

"Getting back together has never been and will never be a possibility. You know that."

He saw her eyes shift to someone behind him, and then she slipped free of his hands and snuggled in close to him, laying her head on his shoulder. He immediately put his hands on her shoulders and pulled her off him. "Sophie—"

Then he realized what must've happened and turned the direction her eyes had traveled to just before she cozied up to him, and saw the back of Avery as she raced away from the dance floor and toward the restrooms.

He left Sophie behind and hurried after Avery, dodging around dancing couples and groups of people still socializing at the edges of the dance floor. By the time he reached the last line of people, though, she had already disappeared through the bathroom door.

Cyriel Wouters, one of the experts who had been judging this competition since he was a kid, pulled him into a conversation he was having with a few other competing marketing directors. He tried to be cordial and respond when asked anything directly, all the while keeping an eye on the restroom doors.

When the bell from the Carillon du Mont des Arts rang on the hour and he still hadn't seen any sign of Avery, he started to worry that she was either very terribly upset, or he'd somehow missed her exit from the restroom.

He excused himself from the conversation and started to look for her, trying not to appear as frantic as he felt. As he passed by Madame Blanchet, she reached out and touched his arm, stopping him. "Who are you looking for?"

"My date."

"Not the woman in red, right?"

"No. The woman I introduced you to earlier."

"Avery Parks, right?"

"Yes," he said, desperate for whatever information she had.

"I think she may have left."

"Left?"

"Or maybe she was just getting away from the reception for a bit. Now before I tell you this, I need you to know that as judges, we aren't as swayed by flattery as you might think. We judge based solely on the chocolates."

"Okay." He didn't want to hear about the competition right now. He only wanted Avery.

"I accidentally witnessed an exchange in the women's restroom between Avery and your mother."

Oh, no. This whole night had gone so much worse than he'd ever imagined. He'd fed Avery to the wolves by bringing her here. "How was Avery?"

"She seemed pretty upset. When I came out of the restroom, I saw her heading toward the gallery."

"Thank you!" he said as he took a step toward the gallery, grateful for a location to search.

Then he heard Madame Blanchet say, "You'd have been proud of her." He turned back to the woman as she continued, "I barely met her, and I was proud of her."

Nicolas gave her a smile of gratitude, then hurried to the gallery. There were so few people there that he immediately knew she wasn't in the room. He pulled out his cell phone and texted, *Where are you?* He knew that she didn't have her cell phone with her, though, because that sleek, fitted dress definitely hadn't had pockets.

He hurried down the steps, across the gallery and outside, looking all around for any sign of her. There was nothing.

He held onto his phone, needing her to text back, then headed back inside to see if she'd maybe just taken a break for a minute then rejoined the reception. He searched through all the crowds of people, worry filling his gut.

Finally, his phone buzzed with a message.

AVERY: I am back at the flat. I am so sorry I left. I made a lot of mistakes tonight. I am very sorry for that too.

NICOLAS: Did my mother say awful things to you?

AVERY: Yes. And I said some equally awful things back. And I'm pretty sure I ruined everything.

NICOLAS: You didn't ruin anything. I'm coming over right now.

He headed toward the doors again, not even caring about letting anyone know he was leaving. But he stopped in his tracks when he got her next message.

AVERY: No, please don't. I'm emotionally exhausted. I just need to sleep.

NICOLAS: Are you sure? I can leave right now and be there in less than ten minutes.

AVERY: No. I am sure. Please just let me sleep.

NICOLAS: Okay. Just know that I am so sorry for everything.

Nicolas slid the phone back into his pocket and closed his eyes, trying to calm his breathing, twisting his watch around and around, feeling like everything was crumbling down, yet feeling completely powerless to do anything about it.

Chapter Twenty-Five

AVERY

Avery finished packing her suitcase, wishing Riley was there to sit on it for her while she zipped it. She was heading home with more than she'd brought—she'd have to leave a note for Jacques asking if he would ship everything that wouldn't fit in her suitcase home for her.

She walked to her full-length windows and stared out at the city she had come to love, not even a single tear left inside her after the night she'd had, but still feeling sadness at leaving. The sun wouldn't be up for more than an hour, but the first signs of the sky lightening could be seen in the silhouette of the Brussels skyline.

She had hardly slept at all during the night. She'd spent plenty of time buried under the luxurious bedding, crying into her pillow, but as exhausted as she was, sleep wouldn't come. Only a replay of everything that had happened. Everything she'd experienced in Ghent and Brussels. Every moment she'd spent with Nicolas. Every little touch, every kiss, every time he made her smile and laugh, every time he whispered in her ear. Everything she'd experienced with his parents, Margaux especially, and with his brother, Maxim. Everything about the IRCA reception down to the last detail.

Emotion after emotion kept hitting her, knocking her down, keeping sleep far from her.

Eventually, she knew that she needed to leave, and cried in relief at finding an open seat on the next flight out.

She had separated her belongings—everything that she would need as soon as she arrived in South Dakota was packed into her single small suitcase, and everything she wouldn't need immediately was stacked neatly on her bed and would hopefully be shipped to her before long.

She picked up the little figurine that Nicolas had given her last night, gave it a tight squeeze, then slid it into the shoulder bag that she would be taking with her on the airplane.

It was just after five a.m., so she lifted the suitcase off her bed and placed it on the floor as quietly as she could. Then she put her bag over her shoulder and took one last look at the room before she turned and wheeled her suitcase out of it.

As soon as she came to the end of the hallway and

rounded the corner into the main living area, she let out a soft yelp. Nicolas's grandfather was sitting on one of the armchairs in the recessed living room, facing her direction, drinking a mug of something steaming.

"I'm so sorry—I didn't think anyone would be up." The early morning was letting just enough light through the uncovered full-length windows that she could see everything.

"After a night like last night," Nicolas's grandfather said, "I'm surprised I am, too."

She had hoped to avoid talking to anyone, but since he was awake, she couldn't exactly wave goodbye and just get on the elevator. She left her suitcase where it was and sat down on the couch across from him.

"Last night got a little intense," he said.

She nodded.

"I take it that you've packed your suitcase and are sneaking out before the sun rises because you're flying home early?"

She swallowed, then cleared her throat. "This isn't a world that I'm equipped to be in. I ruined things for Nicolas and probably all of Oma Servais, and I feel like if I stick around any longer, I'm just going to ruin more things for him."

Because now that several hours had passed since she'd confronted Margaux, she felt a little differently about the exchange. She was still worried about the trouble she'd caused for Oma Servais, but as far as what she'd said to Nicolas's mom—she still meant every word. And if she stayed, she couldn't guarantee that she wouldn't say something similar again, if the situation arose.

It was strange to realize that as non-confrontational as she had been for the bulk of her life, she was most worried right now that she would cause problems by being confrontational. But she wasn't willing to be Margaux's lapdog, like Sophie was, and do whatever bidding Margaux requested. If Margaux needed to be stood up to, she was going to stand up to her.

Which meant that if she stayed, she would likely cause even more problems for Nicolas and the career that he loved. And she loved him too much to do that to him.

Nicolas's grandfather nodded, looking thoughtful, and she could tell he had something he wanted to say, so she stayed sitting, even though it was hard to face him and own up to her mistakes.

Finally, he said, "You love him." As a statement, not a question.

Avery looked down at the fibers of the cream-colored carpet. "Do you think it's stupid that I'm leaving?"

"I think you have to go with your gut at times like these. No one else can make that decision for you." He paused for a moment, then said, "I've seen enough through my life to believe that if things are meant to work out, they will. And if they're not, they won't. Any extra worrying about it—or worrying what other people think about it—won't change that outcome."

Avery looked up and met his eyes again.

"I think Margaux has her reasons why she's holding onto Nicolas especially tight right now. Not that it excuses any of her actions and behaviors, mind you. Just that it explains them. And I think it's hard to step away from a company that you've been running for seventeen years. She and Nicolas have much to work out."

That only confirmed that Avery leaving was the right thing to do. Staying was only going to make everything more difficult for them to work through. "I should go."

He nodded slowly, and they both stood.

Avery wanted to ask him to give Nicolas a message from her, but she couldn't think of anything even remotely okay as a message not delivered by her in person. "Do you mind telling the staff goodbye for me?"

He glanced behind her just then. She turned to see that all three of them—Jacques, Delphine, and Rania—were walking out from the staff hallway, Rania hopping as she was putting on her second shoe and Delphine sliding her arms into a cardigan.

Rania pointed a finger at her. "You weren't planning on leaving without telling us goodbye, were you?"

"I'm sorry I woke you up."

"You be glad that Jacques is a light sleeper," Delphine said as she wrapped her arms around Avery. "Or you would've had three very upset Belgians hunting you down at the airport."

Jacques clasped his hands behind his back. "And I would be offended if I wasn't the one to drive you to the airport, Ms. Parks."

"Rania and I are coming, too," Delphine said.

She looked at all three of them, shocked that they were acting like they usually did around her and not showing the formality they always did around "Master Servais." She knew it was for her benefit and that must've been difficult for all of them. "Oh, I'm going to miss you all so much!" Avery pulled the three of them into a group hug.

"We'll play Nertz in your honor while you're gone," Rania said, her voice coming out muffled from their tight hug.

Jacques nodded. "And we'll be sure to let you know who won."

Avery laughed and wiped at a tear that threatened to escape. Then she turned to Nicolas's grandfather. "Thank you again for letting me stay here. And for coming to my rescue last night."

"It was my pleasure."

Jacques grabbed hold of the handle of her rolling suitcase, and they all headed to the elevator. Just before she stepped on, Nicolas's grandfather said, "Oh, and Avery?"

She turned.

"I think you're perfectly equipped to be in this world."

Avery looked at him for a moment, then hurried forward and gave him a quick hug. He awkwardly patted her back twice before she pulled away and smiled at him. Then she stepped onto the elevator.

Chapter Twenty-Six

NICOLAS

Nicolas stayed insanely busy all week during the International Royal Chocolatier Awards. He split his time between the office and the venue for the competition, making sure that their social media was keeping everyone up to date on how the competition was going, that their paid ads were covering everything, and ensuring everyone had what they needed when and where they needed it. The competition had kept everyone at Oma Servais hopping, especially him as the marketing director.

It had been busy enough that he mostly managed to keep his mind off Avery. Until he went home each night, and he'd nearly pick up his phone to tell her something about his day before remembering that she was gone. And anywhere he went, he'd long to have her by his side.

And when he climbed into bed at night, hoping for sleep to blissfully consume all his thoughts, everything would replay in his head. Then he'd start missing her so badly that he'd bring up the picture on his phone that he'd taken of Avery that night on the red carpet. It showed the smile on her face before everything had gone bad, and he'd imagine all the ways he could've handled things differently so she'd have kept that smile on her face for the entire evening.

He could have thought ahead enough to realize his mother's plan with Sophie and stopped it before it even happened. Or he could've come up with his own plan. He should've anticipated it.

He could've stood up to his mother at the reception and insisted that he was going to stay with Avery and deal with fixing the damage that Sophie had already done. Avery had stood up to her that night. Why had he thought he couldn't?

He could've just told Sophie to leave. He could've taken Avery's hand and the two of them could've left the moment he saw that Sophie was there. If nothing else, he could've gone to his grandfather's flat that night and talked to Avery, even though she'd told him not to, and convinced her to know that she had done nothing wrong. He analyzed over and over why he had felt like he had no choice in the moment. And he made plan after plan of how he could make changes so that he'd never feel that way again. He would do whatever it took to keep Avery from ever being in a situation like that again.

He wasn't sure he'd ever get another chance, though.

And sometime late into the night, he usually managed to fall asleep, dreaming only of her.

The competition had helped him get through the week, but then the weekend came. That was when everyone at Oma Servais typically crashed—IRCA week was exhausting for all of them. And despite everything, they'd won the competition. The judges had announced the winners on Friday. That same day, he and his team had turned in their final ads, which were now running on all social media platforms and would be releasing in online and print magazines for the next several weeks. Sales had already skyrocketed. Their production teams were prepared for another long stretch of busyness.

But not having work over the weekend meant that Nicolas had two full days of nothing to distract himself from the pain of missing Avery. His grandfather had texted him the morning that she'd left, but after her plane had taken flight. He'd immediately regretted not fighting for her and had been kicking himself ever since.

He'd managed to mostly avoid his mother except in a professional capacity, and only when the situation required it. He hadn't gone to their usual Monday family dinner last week and wasn't going today, either. Not only had he not wanted to see her, but he hadn't trusted himself to not say things he'd regret later.

This morning, though, at the start of a new week, he woke up at five a.m. and couldn't handle facing more time spent painfully longing for Avery, so he'd headed into the Oma Servais kitchens bright and early to make chocolates and clear his head. He was the only one there for quite a while. This time, he wasn't there to create a new flavor— he needed the comfort that only came from making one of his grandma's traditional recipes. A salted caramel praline.

Hours later, Jean-Pierre was the first person to walk into the kitchens, holding a stack of papers in his arms. Nicolas glanced up just as the Chief of Product Development set his things on an empty table and leaned against a counter across from Nicolas.

"I wondered if I would find you here this morning." He leaned forward to see the chocolates Nicolas was just finishing up. "Is that your grandma Servais's praline?"

Nicolas nodded.

Jean-Pierre stayed quiet for a moment, then asked, "Have you heard from Avery?"

Nicolas shook his head. There had been so many times he'd wanted to call her. He felt awful that he'd put her in that situation, not thinking ahead enough to know how volatile it could be and that it had such potential to harm her. He worried that by calling, he'd make her feel like he was trying to get her to come back to a situation that had hurt her. He wanted her in his world, but he knew how selfish that want was.

"Are you going to just let her go?"

Nicolas looked up from his work, releasing a long, slow breath. Then he leaned against the workstation behind him. "I don't want to."

Jean-Pierre moved some of the papers in his stack and pulled out a magazine that said International Royal Chocolatier, and Nicolas leaned forward a bit. Was that the new issue?

"This just came out this morning." Jean-Pierre opened it to the centerfold and held it so Nicolas could see.

Both sides of the two-page spread was a big picture of Nicolas, taking a photo of Avery on the red carpet. It was the opening image that led to the entire article about the competition. He was surprised, especially because it wasn't even of the two of them posing in typical red carpet fashion. It wasn't a picture of any of the chocolate creations in the gallery nor the auction afterward. It wasn't the chocolates, or the competition itself, or the chocolatiers who competed, or even of what went on inside the reception.

It was just a picture of him, taking a photo of Avery.

"Tell me what you see here," Jean-Pierre said.

Nicolas took the magazine from his hands and stared at the woman he'd been looking at on his phone every night since she left ten days ago, just from a slightly different angle. "I see a confident, exquisite woman. A woman whose beauty gives a hint at who she is inside. Someone thoughtful, caring, smart, funny, humble, and who cares deeply about people."

Jean-Pierre nodded. "Indeed. Now let me tell you what else I see." He tapped two fingers on the photo of Nicolas. "I see a man so in love with a woman that he's never going to be satisfied with anything else in life if he just lets her go. The IRC sees it, too, or they never would've chosen this picture as their headline image."

Nicolas stared at the picture for a very long time. Jean-Pierre was right. All the love he had for Avery was right there on his face, plain as day.

"Can I give you some unsolicited advice?"

"Please."

"Figure out what you most want and how you want it. And then go for it with all you've got."

Nicolas let out a quick breath of air. Jean-Pierre made it sound so simple.

But maybe he wasn't wrong. Maybe it was simple.

Jean-Pierre gathered up his things. As he was heading out of the room, Nicolas said, "Out of all the images they could've chosen for that spread, why do you think they chose that one?"

"My guess? Because they want people to look at chocolate the way you're looking at Avery."

Nicolas smiled. "Thank you for everything, Jean-Pierre."

———

WHEN NICOLAS WALKED into his office suite at nine, Finn stood and said, "Your father is waiting for you inside."

"Did we have an appointment?" He suddenly didn't remember what was on the docket for today at all.

But Finn shook his head no.

Huh. His father was much more willing to stop by his office just to say hello than his mother was, but it still wasn't a common occurrence. He walked into his office and found his father seated on one of his couches.

"Good morning, Father," Nicolas said as he set his things down on his desk. "What brings you here this morning?"

"I just want to chat about Avery."

"Oh." So this was something serious. He pressed the button to turn on his computer, then went over to his seating area and sat down in an armchair directly across from his father. "What do you want to know?"

"Mostly how you feel about her. Do you love her?"

"I do." He ran his hands over his face before resting his elbows on his knees. "But she left after experiencing mother's very clear disapproval of her."

His father was quiet for a moment, then said, "Did you know that your grandfather didn't approve of me when your mother and I were dating?"

Nicolas's eyebrows rose. He'd never heard that before.

"Not even a little bit. He all but forbade your mother to date me. But she stood up to him, and it all worked out in the end."

"I don't recall Grandfather disowning any of his children because they didn't do what he wanted, though. I think we can count on my mother's reaction being a bit more extreme."

"Oh, make no mistake—she's not going to be happy. But the right thing to do isn't always the easy thing to do." He paused for a moment, then, more quietly said, "Just ask your mother."

Nicolas tried guessing what his father was trying to say without actually saying it, but he came up empty.

At Nicolas's confused expression, his father said, "She's known for a dozen years that repairing things with Maxim is the right thing to do. But it's hard. It's hard for me, too. And we've both let that stop us. Don't let the fact that something is hard stop *you* from doing it, son. Don't let your life be less than it can be."

The last bit of advice that Jean-Pierre gave him rang in Nicolas's mind. *Figure out what you most want and how you want it. And then go for it with all you've got.* It was like his father was adding: *And don't let hard things stop you from doing it.*

His father got up and walked to the door, but hesitated in the doorway. He turned back to Nicolas and said, "My guess? Your mother doesn't want to lose another son. I know I don't."

He thought back to when Avery had talked with him about worst-case scenario and most-likely scenarios with his mother, and about how he had experience with really disappointing his mother and surviving it. He'd had his answer longer than he'd realized.

Chapter Twenty-Seven

AVERY

very was running the day's batch of college applications while talking to Joy, who currently sat on the edge of Avery's desk, mug of coffee in hand. All of last week had been so busy, trying to catch back up with everything that had fallen behind with Joy trying to do the job of two people, and the end of the year for her student employees. She only had two who worked through the summer semester.

In getting caught up, she finally got a moment to really talk to her friend about her trip.

"You know, I always thought that when I was in danger, I'd be a 'freeze' kind of person. If a bear came after me? I'd freeze. If someone tried to rob me? I'd freeze. If Shelly jumped out to scare me when I came home after dark? I'd freeze." Avery thought back to the night of the reception and the incident in the restroom with Margaux. "It turns out I'm a 'fight' and then 'flight' kind of person."

Joy lifted a shoulder. "Maybe it's one of those things where you do something different based on what the situation called for. It sounds like that one called for fight and flight."

"Maybe it called for the fight. But I'm not so sure it called for the flight. At the time, it felt like it was the right thing to do. The *kind* thing to do. The way that would make things less difficult for Nicolas. And for me, I guess. But now, I just keep thinking that if the roles had been reversed, no matter how much harder it made things, I would've wanted him to stay and say goodbye first. I wish I could go back and change things. Do it differently."

She felt like her insides had been gutted, and she'd been the one to leave, not the one getting left. It had to have been awful to be in Nicolas's position.

"Regrets are a hard thing to live with."

They really were. There hadn't been a moment since she'd left Belgium when Nicolas hadn't been on her mind, regardless of what she was doing or how hard she was trying to focus on anything else. There was a pang in her heart. A longing deeper than she knew how to manage, and it was there constantly. She'd never known she could miss a person so much.

"Avery."

She turned at the sound of her name being called

and looked across the half-wall to where Summer stood in her office doorway, Elle and Deja just behind her, and said, "Come over when you've got a few minutes free."

"Go," Joy said. "I need to get back to my office and get to work."

Avery was finally caught up, so she went through the half wall separating Admissions and the Welcome Center and entered Summer's office.

As Avery walked in, her friend said, "You know that Elle is doing a feature in the school's magazine where she interviews alumni who have been very successful in their field, right?" Avery nodded, so Summer continued. "Her first one came out today!" She held up the magazine, grinning.

Avery grabbed the magazine and looked at the article about a woman who, based on the tagline at the top, had graduated with a degree in film and history and was helping to create short documentaries recreating historical events for teachers to use. The article was pretty long and, honestly, looked so professional. She smiled at her friend. "Elle, this is fantastic!"

Elle smiled, too, clearly proud of what she'd done.

"Now we need your opinion on something very important," Deja said, "because Everett and Brock are being no help whatsoever. Elle has to line up interviews quite a bit in advance, so she already has her next two alumni chosen. We're trying to talk her into interviewing Declan Davenport for her next opening."

"The YouTuber with the amazing voice?"

"Thank you!" Deja said, motioning toward Elle with both hands like she was presenting evidence to back up her claim.

"I didn't say he had a bad voice," Elle said. "Just that I'm not sitting over here wishing he'd read me poetry."

Summer touched her fingers to her lips. "Oh, my. Can you just imagine him reading poetry to you?"

Avery wished that Nicolas was there right now, meeting all her friends, bantering right along with them. She would take him all around campus and show all the things that mattered to her when she was a student there and all the things that matter to her now, as her place of employment. She wanted to show him everything that had changed since he'd last been in Lake Baldwin ten years ago.

In fact, she missed everyone in Belgium, and she suddenly wanted to know what Jacques, Delphine, and Rania were doing right now. Had they played Nertz lately?

Tess Barringer, the associate director over admissions and the boss of everyone except Avery, halted in the doorway with her usual protein bar in hand. "It looks like lots of work is getting done over here."

Last week had been the week of finals at LBSU, and

there had been a distinct stressful buzz running through the entire school. Most of the students had now returned home for the summer, so the halls were practically empty. This week was typically one of their least busy weeks of the year. High school was still in session, but most applicants were heading into all the end-of-year deadlines for assignments, projects, and exams, so they didn't have the free time to worry about college just then. It was a time of the year when both sides of the half-wall got to relax a bit after their busiest seasons.

"Oh, you know it," Deja said. "We are trying to talk Elle into interviewing Declan Davenport as her next alumnus for the school magazine."

Tess's eyes widened. "Can you imagine if he'd been a student ambassador when he'd gone here? We could've just had him do all the talking during the school tours and presentations, and we'd have had every single visiting student fill out an application before they even walked out of the building."

Elle threw her hands up in defeat. "Maybe I should just see if I can line up an interview between him and all of you."

Avery laughed as every single person in the room sat up straighter or stood taller, leaning slightly toward Elle, excited at the mere thought of that happening.

Tess turned to Avery. "I haven't gotten a chance to ask you—how was your trip?"

"It was great!" By answering the question multiple times now, she'd found that if she focused on the sites she saw, especially the ones she went to with Riley and not Nicolas, it was easier. She just had to focus on the good stuff and not all the parts where her heart was in pieces because of the way she'd left things, and because Nicolas was no longer in her life daily like he'd been over there. So she told Tess about the magic of the country that she now loved.

"And how was your friend who lives there?" Tess asked. "Did you get to see him much?"

From the corner of her eye, Avery saw Summer motioning to Tess to cut that line of questioning, and Tess immediately reacted.

"I apologize. It seems I've stepped into a painful subject. Oh, look—Pavani is back. Pavani!" Tess waved her in, seeming grateful for something that could change the subject, and Avery was grateful, too, because things had just turned very awkward.

Tess moved away from the doorway, allowing Pavani to join the now very crowded office. Everett and Brock must've realized that the focus was off Declan Davenport and onto Pavani's news because they both came to the doorway as Pavani lifted the strap of her bag over her head and set it on Summer's desk.

"We heard the heartbeat!"

Everyone shared their congratulations, and Avery and Tess—the two closest to Pavani—both hugged her.

"The baby's due date is around Thanksgiving, so that'll be so much fun."

Their chatting was all babies and getting ready to have babies and Pavani getting ready for her baby. And then it turned to school getting out and summer plans and work things that happened only during the summer months when everything was less busy.

It felt so strange to see life going on like normal for everyone else when Avery's had changed so drastically. The way she looked at everything had changed. The way she looked at her job had changed—her outlook, the freshness of it. And she realized that she was ready for something more. She was ready to step outside of her comfort zone and stretch and grow. She had found what she'd been looking for.

She'd just also found something she hadn't been looking for—she'd never expected to come back home with heartbreak.

Instead of heading through the opening in the half-wall back to her desk, she walked out through the Welcome Center doors and down the hall, turned down the next hall of the L-shaped building, then circled around outside, taking in the spring sunshine before entering back into the building through her normal door. She'd hoped that the fresh air and movement would help clear Nicolas from her mind, but it had only given her more time to think about him.

Just like she'd done every time since getting back, even though there were so few faces in the halls now, she looked at each one that she passed as she headed back to her office, aching to see a familiar face from Belgium. Grasping for anything to get a connection to that magical place, even though she knew full well that she wasn't going to see anyone.

She returned to her desk and pulled from her purse the little figurine of the young girl holding a star that Nicolas had given to her the night of the reception. She held onto it tightly, like it was a lifeline, keeping her tethered to him.

After a few moments, she set the figurine standing up just in front of her computer monitor and opened a web browser before typing in the address for Oma Servais's website. She stared at the new award badge that had joined the others just below their company name before she registered what she was seeing. Had she somehow *not* destroyed that chance for them?

She sat back in her chair, stunned. They must've done well at the competition to have won despite the obstacles she'd thrown in their path.

All the damage she caused aside, it was probably a good thing that she'd gone to the reception with Nicolas. And that she'd experienced all of what was causing her heartbreak. It was important that she met Nicolas's parents and went to an event with them that she'd been so unequipped to handle. Someone had once told her that sometimes you had to make the wrong choice so you could *know* that it was the wrong choice. Because if you only made the right choice, you'd spend your life wondering if the other choice might have been the better one.

She wouldn't have known that she could never make it in their world if she hadn't tried. So she was glad that she had.

———

"CHECK IT OUT," Riley said the moment that Avery walked into their apartment after work and hung her purse on the hook. "I got back early enough to make dinner for once. Chicken fajitas!" She motioned to the table, where everything was set up. "Shelly has to work late, so she just wants us to save her some."

"How's Sara?" Avery asked Riley as she walked up to the table and breathed the fajita-y goodness in deeply. Riley had been busy running Under the Arch by herself since Sara's accident, but she took every chance she could to go visit her friend—at first in the hospital and now at her home. And Avery knew she'd gone to see her this afternoon.

"Good. She's going to physical therapy every day, and

they told her she's making amazing progress. After another week or so, she'll be able to come back to work part-time."

"Oh, that's fantastic news." She tried to focus on that. On everything that Riley was saying. It helped with the regret a little.

They both sat down, and Riley handed her the tortilla warmer and asked, "How are *you* doing?"

Avery shrugged as she pulled out a tortilla. "Work feels very different now. I'm more ready to take on new things, and it's helping me realize how much I've changed. I headed off to Belgium to kick myself out of my comfort zone, broaden my experiences, and grow and become something more, and I feel like I accomplished just that. But I'm having a hard time reconciling being happy about that with being sad about the loss of Nicolas."

Wow. That was probably way too deep for not even having finished getting the chicken and peppers on her tortilla.

"Have you talked to Nicolas yet?"

Avery shook her head as she put the cheese, salsa, and guacamole on her fajita. "After that Friday night at the reception, I think we both knew that I wasn't cut out for that world. And knowing that it can't work out just makes it too painful. I don't think either of us could handle talking yet. I don't know. Maybe I just wasn't ready for a relationship."

Riley rolled her eyes. "You're just saying that to make yourself feel better."

"Maybe I am," Avery said, and Riley's eyebrows rose, like she was surprised that either she'd admitted it, or that she'd agreed with Riley's assessment.

Avery had realized that she still hadn't fully become who she wanted to be before finding someone to share her life with. But she also realized that she didn't have to be perfectly there before finding him. It wasn't something that could just happen by the time she was twenty-seven—it took a lifetime of work. And if he was the right person, then they would get there together.

"I decided that successful relationships are all about finding the type of person where you could develop a relationship of supporting each other in reaching your goals and becoming who you wanted to become." She paused for a long moment, then said, "And Nicolas felt like that person."

She picked up her fajita and took a bite. It was pretty good, which was impressive, given Riley's lack of experience in making them.

Riley put her fajita down, then said, "It's pretty clear that you love him and he loves you. So why are you not trying to make this work?"

"How?" Avery asked. "How could it ever work? He lives on the other side of the Atlantic. He has a life there. A job that he loves. He's about to become a brand new

CEO of a company, and he'll have so much to learn and do that there won't be time for travel. And I have a life here. A job I love, too. I love Belgium, but I'm not okay just giving up everything here, either."

She wanted a life with Nicolas. But he lived in a world that felt impossibly out of reach for her—even more so now that she was back in her own world.

Chapter Twenty-Eight

NICOLAS

Nicolas went into the men's restroom closest to the conference room on the executive floor and splashed water on his face, then grabbed a towel and dried it off. He had made some major decisions and was about to do something that could impact his entire support system, and he was feeling the weight of it. Except for Maxim, every bit of his support system—parents, extended family, friends, colleagues— was tied to the business, which was tied to his parents' wishes for him and the company.

He had felt so torn between those two loyalties—his family, including the family business, and Avery. But now he knew without a doubt that Avery was his number one. He needed to do everything he could to be her number one, too. And that meant adjusting his life to make room for her.

He had planned to talk to his mother about it in her office two days ago and then again yesterday, but she'd taken most of the last couple of days off work. It was unusual for her to take any time off. They'd all been working themselves to the bone during competition week last week, so it made sense that she was taking time off. But now that he thought of it, he realized she had been taking partial days off quite a bit over the past several weeks.

So he scheduled a meeting for today with both his parents and invited his grandfather. Since he was the Chairman of the Board, this would impact him, too.

When it came time for the meeting to start, he walked to the conference room door, shook out his hands, hoping to stop the trembling, then took a slow, deep breath and turned the knob.

Across the room, his mother, father, and grandfather were all seated around the table. Which was surprising—he'd expected his mother to be pacing the room, demanding to know why he hadn't been the first to arrive since he was the one who called the meeting.

He thanked them for coming, especially his grandfather since he had to travel so much farther to attend. And then, since his mother preferred when people got to the point quickly instead of easing their way into things, he jumped in.

"Avery is important to me. And not just a little bit—she's everything."

He ignored his mother's partial eye roll as she looked out the windows like there wasn't anything important going on in the room.

"There are many reasons why I want to make this request and why I've wanted to for years, but I'm making it now primarily because I want her in my life."

His mother kept her focus on the windows, but she could no longer pretend that she wasn't interested in what he was saying.

"I don't want to be the CEO of this company right now. I would like to stay in my current position for now and then move into the position of Chief of Product Development when Jean-Pierre retires. I think that's where the company can best use my talents."

His mother turned her focus back onto him. "That's not going to happen."

"I think you should name Christophe Mertens as CEO."

She slapped her hand down on the table. "The name of the company isn't Oma *Mertens*. It's Oma Servais because it's a family company and should stay in the family. I've raised you for this position your entire life!"

"Not my *entire* life—just since I was thirteen. You raised Maxim for it his whole life until he was eighteen." He didn't know why he felt the need to point out that he had been her second choice. Or that she had experience with the person she had in mind for the position not working out. "And why turn it over to me now? I'm twenty-seven, almost twenty-eight. You didn't take over as CEO until you were *thirty*-eight."

"I wasn't needed until I was thirty-eight. You're needed now. And if you insist on dating Avery, you can do it while you're CEO."

"Mother, you know I'll never have time for a relationship with Avery if I become CEO now. If it's so important to you to keep it in the family, why don't you stay on? I know that you care about the non-profit you're going to help run, but I know you don't care about it nearly as much as you care about Oma Servais."

"The non-profit is a cover."

"What?" The words didn't make sense. He looked to his father and grandfather, but neither of them looked as confused as he felt. Whatever she meant, they knew.

"I can't stay on as CEO," she clarified.

"Why?" He asked, but now he was dreading hearing the answer.

She stood from her chair, like she was too angry to stay seated, and walked over to the window. Then she turned to his father. "I don't want to do this."

"He deserves to know."

She let out a breath in a huff. "Fine." Then she turned back to Nicolas. "Do you remember when I got breast cancer when you were just starting primary school? We found out back then that I have the cancer gene. So I've known that cancers could show up at any time again. I've been trying to prepare you—and Maxim, back when he lived at home—for quite a while in case one does." She paused. "I've been trying to prepare you for now."

"*Now*? You have cancer?"

"Yes," she said like it made her mad that she couldn't just threaten the cancer and force it to go away. "I've been getting treatments, and I've managed to keep it hidden from everyone so far. But my doctors tell me that we're going to have to fight it more aggressively and things are going to get pretty tough for me. And I'm not about to stay on as CEO and come into work sporadically, looking weak and incapable of running a company as big as Oma Servais when I do."

"Oh, Mother. I'm so sorry." It felt like the room was spinning—both out of grief for his mother's diagnosis and because everything his mother had done throughout his life, all their disagreements, all the times she pushed him, were suddenly being reframed in his mind.

"Stop! I am not telling you this because I want pity. I'm telling you this because it's an obstacle we're facing that needs to be addressed."

"I'm not saying 'I'm sorry' in my capacity as someone

on the executive team of Oma Servais. I'm saying it as your son."

She paused a long moment, pursing her lips. Then she met his eyes and said, "Thank you."

In that one moment of softening, he could see the worry in her eyes. The very human emotion of knowing that she was facing a battle with a strong foe. He walked over to her and wrapped his arms around her in a hug. She stiffened at first, but then relaxed a bit and eventually put her arms around him and gave him a squeeze. It was the first real hug they'd shared in more than a decade.

The moment he released, though, she was back in her professional capacity. "So we need to address this obstacle."

Nicolas nodded. "Okay, so you will definitely want Christophe Mertens as the CEO, then. He has more experience than I do, so he'll need to go to you for help on fewer things than I would."

She shook her head, arms crossed, and looked out the window again.

He softened his voice just a touch. Not enough to make her think he was pitying her in any way. "I know this is hard for you. You love this company, and it's going to take time to come to terms with someone leading the helm who isn't a Servais. Christophe will make an excellent CEO. But I'm pretty sure you know that after working with him for the past nine years."

"I agree," his grandfather said, the first words he'd uttered during the entire meeting.

"I love this company too," Nicolas said. "I've given it my all since I first started helping out in production when I was fourteen, and I continue to give it my all in every capacity that I serve here. You've raised me for this position, and there will come a time when I am very ready for it. Like when I've started a family and they've had a chance to grow up a bit.

"But for now, Oma Servais will be in good hands. I will still be here. Father will. Grandfather will. And you'll be on the board. And so many of our Servais extended family are here—my uncles and aunts and cousins—in nearly every single department. It will still be a family company."

She turned back to him, throwing her arms out. "All this, for a *girl*?"

Nicolas's grandfather had been so quiet through the meeting that he wondered if he was only going to say a word of agreement or disagreement here or there. But he surprised Nicolas by clearing his throat and speaking. "She's not just 'a girl.' After talking with her a bit and seeing her actions, I stand up for Avery, and my staff will vouch for her, too. They have demonstrated extreme loyalty to her, so the 'girl' has proven that she can engender that in others. That's a valuable trait to have. It's not surprising that she has Nicolas's loyalty, because he's an extremely loyal person." He paused for a moment. "But she also has mine."

Margaux stared at Grandfather for a long time, and Nicolas wished he could tell what she was thinking. But, as she often did, she kept her face an unreadable mask.

Then she said, "I think it's foolish that he's wanting to throw away everything we've worked for, all for a girl that he's smitten with."

"She's a *woman* who makes me a better man," Nicolas said, "and I think that's what you've wanted for me all along."

"I agree," his father said.

His mother's eyes flew to his father's. "Et tu, Brute?"

"Did you think I wouldn't have Nicolas's back on this? What if you had never stood up to your father when he said he didn't think you should throw everything away for 'a boy' you were smitten with?"

Nicolas's grandfather met her gaze. "He's got a point."

"Is she worth all of this?" his mother asked.

Nicolas gave a single nod. "She's worth so much more than this."

"Do you know if she even wants any of this?" she asked. "What if you go to her with your grand plans and she wants nothing to do with them?"

The mere thought of that outcome sent a stabbing pain to his heart. "I don't know what she wants for certain, but I have a great deal of hope. All I know is how much I want this and how much I'm willing to do everything possible on my part to make a relationship with her work."

His mother turned back fully to the window, staring out, arms crossed, for a very long moment. Nicolas hoped that she'd understood that dating Avery and not being the CEO were not negotiable. And he hoped that she wouldn't be so inflexible that she'd turn him away, just like she had Maxim. But even if he had to leave the company that he loved and find a different job—and a support system—outside of Oma Servais, he would.

After several excruciatingly long minutes, Margaux turned around, looking resigned. "I guess I need to come to terms with Christophe Mertens being at the helm of this company."

Nicolas felt his smile all the way in his heart.

"I think it's a good choice," his grandfather said. "I'll back the vote for him to the Board of Directors."

His father nodded. "And we'll need to start the search for a new Marketing Director who can start when Jean-Pierre retires in a couple of months."

As much as Nicolas wanted to cheer or shout for joy, there was another issue of equal importance. "One more thing we need to discuss. I don't want you to ever make Avery feel less than the incredible person that she is, Mother. I can only bring her here if it's a safe place for her, and if it's not, then I can't stay."

Considering who his mother was, that was a sizeable

ultimatum, and he could barely breathe as he waited for her response.

She paused for a beat and then gave a single nod of acceptance.

Nicolas took a big, deep breath that felt fresh and free.

Now he just needed to show Avery how much he wanted her in his world and how much he wanted to be in hers.

Chapter Twenty-Nine

AVERY

very sat in front of her desk at work, her mind running in a loop of how she could possibly make things work with Nicolas—a loop that always ended in a fail—while trying to keep her mind on her actual job, which at the moment was approving paychecks for her student employees.

Her phone rang and she glanced over at it, assuming it was a telemarketer. When she saw the 32 of Belgium's country code and the 02 of Brussels' area code, many emotions ran through her at once. Elation. Confusion. Hope. Fear. Anticipation. Desperation to hear from anyone in Belgium. And an intense desire to not let any of the positive emotions get too big, for fear of the imminent letdown being too great.

It wasn't the number she had in her phone for Nicolas,

though. Fleur had called her several times since she'd been home, but it didn't show Fleur's name on the screen. She had Jacques, Delphine, and Rania's phone numbers all programmed in, too. This number was one she didn't have.

With curiosity and wariness, she pressed to answer the call. "Hello?"

"Avery Parks?" a woman with a Dutch accent said. When Avery told her yes, she said, "Please hold for Margaux Servais."

Shock and worry flashed through her like hot irons. Had something happened to Nicolas? Or was she simply calling to demand an apology from Avery? Would she give it? No, she realized. She wouldn't. Not for the words she'd said. She stood and started walking back toward Grant's or Joy's offices, hoping one of them was vacant, preparing herself to withstand whatever tirade Margaux was about to send her way.

"Avery?" Margaux's voice sent a chill down her spine, and she had to remind herself to breathe.

"Yes?"

"Margaux here. I need to apologize."

Wait. For real? Margaux was calling to *apologize*? She stopped in her tracks, in the hallway leading to Grant's and Joy's offices.

"I thought you were a pushover," the woman continued.

There was a long pause, so Avery waited for the part

with the apology before wondering if that may have been the apology.

Margaux let out a frustrated breath in a huff, almost like it physically pained her to say something nice to Avery. "I wrongly assumed that you were someone who could never make it in our world. But after that night of the reception, I began to see that maybe you have convictions, passion, and a willingness to fight for what matters to you. And I was especially impressed that you stood up to me."

She was? Was she referring to the conversation in the restroom? Because the look on Margaux's face during that conversation hadn't been anything close to resembling being impressed. "Thank you?"

"And as much as I hate to admit it, I can also see how having someone who brings people together can be a helpful thing. Maybe we could use more of that calming influence."

Avery leaned against the wall in the hallway, needing its support. "Why are you telling me this?" She couldn't help but ask the question, because Margaux seemed like she wasn't particularly enjoying saying that she appreciated aspects of who Avery was.

"Because it seems you've rubbed off on Nicolas."

Avery had no idea what she meant by that. Standing up for herself? Bringing people together?

"Apparently, you've got a lot of people here on your

side, so I guess I need to be, too. I've been re-examining my opinions on a few things. I have to say that I fully thought you were a bad influence on Nicolas. I'm still not convinced that isn't the case, but in the past couple of weeks, I've seen how not having you in Nicolas's life is what has been bad for him. It has taken me a while to accept that."

Avery swallowed, emotion welling up in her throat.

"Nicolas doesn't know that I'm calling, but I'd like to request that you consider giving him a second chance."

"Oh!" Of all the reasons Avery could've guessed that Margaux might be calling, she would've never thought that would be it. Margaux had made her feelings toward Avery pretty clear at dinner and the reception. It never occurred to her that winning Margaux over was even a remote possibility. She found herself without words.

Margaux's voice throughout the entire phone call had been brusque and begrudging. Almost gruff. But after a moment of silence, her voice came out softer and quieter. "And I'd like to acknowledge your not-so-gentle nudge in regards to my relationship with Maxim. Apparently being reprimanded by a farm girl from South Dakota was exactly what I needed to take the first step there. It's because of that nudge that I now know that I am going to be a grandmother."

Happiness washed over Avery, causing goosebumps to rise on her arms. "Oh, that's wonderful! Congratulations!"

"It's going to take years to repair the damage, but the first step has been taken." She heard an audible swallow on Margaux's end of the line. Then, in an even quieter voice, with the tiniest bit of emotion peeking through, she said, "Thank you."

When Margaux ended the call, Avery held the phone in her hand for a long minute, too blown away to move from the spot where she still leaned against the wall in the hallway.

Since coming back home and getting some distance from the trauma of the reception, she had realized how proud she was that she had stood up to Margaux that night. She hadn't avoided conflict like she normally did, and she had said exactly what she'd felt she needed to say.

It wasn't like it had been the first time she had ever stood up for anyone and put herself in the line of fire or anything. Yet she still felt like she had leveled up that night.

And yeah, it had worked out in this instance. But it could've just as easily had the disastrous consequences that she'd thought in the moment that it might have. But she'd done it. Which meant that she could again.

It wasn't just about standing up to people like Margaux who were making her life or someone else's life miserable. It was also about standing up for what Avery had figured out that she wanted. She'd gotten better at figuring out what that was, too, instead of always bending to what everyone else wanted. And if the past couple of weeks had taught her anything, it was what she wanted most. And that was Nicolas.

It was time to put that new *standing up for herself* skill to more practice.

Instead of heading back to her desk, she went straight to Grant's office and knocked on the frame of the open door. "Do you have a minute?"

He nodded and said, "Come in."

So she shut the door behind her and took a seat. She told her boss about how she loved her job and her life here, but that she also had fallen completely for Nicolas, and that she wanted with everything she had to make things work out with him.

Then she told Grant about an idea that she'd had bouncing around in her head for the last couple of days as her mind had run in a loop, trying to figure out how to make a life with Nicolas possible. She brought up the idea of a job share situation. The admissions department as a whole, and especially her position, was super busy half of the year and not so busy the other half. If they were to find someone willing to only work the slow months of the year, then she could work the busy ones and have half the year to spend in Belgium.

"Of course, it might end up not being needed." She knew that even if Grant did approve her request that it might come to nothing—she was only half of the equation in her relationship with Nicolas, after all—but she wanted to do everything she could to make a relationship with him possible. She wanted to stand up for what she really, truly wanted.

"He sounds like a great guy, and it sounds like you've fallen for him. I'd have to bring your proposal up to the Assistant VP of Enrollment and get their approval, but I think it would go through. We'd miss you six months of the year if it does work out, and I sincerely hope it does."

She gave him a grateful smile. It felt like she'd just taken a big step in Nicolas's direction, and it thrilled her. Now she just needed to figure out how to show Nicolas that she did want to be in his world.

A chatter arose in the distance, and she reached back to open Grant's office door. It sounded like it was coming from the Welcome Center side of the wall—sometimes they got very excited about things over there.

Then it sounded like it was spilling a bit into the Admissions side. At first, she assumed one of the sports teams was walking down the hallway, celebrating a victory or getting pumped up for an upcoming game, but school was out for the summer. Did they have any groups doing a camp this week?

As the sound of exclamations and awe grew, both she and Grant leaned to where they could see Avery's desk and the main area through his open door. The few student employees working in Admissions were turning back to look at Avery and Grant.

Then Julia waved for Avery to come and see.

Curious, both she and Grant stood up and walked to the main area to look at whatever everyone else seemed to be looking at. She glanced over at the Welcome Center side to see every single employee out of their offices and craning to see through the glass front of the Admissions department.

And then she saw a beautiful bouquet of a couple of dozen flowers in a vase, sitting on the front counter at Julia's window. "They're for you!" Julia said as she waved Avery over more urgently.

Avery hurried to the front area and marveled at the flowers until Julia said, "There's a note."

Avery pulled it off the cardholder and opened the envelope, immediately recognizing Nicolas's handwriting. Had he mailed a local florist the card to put in flowers they had delivered? Then she read the card.

Come to the parking lot nearest the Student Center.

Her stomach flipped and the world seemed to stop for a moment. Was Nicolas here in Lake Baldwin? She hurried through the main door out into the hallway and looked both ways. Joy, Julia, and Grant were right behind her, and everyone in the Welcome Center practically burst through their door and into the hallway.

"Was that him?" Summer asked.

"Who?"

"The guy who dropped those off!" Pavani said.

"Hot guy," Deja said, "in a suit. Please tell me it was him. It had to be him."

Avery looked down the hall in both directions again. Nicolas couldn't be there. She shouldn't get her hopes up so much that he might be. He was 4300 miles away. And today was a workday for him, too.

"What does the note say?" Elle asked, taking it out of Avery's hand and reading, "'Come to the parking lot nearest the Student Center.'"

"Go," Grant said.

"I'll cover for you," Joy said.

"Okay. I was just approving the—"

"Go!" everyone yelled, practically in unison.

So she did. She took off running down the hall and out the main doors and kept running across the campus sidewalks to the parking lot where she normally parked.

And there, right at the front, was a green, shiny, new model John Deere 9620R Tractor. It was a big tractor with double wheels, so eight massive, yellow-rimmed wheels total. And Jacques was standing right in front of it, wearing the same uniform he'd been wearing when he'd picked Avery and Riley up from the Brussels airport on that first day.

A laugh burst out of her and she wiped a tear that came with it. "Jacques, what are you doing here?"

"I came to pick you up, Ms. Parks. Are you ready?"

Was Jacques really here? In South Dakota? "Yes."

He opened the passenger's door of the tractor, then held out a hand for her as she climbed into the monstrosity. Then he went around to the driver's side and climbed in himself. After starting the tractor, he took a moment to make sure he had his hands and feet where they belonged, then slowly pulled away from the curb and gradually made his way through the parking lot and toward the exit.

"You'll have to be patient with me. This is a little different than what I'm used to driving." He winced as he went over the curb while turning onto the road. As they neared the top speed for the tractor, he added, "A little slower than I'm used to, as well."

With as uncomfortable as he seemed in the driver's seat of the big tractor, slow was probably good. A car passed by them, and after a glance at it, he pulled the steering wheel to the right, sending half of the wheels off the edge of the pavement, driving in the weeds.

"This thing has good power, but it's the opposite of a limo—instead of being spread out long, it's spread out wide. I fear I'm going to sideswipe another car."

She laughed. "You're doing great. Where are you taking me?"

"To the South Dakota Agricultural Heritage Museum."

That could only mean one thing. "Nicolas is here?"

"I'm sworn to secrecy, Ms. Parks."

Avery leaned back in her seat, smiling. Nicolas was *here*. In South Dakota. She could feel it in her bones.

She looked over at Jacques, who was trying valiantly to negotiate driving in such a massive vehicle. "I can't believe Nicolas had you come to pick me up in a tractor."

"When in Rome, Ms. Parks." He looked around at the scenery, which, now that they were heading away from town just a bit, was already starting to show fields of growing crops. "Your 'Rome' is rather breathtaking. It smells incredible here, too. Those fields are simply a work of art."

She smiled. "I think you'll get along well with my dad." And then she started to get emotional. "Thank you for coming all this way, Jacques. It means a lot."

He gave a single nod. "I wouldn't have missed it for anything."

Chapter Thirty

NICOLAS

$\mathcal{N}$icolas hadn't been able to sleep at all on the long plane ride to South Dakota—he was too excited to see Avery again, and the thoughts of her that had been running through his mind seemed to be on double-speed. He'd spent twice the amount of time as usual shaving and had put on the tie that she'd mentioned once that she loved.

Dropping off flowers at Avery's work seemed to create quite the stir, so Nicolas had ducked quickly into a hallway not far from the admissions department. He was close enough that he'd heard Avery's reaction along with that of all her co-workers. He couldn't leave without being seen, so he waited.

And then Avery took off running down the hall and he'd gotten nervous about the timing for a moment. As soon as she was gone, he slipped through a side door and hid where he could see the parking lot and Jacques helping Avery into the tractor. He hoped she was getting a kick out of his choice of transportation.

The moment Jacques pulled the tractor out of the parking lot and onto the main road, Nicolas raced to his rental car and pulled out behind them. He passed the tractor with no problem driving at normal speeds. Jacques had glanced at him as he passed, but Avery hadn't even looked over.

The museum wasn't far from the college, but he had no problem at all getting there much sooner than the slower tractor. He pulled into the parking lot near the doors of the Agricultural Heritage Museum near where Avery's parents and sister, along with Delphine and Rania, waited.

Her mom came up to him and wrapped him in a tight hug. He had missed those hugs. "Oh, I know I already hugged you, but I'm just so happy to see you again. It's been far too long."

"It really has."

"Oh, and I've been meaning to apologize to you for making you clean our bathroom! I just figured you came from a home where cleaning bathrooms was normal, not one where a maid did it."

Nicolas clasped one of Jody's hands in his. "Please don't apologize. I'm grateful you did. I would've hated not to have a clue how to clean the bathroom in my first apartment. You saved me from that particular embarrassment."

She blushed and Nicolas turned to Avery's dad, holding his hand out to shake his. But Dalton pulled him in for a hug. "I wanted Avery to find someone to date here in South Dakota, but I know you well enough not to be surprised that Avery got all head over heels." He looked up at the building. "And I couldn't be more thrilled that you're working everything out here. Back when you first came to our house as a teen, I told Avery you would like this place!"

"I definitely found it a wonder. And thank you again for helping me to line up the tractor."

Dalton nodded. "Yeah, my neighbor is always buying the newest, most flashy tractors, if for no other reason than to have the coolest. He was happy to help."

Nicolas smiled at Riley. "How has it been running Under the Arch by yourself?"

Riley flexed a bicep. "I got my superpowers!"

"Right on. Congrats. And your business partner is healing okay?" At Riley's nod, he said, "I never really got a chance to thank you for Mini Europe."

"No need to say thank you. A crown or a sash stating that I'm the favorite will do."

He laughed. Then he glanced out at the scenery, especially the nearby flowering trees whose leaves and blossoms had all grown in, and breathed in deeply. "It is so good to be back here." He hadn't stepped foot in this place since he'd flown back home nearly a decade ago. Some things had changed. Most things were exactly how he'd remembered them. "I love the fresh air."

"And the manure smell," Riley said.

He laughed. "And the manure."

Delphine stepped closer to them and said, "They're two minutes out."

He nodded, excitement and anticipation and a little bit of worry building inside him. "We better get back inside." He couldn't wait to see Avery again.

As soon as they were through the doors into the museum, Avery's family and Delphine and Rania both moved off to the side where they wouldn't be seen from the doorway. Nicolas moved to the right in front of the museum's focal-point piece—the steam-powered tractor in the center of the space.

He put the well-worn cowboy hat on his head that he'd convinced the museum manager to let him wear and slipped a short stem of wheat in his mouth, well aware of how contradictory both of those items looked with the expensive suit he was wearing. Especially because he was standing in front of a piece of machinery that, based on the info plaque in front of it, was built in 1915.

It didn't take long before Jacques opened the front door of the museum and Avery walked in. He knew it had only been a couple of weeks since he'd last seen her, but seeing her now made it feel like it had been months. He was a dying man traversing a vast desert, and she was the oasis.

So many emotions crossed Avery's face as her eyes landed on him. Elation. Wonder. Amusement. Curiosity.

She wore a white dress with little flowers on it that fell to just above her knees and a smile that said she was just as happy to see him as he was her. He hadn't known exactly how she would react to him showing up unannounced. But man, was it good to see her now in her own city, smiling like everything was right in the world.

She hurried down the aisle separating them and wrapped her arms around him. He held her tight, breathing in her scent that he'd missed more than he'd known he could miss something. She pulled back and looked at him again. "You're here."

He smiled. "And you seem happy to see me. Which, honestly, is a relief, because I hadn't quite practiced what I would say if you weren't." Although he still didn't know how she would react to what he was going to say.

An eyebrow of hers rose. "You practiced things to say to me?"

"Yes, so don't interpret my suaveness in delivering the lines as anything less than completely genuine."

"Suaveness, huh? No nerves at all?"

"Nope. Nothing."

She grinned at his wrist where he was currently twisting his watch, and he dropped his hand. "Okay, maybe a little."

"Now see how genuine that is?" Avery said, eyes still amused.

Then her smile turned to an expression that looked like it was a mix of adoration and anticipation, and he couldn't help reaching out and running a finger from her temple down to her jaw. She was so beautiful. His heart ached just remembering spending the last two weeks without her. All the times when he'd wanted to show her something or tell her about something that happened at work or on the drive home. All the times he'd wanted to be by her side.

He opened his mouth, and all the words he'd thought of during the entire plane ride fell from his mind. So instead, he just spoke from his heart. "To start, I need to apologize for not standing up to my mother sooner, and especially for not standing up for us at the reception." He hadn't stopped wishing he would've done everything differently.

"I understand why you didn't, and I don't fault you for it."

He rose an eyebrow.

"It was a trauma response, probably rooted in losing Maxim from your family when you were young.

Sometimes you don't know how you'll react to a situation until you're in it."

"Well, I do now, and I promise it'll never happen again." He reached out and lightly ran a finger from her temple to her jaw. "You are an incredible human, you know that?"

She shrugged and winked. "What I do know is that I'll never tire of you telling me that."

He smiled, then reached out to hold her hands with both of his. "Avery, I want to be in your world. I want you to be in mine. I have no idea how we are going to accomplish both, or if you're even slightly interested. All I know is that I love you and I want to be with you, and I want to do whatever it takes to make that happen. I think we are great together. And I am certain that I can't spend the rest of my life without you and still be a happy man."

She smiled up at him, looking like she was drinking in his words. "I love you, Nicolas Servais. I want exactly that too. I want you to be in my world and I want to be in yours."

Did he hear that right? "You really want to be in mine?"

She leaned in closer. "I can't say I'll never be nervous in unfamiliar situations and I definitely can't say that I'll never have awkward moments, but yes. I want to be in yours."

"It's settled, then. We just need to clone ourselves—we'll have one set of us here and one set in Belgium."

She laughed, and the sound made his entire soul happy. "Or how about I only work six months of the year so I can spend time in Belgium, and we work out a way for you to spend some time here?"

"Wait. You can do that?"

"I don't know. My boss is on board. We'll have to see if the director approves it. And then, of course, we'd have to find and hire someone who is okay with only having a job half the year, and I'll have to train them. But it's in the works."

A warmth radiated through his body as adrenaline coursed through him. He cupped her face in his hands and pressed his lips against hers. She immediately melted into him, wrapping her arms around him, and he wasn't sure he had ever felt more happy and alive in his entire life.

When they broke the kiss, they stayed a heartbeat apart. She put a hand on his chest, and he was sure she could feel his heart hammering inside. He felt like he could feel his heartbeat throughout his entire body.

"I know that we knew each other well as teenagers and that we've stayed in touch a bit over the past ten years, and *really* well over two weeks in Belgium." She smiled, so he gave those smiling lips a quick kiss. "And I know that hasn't been long enough to start planning a future or anything, so I'm not going to scare you off by proposing yet. But just so you know, it's on my mind." Maybe he should have given her a "spoiler alert" warning on that bit of info. He hadn't planned on saying that.

But then she leaned in close, her lips right next to his ear, electricity zinging through all his nerve endings, and whispered, "And just so you know, I wouldn't have been scared off."

He pulled back, feeling dizzy and tingling. "Wait. You've been thinking about it?"

"Nicolas, it's *you*. How could I not?"

He nearly opened his mouth and proposed right then. But he stopped himself just in time. He wanted to do this right. To make it memorable. And he wanted to do it after they'd had a chance to date each other for longer. He didn't want the thrill of a new relationship to be the reason she said yes. He wanted the thrill of an established relationship across two different continents that was working out well to be the reason she said yes.

He could wait.

Chapter Thirty-One

AVERY

*A*s Avery and Nicolas got out of the car at Lake Baldwin, Nicolas released a long, audible sigh. "I can't believe how much I've missed this place. I should just quit my job and move here and enjoy it with you every single day."

She gave him a playful shove. "You need Oma Servais and Oma Servais needs you. The same goes for Ghent."

As sweet as it was for Nicolas to involve her family today, and as great as it was to see and chat with Jacques, Delphine, and Rania again, she was grateful to have found a moment when the two of them could slip away. The sun had set and stars were just starting to dot the sky as Nicolas put his hand in hers, leading her toward the shore of Lake Baldwin.

"I told my mother that I didn't want to be the CEO."

Avery felt her eyes widen. "You did?" They stopped walking at the edge of the lake and she looked up at him. Was that what his mother had been referring to when she said that Avery had rubbed off on Nicolas—that he'd stood up to her, too? "What did she say? There's no way she was okay with that. Right?"

"She was not. For now, though, she's okay enough. Well, she's working on it. She's got a lot on her plate right now—some things she doesn't want me to share yet—so it'll take some time for her to get okay with it. Actually, having so much on her plate might help her to be more okay with it sooner. But she's going to name our Chief Operations Officer as CEO. The board already approved it."

"That is incredible!" She gave him a tight hug, and then he kept an arm around her as they looked out across the lake. She knew how much he'd wanted that outcome, and it made her entire body feel lighter just knowing that he got it. "I did not see that coming. Are you relieved? Happy? Surprised? A little sad that you won't be doing something you had planned to do for so much of your life?"

Nicolas chuckled. "I'm pretty sure I've experienced all of those. And more. Oh, and for something just as unbelievable, my parents went to see Maxim!"

"That is truly wonderful." Her heart got all warm and happy just picturing the reunion. As awful as Margaux had been to Avery, she'd glimpsed how important her children were to her. Acting tough or not, she was sure that seeing Maxim again thrilled his mother. And to know that Avery had played a part, even if it was the slightest part, in making that reunion happen not only made her elated, but it also gave her hope in her future relationship with Margaux. "How did it go? What did Maxim think of it?" Avery already knew that there had been some kind of reconciliation between them from talking to Margaux earlier in the day, but she didn't want to take away from Nicolas's excitement at telling the story.

"It was so great. I mean, it was awkward and kind of painful to watch, honestly, but so great. They've got miles to go, but at least now they're on the road together. And now my parents know they're getting a granddaughter and finally got to meet Léa.

"When they found out that Maxim is a paramedic and a helicopter pilot, my father looked impressed. Like he respected that choice and that he was happy for him. My mother just looked like herself, but she didn't look disappointed, which is huge. She might've even had a smile on her face."

It was so fun to see the excitement coursing through Nicolas as he talked about things changing in his family. Fierce mother or not, it was clear that Nicolas loved his family and would always be happy anytime they became closer. It made her love him even more.

"She called me today," Avery finally said.

Nicolas looked confused. "My mother?"

She nodded. "I think it's possible she doesn't hate me."

"Oh, she doesn't. She may be harsh in her judgments, but she's also smart. Which means she's smart enough to see that you are amazing. The more she gets to know you, the more she'll love you."

Avery wasn't sure what the future might bring in regards to Margaux, but it didn't matter as long as she had Nicolas. "Does this mean there won't be any raw meat in my future?"

Nicolas chuckled. "I'm not saying you should expect her to give you proper hugs or ask you to meet her for lunch and an afternoon of shopping—that's not her style. But she might put her hands on your shoulders and give you an air kiss and mean it, or invite you to a family dinner and not belittle you the entire time."

Avery laughed. "I'll take it."

It felt so perfectly right to just be with Nicolas, chatting about their lives. She had missed this so much. She had missed him so much.

She looked out over the smooth lake and the many stars that were now reflecting on its surface. How was she going to be able to handle a long-distance relationship with this man? She wanted to be with him all the time. When she had asked Grant about the possibility of spending six months in South Dakota and six months in Belgium, it hadn't hit her how hard it would be to go six months without seeing Nicolas. Now that he was here with her again after only two weeks apart, a full six months seemed impossible.

"I haven't even shared the really exciting part yet," Nicolas said. "I told my mother that I wanted the position at Oma Servais that I've been dreaming about my entire life. And when Jean-Pierre retires in about three months, I'm going to get it."

"Nicolas! Oh, I'm so happy for you!"

He was beaming. He had talked about how much he loved product development so often while she'd been in Belgium and his passion for it had always come through. It seemed like he was uncommonly skilled at it too.

When a breeze blew a lock of her hair across her face, he reached out and brushed it back behind her ear. "Not only is it where I think I can do the most good and what I most want to do, but it has definite busy times of the year and definite lulls." He smiled broadly. "And during the lulls, I could absolutely spend some time working remotely."

Avery gasped, her eyes wide, her heart racing as a warmth radiated through her entire body. She felt like running. Jumping. "For real? And you could come here?"

He grinned.

She wrapped her arms around him in a hug and he swung her in a circle. When he placed her feet on the ground again, he said, "And you can bet I'll be here with you every moment I can. We can even go get some very well-done burgers. Bison, even, if you'd like."

She laughed, and then in amazement said, "We're going to make this work."

He nodded. "Yes, we are."

Epilogue

Excitement ran through Elle Markle as she carried a stack of totes up to the front door of the Parks' farmhouse, Summer carrying her own load of totes by her side. Elle had heard her co-workers refer to her as the "wedding planner of the office" several times. Being the event coordinator at LBSU was more up Elle's alley than actual wedding planning would be, but planning this last-minute engagement party had been fun.

Okay, more than fun. It had been exhilarating. All the coordinating, details, planning—she loved it all. Doing it for Avery and Nicolas made it even better.

Avery's mom, Jody, answered the front door with a wide smile and invited them in. Avery's sister, Riley, and her dad, Dalton, both helped take totes from their arms and carried them back to the big great room at the back of the house.

The Admissions department had found and hired Mariana—someone who wanted to job share with Avery—four months ago. She'd asked to switch off with Avery every three months instead of every six. As soon as Avery had trained her, she'd headed back to Belgium.

It had been so fun to get Avery's phone calls at the office over the past three months with updates. A roar of a cheer had gone up on both the Welcome Center side and the Admissions side when she'd told them all that she and Nicolas had gotten engaged last Friday.

And now the two of them were both headed back to South Dakota. Nicolas for four weeks and Avery for three months, and Elle knew they needed to have an engagement party for everyone to celebrate. She'd gotten together with Avery's mom and they'd decided to have it at Avery's parents' house since that was where everything had started.

"You go ahead and just boss us around," Jody said.

Dalton nodded. "You tell us what you want us to do and where, and we'll do it."

"I will take you up on that offer," Elle said. This was where things really started to get fun—when all the planning began to take physical shape in the location.

There were a few elements of her and Summer's jobs at the Welcome Center that overlapped, so they were used to working on big events together and could guess what the other person was thinking. Having such willing help in Avery's family was a huge plus. Soon, all the decorations were up, the refreshments artfully arranged, and the multitude of beverage options displayed. It all looked perfect, and they even finished before the first guest arrived.

Before long, the house was filled with the happy chatter of her coworkers—Joy, Grant, and Mariana from the Admissions side of the wall all came. And so did Pavani and her husband Zain, Brock, Everett, Deja and her husband Trent, and Tess and her husband Dane from the Welcome Center side. And of course, Avery's parents and sister.

And then the front door opened and the noise in the house increased as Avery and Nicolas walked in. Elle smiled as the newly-engaged couple gave everyone hugs. Avery had a look of confidence about her that was stronger than usual like she was completely comfortable in her own skin. And like she knew she was loved deeply. Elle suddenly had a pang of longing for the same feeling.

Then Avery made it to Elle and wrapped her arms around her. Elle gave her friend a tight squeeze back and said, "Congratulations. I am so thrilled for you."

"Thank you," Avery said. "And thank you so much for planning all of this. It really means a lot."

Once they all had a drink in hand, Elle gathered

everyone into the family room and got them seated, then asked Avery and Nicolas to tell the story of their engagement.

"It was last Friday night," Avery said. "We started off the evening all dressed up fancy and went to the restaurant that Nicolas had taken Riley and me to the first time we'd been in Ghent—Trattenuto Andante. I had the barberie duck with beetroot that I loved so much the first time we went. It's the kind of restaurant that doesn't make you feel rushed to leave, so we just sat and talked and had the best time."

Smiling at Avery, Nicolas said, "We really did." He looked back at everyone listening and said, "Then we went for a ride in one of the canal boats and traveled down the Leie quite a distance until we came to a quiet park that we discovered a couple of months ago and loved. It has pathways and trees and lots of flowers and grassy areas. I couldn't have asked for a more perfect night."

Avery nodded. "Nicolas had brought a bag with a blanket in it, and we laid it out so that we could look up at the stars. Then Nicolas said that he brought dessert—chocolates that he had made himself. Get this: it was a bonbon that he named 'The Avery.'"

"Aww," Summer said. "He named it after you? Nicolas, you are one classy guy."

Nicolas looked the slightest bit embarrassed, but then

he looked at Avery again, and it seemed to ground him before he turned his attention back to everyone else. "One of the things that I love about Avery is her ability to bring people together. She can even bring together people who don't seem to want that. Somehow she's always able to find what it is about people that they have in common, and then she helps them to bond over it.

"So I've been thinking about that for a while and thinking about all the flavors that go well with chocolate. Things like cinnamon, sea salt, nuts, chilis, caramel, cloves, ginger, vanilla, star anise. All ingredients I've used before in coming up with new types of chocolates for our stores.

"But I've been dreaming a lot about how they could all be combined. Trying to figure out what they had in common so I could help them 'bond' over it. Some I infused into heavy cream. Some I used subtly—a hint. A nuance of flavor. Others I went bold with, making the taste hit right up front. Others are an aftertaste that lingers on the tongue. I've tried selecting and roasting the cocoa beans in different ways to highlight different flavors. I kept working with the ingredients—how much and how I use them—and tweaking things.

"And eventually I figured it out. I brought all the flavors together in the right way and made a truffle with a complex depth of flavor that will keep surprising you. Just like Avery. And then I gave its shell hints of the deep blue of the dress that Avery wore the night of the IRCA reception months ago."

Elle didn't know if she should wipe away a tear at how sweet that story was, or wipe away drool from the corner of her mouth.

"Dude," Everett said. "What are you trying to do to us?"

Avery laughed. "Okay, I know all of your mouths are watering."

"You got that right, honey," Deja said.

Pavani pointed at Nicolas. "Yeah, it's kind of mean to describe it so well to a pregnant woman who just happens to be having chocolate cravings like all day, every day right now."

Avery and Nicolas shared a mischievous smile, then Avery turned to everyone. "In the interest of not being mean, we've brought some for you all to try."

Elle had never been more ready to try a new food. Avery pulled some boxes from her bag by the doorway and Elle immediately jumped up to help. She started taking them around for each person to grab one.

"This is absolutely gorgeous," Tess said as she held the bonbon up, tipping it to the left and the right, admiring it in the light.

As Elle reached Summer and Brock, Summer whispered loudly, "If there are extras, circle back around to us, okay?"

Elle laughed. "Take it up with these guys," she said as she handed the box containing the last few to Nicolas, right after she took one out for herself.

She bit into the chocolate and immediately moaned as it started to melt in her mouth. Her palate wasn't nearly refined enough to pick out each of the individual ingredients. All she knew was that it was an explosion of flavor and she hadn't known chocolate could taste like that—so smooth and creamy and full of flavors that didn't compete with the chocolate yet somehow enhanced it, making it better than anything she had ever tasted before. And the taste seemed to change as she ate it, each different taste even more exquisite than the last.

"Avery," Elle said, "if you don't marry this man, I will."

"You'll have to fight me for him," Joy said as she gazed at the other half of her bonbon.

"So now that you've tried one," Avery said, "you'll understand when I say that I ate one and I nearly died from experiencing something so delicious. And then I nearly died because Nicolas was the one who made it. And then because he named it after me. And then while I was nearly dying—three times!—he said all the other things he loves about me."

"Like how much I admire her heart and how she looks out for others. And how she can take a high-conflict situation and help people find a way to resolve things. How she listens and helps me see the things that I can't see myself. She supports me when I'm feeling stressed and makes me feel fortified for any challenge. She cheers me on in everything I do. She makes me laugh. She loves me unconditionally. She's my constant. My everything."

He was looking at Avery in a way that made Elle's heart ache. Avery was looking right back at him the same way.

"And then I said all the things I love about him," Avery said. "Like how thoughtful he is.

He's always on the lookout for anyone who doesn't look a part of something and makes them feel included. He's loyal and forgiving and sees the best in people and cares about everyone. He's smart and hard-working. He remembers the little details. He makes me feel important and loved. And he has the greatest smile ever. This whole time, the stars were shining and there was a scent of flowers in the slight breeze. It was a perfect night, at the perfect place, with the perfect company."

"So with all of that," Nicolas said, "I was feeling as confident as could be. I pulled the ring box from the bag and opened it." He paused for a moment. "And then Avery screamed."

Avery held out her hand with the shiny ring on her finger for everyone to see. "Look how pretty it is! You'd have screamed too!"

Nicolas smiled down at it, then looked back at Avery.

"When I realized that there was no danger and my heart calmed, I asked if she would marry me. Before I even got all four words out, she was already saying yes."

"Because even when I haven't been thinking about it, my subconscious has been saying *yes* every moment since I saw him in that suit in front of the steam-powered tractor months ago. That *yes* has been trying to burst free for so long, it just couldn't wait."

They were looking at each other with smiles so big and full of love—Elle couldn't look away.

"To Avery's and Nicolas's engagement," Grant said, holding up his flute of champagne.

"To Avery's and Nicolas's engagement," everyone else echoed, holding their drinks up.

Brock took a sip of his drink, then asked, "So are the two of you going to keep switching between here and Belgium after you're married?"

Avery and Nicolas looked at each other and shrugged. Then Nicolas said, "It's working out well so far. It's been great to experience our relationship in both places."

"Maybe we'll have to choose once we have kids," Avery added. "Or maybe not. We'll have to see. For now, we're just going to revel in it. In a really strange way, it keeps us very balanced."

Avery's dad raised his hand. "If my vote counts for anything, I say either keep switching back and forth or just choose to live here. Heck, we'll even give you some acreage if it means you'll stay close."

Nicolas shook his head, grinning. "I loved being part of your family back when I was in high school. I'm glad that I get to be part of it again."

Avery's dad made his way from his seat on the couch to Nicolas and wrapped his arms around him in a hug. Avery's mom and sister joined in right afterward.

Everyone started socializing in smaller groups. Even as Elle was too, part of her was thinking about her own love life. She had dated quite a bit over the years, but she had never connected with anyone like Avery and Nicolas had.

After a while, they slipped outside onto the patio that stretched across the whole back of the house. They'd said that they had hung out there at night a lot when they were teens, looking up at the stars and chatting and that they wanted to reminisce for a moment.

The patio lights were on, and the guests could all see the happy couple as they leaned against the railing, looking out across the fields of oats.

"Aren't they just the sweetest thing ever?" Deja asked.

There were murmurs of agreement from everyone.

"I want a relationship like that," Elle said. "But what if I never find it?"

Summer wagged her eyebrows. "Maybe you'll get it with a certain deep-voiced celebrity when you finally interview him."

Elle rolled her eyes. Not because she didn't think Declan Davenport's voice was as amazing as everyone said it was because it very much was. She was fine with them all assuming that was why she rolled her eyes, though. The real reason was because she and Declan having a relationship was such a far-fetched idea. What were the chances of anything happening between Declan and her when she interviewed him? Celebrity wasn't exactly the type she normally fell for.

In fact, it was about the furthest thing from it.

Want more of Elle's and Declan's story? *It Started with a Glance* is out now.

IT STARTED WITH A GLANCE

His famous voice and dimples might make him attractive, but his celebrity status makes him anything but.

If Elle Markle learned one thing from her rock star dad, it's to stay far away from celebrities—they can't be trusted. (And that she didn't inherit his voice and therefore should also stay far away from karaoke.)

Declan Davenport would say he isn't a celebrity. His team and the millions of fans on his hugely popular science YouTube channel say otherwise.

When Elle is assigned to interview the star with the incredibly deep voice and irresistible dimples, she reminds herself that she's dealt with celebrities before and this will be no different. When she discovers it's actually an overnight day-in-the-life gig at his house, she resolves to keep the walls firmly up. Like, concrete-and-barbed-wire up. No celebrity is winning her heart. Not now, not ever.

Declan is wary of the mysterious interviewer visiting his home and intruding on his privacy—until he discovers that she's smart and beautiful and exactly his type (if he had a type). They have an undeniable chemistry that surprises even the scientist in him . . . which means she's even more dangerous than he thought.

Because there's one interview question Declan can never answer.

And he's the last person who can give his heart away.

About Meg Easton

Meg Easton is the *USA Today* bestselling author of contemporary romances and romantic comedies with fun, memorable, swoon-worthy characters, and settings you'll want to pack up and move to. She lives at the foot of a mountain with her name on it (or at least one letter of her name) in Utah. She loves gardening, bike riding, baking, swimming before the sun rises, and spending time with her husband and three kids.

She can be found online at www.megeaston.com

Sign up to receive her newsletter and stay up to date with new releases, get exclusive bonus content, and more.

If you liked this book please leave a review. Your review can help other readers find books they might fall in love with.

youtube.com/@megeastonauthor

bookbub.com/authors/meg-easton

instagram.com/megeaston_author

facebook.com/MegEastonBooks

tiktok.com/@megeaston_author